Penguin Crime Fiction
Editor : Julian Symons
The Dresden Green

Nicolas Freeling was born in London in
1927 and spent his childhood in France.
Before taking up writing he worked for
many years in hotels and restaurants, and
from their back doors got to know a good
deal of Europe. When *Love in Amsterdam*,
his first novel, was published in 1962 he
stopped cooking other people's dinners
and went back to Holland. His second
and third novels, *Because of the Cats* and
Gun Before Butter, were published in 1963.
They have all been published in Penguins,
as well as *Double-Barrel*, *The King of the
Rainy Country* and *Criminal Conversation*.
He has also written a straight novel under a
pseudonym. His latest book, *A Long Silence*,
was published in 1972.

Nicolas Freeling

The Dresden Green

Penguin Books

Penguin Books Ltd, Harmondsworth, Middlesex, England
Penguin Books Australia Ltd, Ringwood, Victoria, Australia
Penguin Books Canada Ltd, 41 Steelcase Road West,
Markham, Ontario, Canada
Penguin Books (N.Z.) Ltd, 182–190 Wairau Road, Auckland 10,
New Zealand

First published by Victor Gollancz 1966
Published in Penguin Books 1969
Reprinted 1975
Copyright © Nicolas Freeling, 1966

Made and printed in Great Britain by
Hunt Barnard Printing Ltd, Aylesbury
Set in Monotype Imprint

Writer's Foreword

It happens that a writer – even of fiction – who chooses a theme discovers that other people have, suddenly as it seems, become preoccupied with the identical fact or circumstances, and there is nothing odd about this. A happening that may seem insignificant when lost in the clamour of triviality shrieking daily for our attention will still strike the imagination of many. Even were there no happening to arrest attention, merely a set of circumstances that has been there for years, people have a way of thinking about it, all in different ways, around the same time.

It is, too, a truism that fact copies fiction, but fact has a malicious way of copying the deliberately crooked path taken by imagination. To give a personal illustration, four years ago I wrote a novel, stuffed with improbable and melodramatic details, about a juvenile gang, and called it 'Because of the Cats'. Every detail my imagination supplied has since been reproduced exactly by fact. People in half a dozen lands, and from as far away as Peru, have written to me enclosing clippings 'just the same' – often in terms of naïve congratulation for what seemed witch-doctory. Look look, here is a gang where the girls even called themselves the cats – as though I had made it happen! Of course there was no magic about any of this.

I thought it necessary to mention all this because the bombardment of Dresden, twenty years after, has appeared on the horizon of many minds. A German writer, whom I do not know, has written a book about the bombing, which I have not seen. I wish to say that I have no axe to grind about the bombing. It seems clear now that it was an act of criminal folly. With hindsight it is easy to realize that some persons with great power in high positions held feelings about Germans that some Germans, similarly placed, held about Poles. Infamous wild

5

animals, subhuman, to be stamped on with all available means. Even intelligent people succumb to their own propaganda. The bombing of Dresden was an ignoble stupidity, but not a revolting act of cowardly murder, or unforgivable. Nothing is unforgivable.

I have to say this, because people are far too apt to assume that opinions expressed by characters in fiction must always be the tenets of the writer. The opinions of Louis Schweitzer are not mine. Wars have not become more brutal; neither has mankind, and if the destruction of Dresden was on a larger scale than that of many a town in the Thirty Years War, and the destruction of Jews more widespread and 'efficient' than that of Huguenots, or Cathars, it is without especial meaning. Communications are better nowadays; earlier centuries lacked our advantages: they had no radio and no national daily press.

I chose to take the city of Dresden not as an example of senseless and bestial destruction, but as the exact opposite, a symbol of artistic endeavour, and by art I mean neither more nor less than a manifestation of human dignity and nobility. Dresden was always known as a centre of every kind of art in this sense that our European civilization has ever produced. To a painter it was one of the finest collections, to an architect a group of buildings of astonishing richness, and so on. I never saw the town in reality, but to me it has meant all these things, and most of all perhaps opera.

For this reason as the least of many, I wanted to dedicate this book to Erich Kleiber. He wanted to make not only a bridge over the 'Iron Curtain' but a breach in it – a breach made by music, he thought, could not be closed. So he tried to revive the Berlin Staatsoper, and as we know he failed, and it killed him. I like to think of this, just as I like to think of him going to Dresden in 1952, where the first thing he did was to buy flowers to bring to the grave of Carl Maria von Weber.

But EK is dead, killed perhaps by our now universal love of mediocrity. So that I can do no more than offer this book to his memory, and not only the memory of a great musician but the man who travelled with 'a laundry basket of detective stories'.

I am not going to be robbed of my dedication. This book is for my greatly valued friend, EK's wife, Ruth Kleiber.

Not to her only. This is the feast day of ALL Saints, November first, 1965, as I write these words, which gives me the right to ask for a pause – the musical sign for a pause is engraved upon Kleiber's tomb in Zürich. A pause to say a prayer for all who died in the bombardment of Dresden, and all the other bombardments . . .

As for the green diamond, it is either lost or 'buried in the cellars of the Louvre where no human eye will ever again behold it', but it would be wonderful, and I should be delighted, if by some sympathetic 'magic' the world were again to hear of it.

One more word. In our lifetime practically every major city along a rough line drawn between France and Germany has become the seat of some well-meaning if often incoherent organization devoted to Unity and to Peace, to Disarmament, and to Putting an End to It All. We think at once of Brussels and Geneva, or Luxembourg, and my own home town of Strasbourg. Not to speak of the United Nations in New York, Addis Ababa, Algiers. . . . Nobody will blame me for inventing an imaginary town somewhere in the Jura containing yet another of these buildings, and nobody will blame me either for making my central character the slightly misled servant of another – totally imaginary – organization of this nature. I am forced to mention this too because someone might easily think that I was attempting a vulgar caricature of the European Parliament. I have not; I have never even visited the building in Strasbourg that is its seat.

Nicolas Freeling
Wolfisheim: Strasbourg
Toussaint, 1965

Part One

Thursday Evening

Louis Schweitzer walked slowly down the wide flight of steps at the front of the Europahaus. His knees had seized up, after a four-hour spell in his little sound-proofed cabin, and he flexed them going down, to loosen the rigid ligaments. Six thirty of an evening beginning to feel like spring, and he breathed strongly into the air that was fresh instead of being conditioned to exactly fourteen degrees and seven per cent humidity. Out here it was at least three cooler and five damper; the grass and earth were aware of the fact, and there was a nice smell. The gardeners had mowed the odious little formal lawns for the first time this year, and tidied up the beds where the daffodils from the Scilly Isles, present of the English delegation, had just been replaced by the tulips from Hillegom – present of the Dutch delegation. And after the tulips France would have her turn with early roses from Provence. A gift to the cause of European peace, said the neatly lettered plastic plaque that stayed all the year: under came 'from the people of' and a slot for every country in turn to slip into.

Louis had been talking to one of the Russians, and Delegates used the front door, with its steps that had been put in as a sop to photographers, and were used for impromptu press conferences. So now he had to walk all the way around to the side. He surveyed the building as he walked, with his careful balance of tolerant amusement and cold hatred, hunting in his pocket for the key to his bicycle lock and smoking his first cigarette since two thirty with pleasure.

It was exactly like all official architecture, but more wide than high, since there was plenty of space up here north of the river: the quarter had, indeed, not even existed before fifty-five. Concrete and glass, rigid, unimaginative, ugly. Corbusier had turned the commission down: wisely, since they would have messed up his design anyway. They had tried to humanize the insurance-company look; there was plenty of symbolic statuary, friezes, high and low reliefs, and inside were endless frescoes and tapestries, courtyards and fountains, all presented as well, of course, by delegations. The entrance hall was high enough to hold even the colossal Christmas Tree the Norwegians sent every December.

On the lawn outside – Louis was just passing it – was a rugged concrete Europa with bulging muscles and a faintly thalidomide look, suckling wolves – or was it trampling on them? one could not be quite sure – and a bit further, by the entrance to the official car park, there was a huge bad bronze, Hercules wrestling with snakes, or at least Louis *supposed* it was Hercules; his classical education was patchy. It had been presented by the municipality at the suggestion of the local museum, which had jumped at the chance of getting rid of it.

Bicycles were concealed in a small nasty shed with a furtive look, next door to the police post: the architect, with a feeling that bikes were low, had suppressed them. Admittedly even typists now had autos, and sheep were separated from goats by minatory notices saying 'Permanent Staff' and 'Delegates only' while at the front was a plushy rank too snobbish to have a board: chauffeur-driven jobs for heads-of-missions, diplomats, visiting ministers, *observers* – anything, this, from a Papal Legate to the latest Nobel Peace Prize.

Louis was the only senior member of the staff to have a bike. He shook hands with the policeman on duty, who was strolling with his cape on, since there had been rain all afternoon and the street was still shiny. It was M. Gérard today, who came from Perpignan, right over the other side of France: he had a squat, bowlegged Pyrenean build and a bristly Brassens moustache, and Louis had a kinship with him, for he had no great opinion of Peace Palaces. Why, there had been you knows and nattohs and seetoes, for which nobody gave a damn, and there was the Eurocon, and the Economicon, and the Atocon: bleeding saints, said M. Gérard crossly, the whole frontier was packed with the rubbish and what this one was good for he didn't see. Louis sat there all day giving simultaneous-translation: did he know?

It brings prosperity to the shopkeepers, explained Louis. And it is even more European than the others. Finns and Bulgars and Portuguese and all, but no tiresome Chinese or Arabs. Even the Irish were in on this one: that was progress, he supposed. The tiresome thing about the Irish was that they would insist on talking Irish, which added to the burden of the translators. A fellow with one of those warm caressing Dublin accents put it into English, from which Madame Mishposh, sighing, put it into Russian. Louis, senior of the French-Russian group, could take his set off and meditate: the Irish spokesman tended to be prolix, especially if it were cows or sugar-beet.

Louis pedalled; it loosened his muscles and refreshed him, which was even better. He liked coming off at this time of the evening; the office crowd was already finished, the streets were quiet but the smaller shops were still open and one could buy one's supper in peace, without that knock-down stampede at the charcuterie there was at six. Movement, fresh air, soothing flick of light from red to green; nice, after verbosities of delegates: heaven, what a swarm of tiny vanities had been unmuzzled since the opening of the Permanent Parliament, known locally as the Palais de Paix, by all the heads of government, from Atlantic to Urals (what a headache there had been over precedence).

He had about a kilometre to go, to get home. From the pompous Europa quarter, Place de la Concorde, Rue de Moscou to the University quarter, Rue des Étudiants, the Sciences-Po bridge to the old town. It wasn't the old town at all; Second Empire every scrap of it, but it was classed now as old town. Louis was fortunate to live there for it was much sought after: the old town, the real old town with markets and fishwives, Cathedral and Hôtel de Ville, was across the second bridge in the loop of the Doubs, very medieval, tourists' delight and municipal nightmare; streets like small and large intestines wound up in a hopeless tangle and crammed into the city's pelvis.

Louis had lived for six years now on the seventh floor of Number Ninety-six, Avenue de Jura; one of a great heavy row in a characteristic grandiose boulevard. Thank heaven for

Haussmann; the street was wide, which released much of the echo of traffic, and the double row of plane trees minimized what was left. Louis pushed the heavy door, murmured a good evening at the hovering concierge, a thick woman hovering no doubt to catch someone for a gas bill (he kept on diplomatic good terms with her), wheeled his bike between jade-green and cream tiles, horribly highly glazed, with strange Assyrian black patterns in a belt at top and bottom, and kicked the swing door into the courtyard. Here he parked his bike, between the concierge's handcart and Madame Zbrowski's pram. He took the three small parcels for supper and put them in his raincoat pocket, picked up his pedal bin (emptied that and every morning into one of the big dustbins) and put it on the rope lift, hauling away till he saw it sail up to the row of plants projecting over his kitchen balcony. Had all this any importance? No, except that Louis did exactly the same things every day; a creature of habit.

He started back inside. There was no lift, which was one reason why his mansard flat, at-the-back-opposite-the-students, was cheap. There were six students, and only one of him in the same amount of space; he found it worth it. He didn't mind the six flights of stone stairway, either. Like the bicycle, it was good for wind and muscles. Louis was nearer fifty now than forty, but had strong legs and no bulge in front, despite hours in glass phone-boxes: he was not out of breath at the landing between the students and himself.

A wide passage, and a row of servants' rooms. Two had been knocked into one to make a fair-sized living-room, with two doors and two little windows. One was a kitchen-and-bathroom, to simplify the plumbing. One was his bedroom, leaving two rooms too many, into which he had pushed all the junk. Mouldering trunks, packing-cases, an immense porcelain stove – how had they got it up there? – he locked the doors on it and forgot it existed. The passage was now free, with chaste grey-green matting, a table, a coat-rack, and one of those collapsible wardrobes made of plastic shower-curtain, in which lived the floor-polish, the dustpan-and-brush, and the vacuum-cleaner. It had all straight away an old-maidish look; anyone would have said unhesitatingly that a chalky bachelor civil servant lived there alone, and the anyone would have been very nearly right.

The first thing he always did was to change; he hated suits. It was still his winter-weight worsted one, dark brown; on the hanger with it. Shoes under, so; shirt would do another day – so. He put on a checked viyella shirt and corduroy trousers, went into the kitchen, and unpacked noodles, a slice of ham, and lettuce; he turned the gas on under the beans for soup. He peeled an onion; he got a branch of parsley and a bottle of white wine out of his little fridge. When the soup was simmering he poured a glass and took it into the living-room, where he felt the electric-oil radiator with his hand and adjusted the thermostat.

There was no radio or television; Louis despised both, but there was a record-player with an extension speaker. Louis liked music and held a season ticket for the opera, but the season was nearly over: April at last – it had been a long winter. He put his wine on the table, himself on the sofa, and picked up his book: he always read for half an hour before supper and generally for an hour in bed before the light went out.

Of course the room was tidy; it was not hard to keep tidy, for there was not much furniture. Two smyrna rugs on the polished wooden floor, that he had made on winter evenings listening to the gramophone; he liked to occupy his hands. They had vague Afghan patterns sold by the wool shop. The walls were painted what paint firms call ivory, and there were pictures; colour reproductions from calendars or magazines. When he liked them he framed and hung them: if he got tired of them or took-a-dislike they were easily replaced. At present there were fishing boats by Carzou, elegant in dark green and vertical black lines, the Jura in autumn, unsweetened, and a most peculiar vision of a Loire town, spidery dots and pale wash colours, that appealed to him; he had no idea how or why.

On one table his drink, his book, his ashtray, his rubber plant; on the other a half-finished rug folded, with the little lengths of wool underneath in a retired pillow-case. There was a bookcase, with four or five hundred paperbacks, some of which he had read several times before deciding to keep them;

they were carefully purged every six months. The only two big pieces of furniture were very big; they were indeed inherited with the junk and were lumpy, ornate, and oak. A big sideboard and a quite ministerial bureau. He did not dislike them and kept them perfectly polished, for between them they held everything that was him. Botany albums, gramophone records, tax and insurance papers, chemists' bills and a social security number. There were no decorations, ornaments, photos, or souvenirs.

The soup smelt good; he was hungry. He put the noodles on and made salad while waiting for the soup to cool. He had brought his glass with him and had another glass of white wine with the ham. He ate neatly, without dropping crumbs, and with pleasure, thinking about what he was doing: he did not belong to the family of solitary eaters that have a book propped against the plate and get tomato sauce on the page.

He washed up and did his housekeeping, which does not take long when one is *disciplined*. He did it every day, there was no one to disturb him, and it took less than an hour. It even included washing his own underclothes, laundries in Louis' mind being nearly as bad as peace palaces, and when finished he lay peacefully on his sofa and smoked a cigarette with a feeling of satisfaction. There were no armchairs in the sitting-room; he hated sitting, having enough of that at work. It was not yet nine o'clock; he went back to the kitchen, turned the heater on and had a shower.

At this time, usually, he put on pyjamas, thick cotton ones cut like a tracksuit and like a tracksuit fleecy on the inside, and then he would settle down to whatever occupation he had chosen for the evening; but tonight he dressed again, not in the good working suit, and certainly not in the prim white poplin shirt. He had a silk shirt, a beige shetland pullover, and a suit of soft oatmeal-coloured tweed. He stepped out on to the kitchen balcony; it was not raining, the sky was clear, and the air, though cold still from the near-by mountains that still had snow on them above the thousand metre level, had a promise of spring: there was a faint, kind southerly wind. Louis took no raincoat, nor an umbrella – he didn't *have* an umbrella. But he tucked three little cigars in his breast pocket, and ran down the stairs in what any observer would have taken as a most eccentric way: he would have been written down as the bachelor civil servant that is quite given over to toy trains, building Eiffel Towers from matchsticks, or even naughtier hobbies, whereas he was really a well-balanced person on the whole. He went down in irregular jumps on alternate feet, two, three, or even four at a time, pausing an instant on one foot every few jumps; it was only a ski exercise: Louis was a very fair skier.

In the hall he walked sedately, shut the heavy outside door without noise, and stepped along the street in a delicate strolling tempo, a man on his way towards enjoying himself. He had not very far to go, but 'made the most of it', stopping with artificially intense interest to study the stationer's window, crossing the street unnecessarily three times, paying a singular attention to lamp-post design, auto number-plates, and the names printed in little slots opposite rows of bell-pushes. He crossed the Avenue de Constance, went a block along the Rue du Maréchal Franchet d'Esperey, and turned into the Avenue de Neuchâtel. The streets, and the houses, were just like his own, giving a pleasant sensation of familiarity, of being at home in one's quarter: he knew, indeed, the quarter as well as the thousand or so men of his age who stroll along these blocks every night around the same time to let the dog do its business. Louis had no dog, but something just as good.

The house, like at least three hundred in the quarter, had a doctor on the ground floor; diseases of the lungs and respiratory passages, said the plate. And the first floor had a rather dreary printer; mechanisms for offset-and-litho-reproduction. Louis pushed the street door, which gave on a cavern of darkness, but when he shut it again a little light went on, a chaste double bracket on the wall with burnt-orange shades. He stood waiting because he knew that in the door at the end there was a tiny hole ten millimetres wide, with a lens in it giving a hundred and seventy-five degrees of vision. He waited a little more than one minute; the door opened and a woman in a housecoat switched on a charming smile.

If there had been television announcers twenty years before she would have made a good one. She was very carefully presented: *coiffée*, *habillée*, *maquillée*, *rangée*, extremely *soignée*.

She was tall, thin, rather meagre. A white elegant hand with beautifully almond-shaped cherry-pink nails was laid conspiratorially on his sleeve and a voice with a sinuous appealing warmth said, "Dear friend: good evening to you."

Louis gave her a brotherly smile. Looking at him now he seemed younger. Even in the burnt-orange light his face was tanned and healthy, and his eyes were electric-blue; one would have said no more than forty, and not been surprised to learn that typists at the Peace Palace had sometimes given him seductive smiles and been quite upset at his way of not noticing. But Louis liked his relations with women to be carefully professional. He disliked shades of meaning; he had a perfect terror of *involvements*.

The smile now had force as well as malice. He had the air of finding the thin woman a good joke, and something nice to eat, as well as a not-quite-friend. He kissed her hand in rather a theatrical way.

'Seems a long time,' he said amiably.

'Diane will be delighted. Or perhaps Christiane? She's free this evening and she has a new hairstyle too – she'll be dying to show it off too.'

There was a lift in this house. They had the second floor, front and back. The front was very conventional, with mahogany and dark green plush. The back was brighter, with five girls, several looking-glasses, three bathrooms, a Polaroid camera, a projector for home movies ('Just *look* at Danièle eating ice-cream on the beach: no no, Naxos – or was it Lesbos?'), and haughty but quite pleasant ways. The girls all enjoyed horses, swimming, and skiing, kept healthy with all this outdoor exercise, and enjoyed some little attention even more than their ten-franc tip: something childish like smoking one of Louis' cigars. Marie-Claire was admirable; one gave her a hundred francs and was free for three hours in considerable comfort. Two girls together cost a hundred and eighty, which was extravagant, and Louis went to the bother only occasionally, after a tedious and nerve-fatiguing debate at the Palace. The girls all liked him because he made jokes and took an interest in their clothes; they showed him all their new buys and put them on for him to admire. You didn't leave feeling cheated: this is so rare nowadays either in a restaurant, a brothel, or a shoe-shop, that Louis always felt well there. Sometimes he even recommended Marie-Claire to delegates: she was most scrupulous, and always gave him ten per cent commission, which immoral earnings made him laugh and were used to buy gramophone records. This evening he had Christiane, rather a dumpy girl with sturdy peasant calves whose real name was Jeanne and who had an irritating high squeak of laughter.

Three hours later, much refreshed – he had smoked two of the three little cigars, drunk a large cold glass of Chambéry vermouth and two little warm glasses of cherry brandy, besides making several jokes – Louis was strolling home again, sniffing happily at the warm windy sky. It would, he thought, be a good day tomorrow. And he was free; his hours were irregular, but fairly easy on the whole. He did about thirty-six hours, and the schedules lumped the turns of duty as far as could be over four days, so that he could generally manage three free days in seven. When there were extra-plenary sessions, as the jargon had it, or a harassing debate about a well-known death-trap like the Oder-Neisse line, a translator might well be called to do forty-five hours or even more, but one made up for it by repose later, since delegates, haggard after having their ears banged, not to speak of the conspiracies in committee-rooms, were fond of repose themselves.

Louis went out on to the kitchen balcony, where his socks were out to dry beside the geraniums, and tapped his barometer. Slow but steady rise – good. Temperature at midnight eleven degrees – good. Yes: he would have a day in the country.

Friday Morning

It was bright at breakfast. The southerly wind was blowing steadily, rolling harmlessly high fluffy clouds with a strong glary sun in between, and the glass was still creeping up. Louis took his shooting jacket, which was rainproof and had the most

19

pockets, his little flask with cognac in it, his flower-press, magnifying-glass, scissors, knife, cigarettes, binoculars, little trowel: that would do it. Down in the street he got across his bicycle and stopped to look at the Jura, looming up at the other end of the long avenue. Yes, a clear soft outline, not too bright, not hard, sun on the snowfields and a gay plume of cloud off the peak of the Mont d'Or right over in the distance, on the Swiss frontier. He pushed off feeling exhilarated, stopped at the dairy on the corner for a piece of cheese, celery remoulade salad. Bread next door, mineral water, cold roast beef, two big gherkins: ready for the day.

The naggy feeling that after all it was not going to be a good day, even that it was going to be a *bad* day, started before he had even properly set out. He had to go through the old town since they had started this one-way-street nonsense, and even so within the loop of the river it was always congested. Louis had to stop at the Place De Lattre for the policeman; he leaned his foot on the pavement and studied this policeman with dislike. A military, militaristic look that he did not care for: his feeling had grown into resentment – no, even an absurd *rancour* – before the gloved hand dropped and the arm waved him on.

Was it that the policeman was *handsome*? He was about thirty, built more like a fencer than a boxer. His uniform was fresh and pressed, his gauntlets, belt and cap-cover sparkling white: persil-white, omo-white, muttered Louis crossly. He stood in his little wooden pulpit with boredom, but did not droop, and his stomach had not been thickened by nipping at the gentian bottle. Upright, supple, easy, no moustache: he had taken the whistle out of his mouth and was playing with it, leaning over to say good morning to some friend: Louis and the traffic could wait.

Louis leaned his elbows on the handlebars with ostentatious patience and stared hatingly. He could not see the eyes behind the dark glasses but knew they were clear and healthy, commanding the Place De Lattre, with insolence, but without malice and without strain. There was nothing soured in his gestures. Twenty years ago, thought Louis, I was exactly like that.

The arm waved the wedge of traffic on amiably, knowing

that nobody would be angry at the extra minute, not on that lovely sunny day. It was childish, but there was a shadow on Louis' spirit.

And much worse was to come. On the bridge they were all held up again, and for longer, this time for a column of soldiers marching from the barracks with their music. They would be on the way back to the Place De Lattre and the memorial, for they were in parade dress – there must be a grand general come down to make a speech, invoke the Immortal Memory, probably distribute medals. It would be the anniversary of some damn thing – a marshal's birth, a marshal's death, loss of a marshal's virginity.

A crowd formed on the bridge approach; two gendarmes stood slackly at the bridge pedestrian-crossing – fat ones these, *with* moustaches – and everyone watched the soldiers approach without bad humour. Young conscripts, smart and even proud in their best uniforms, a bit self-conscious between the eyes of damned civilians. A few metres from the bridge the band struck up a fresh march; like all French marches rapid and vivid, with a gay irregular beat. The tune is known to everyone in France and to Louis too. 'En passant par la Lorraine avec mes sabots . . . ' – children sing a nursery rhyme to it: there you were, a woman by his shoulder, holding up her three-year-old to see, had started to go la-la. The child knew only the last line and sang that. 'Oh, oh-ho, a-vec mes sa-bots.'

The two gendarmes smiled, the crowd laughed, amused by the child, and started to sing too and stamp their feet, partly because they liked the verve of the rhythm, partly out of mockery, partly out of sympathy for the downy boys' faces trying to look grown-up and solemn under the tilted berets, partly because a French crowd has sometimes a certain jeering affection for the soldiers.

A sergeant marching alongside the column, an old pro with Indo-China and Algerian medals, mitraillette rigidly horizontal, steel along a steel forearm, winked at Louis as though he had seen a kindred spirit. Louis felt a quite illogical moment of shame. He turned his eyes aside and they rested on the child, still singing happily. Three years old; the shame changed to a dull, ground-down misery.

He closed his eyes; when the column was past a fat man in an auto behind him tooted angrily before he remembered to start and a hundred metres further a beat-up deux-chevaux van, all clatter and corrugated iron, cut in on him from the left and he nearly lost balance. No, not a good day. In fact a day that Louis dreaded above anything else. A Dresden day.

He started to ride fast, furiously, putting the bicycle in high gear deliberately to force himself to make an effort that would punish his knees and calf muscles. Good skiing exercise. He was ten kilometres out of the town, in the Jura foothills, in twenty minutes, over hill, under hill, and got off the bicycle staggering a little with breath coming heavy and knees yapping at him. A café had an inviting terrace under a chestnut tree, with asparagus fern all along a wooden balcony railing, and one of the little hill rivers pishing and chukkering under a bridge opposite. This all felt properly healing and he stopped for white wine and a look at the map. He was on the edge of the 'Good Land', where the corn was sprouting and the vines filling the terraces with young greenery, and the woodland of the dark pines. Since leaving the town he had been climbing steadily, but from now on the climb became steeper and sharper, the mountain streams that are the charm and delight of all the Jura more noisy and abrupt, breaking constantly into fan, ribbon or horsetail in their short cuts over rock.

A few more kilometres and a path he had been watching for opened on his left, a path he recognized and liked; he felt much better on it. The glass of wine, tart and young, had helped too. The path ran along a ridge. To climb higher, up to the watershed between the two rivers, one had to leave the bike and scramble over the slippery turf on foot, though it was worth it: it had been up there that he had first found wild cyclamens.

The path itself was just wide enough for a tractor, and the farmer had hardened it with rubble over the years till it had a ribbed rocky surface broken here and there by potholes still full of yesterday afternoon's rain, drying off now quickly in the hot sunlight. The path ran between hedges, rough windbreaks growing anyhow of hornbeam and bitter cherry and the all-invading acacia. Louis got off his bicycle at a gap that looked inviting, shoved his bicycle in among the mess of unpruned acacia, and looked up the long slant of hillside with pleasure; fields of mowing-grass in strips between the rough pasture and the spinneys of close woodland that were thick with untouched undergrowth, alive with game. Over his head the electricity cables drooping up towards the next pylon along the ridge made an alive keening noise.

Louis had respect for the mowing-grass, and followed the track where the soft turf had been rutted by the farmer's deux-chevaux, the only kind of mechanical thing that felt happy on this terrain. It was dotted with rabbit-droppings, feathers – a hawk had had dinner there. A grass-snake that had been enjoying the sun slid away terribly frightened and a hare lolloped for cover but was overcome by curiosity half way and sat up to inspect him. Louis went on uphill; the slope ended in a ridge that fell away in a confused way on the far side before climbing again to a higher, steeper peak: the top was crowned with a spinney which at this height was not just pine-trees, but a close mass of mixed timber that had never been thinned. Birch, thorn and pine, elm, dwarf oak and the ubiquitous acacia were all crowded together in a scrubby straggly tangle, full of rubbish, undergrowth and animals. There would certainly be a badger, and probably a fox to make war on the pheasants. The upper branches were already full of rooks, all talking at once as they do; they paid no attention to Louis, simply because he was not carrying a gun.

It was pleasant up there in the sunshine, away from the zing and crackle of the cables. The mowing-grass stopped and left a strip of rough turf broken by rocky outcrops that had stopped the plough being pushed up to the spinney. On the far side of the spinney the ground was rocky and too broken for any sort of cultivation, and it was there that Louis hoped to find maybe a few flowers. The farmer kept his ground neatly; the spinney had been lopped for firewood and a rough ditch around it kept the trees within their bounds. The farmer should have taken a billhook to this ditch last autumn but hadn't, and it was beginning to get insolent with brambles and barren strawberries. A wood-pigeon went off with a noisy fuss as Louis, a bit out of breath, came up the last of the rise. As he reached the ditch a most peculiar thing happened. A voice said, 'Thirst.'

Any sort of voice was unexpected, and a shock, up there, but this voice was more than shocking; it was frightening. A hoarse, plaintive, feeble voice, that of a man in pain who has already been many hours in pain, whose voice, even, has nearly ebbed away to coma and whose life is beginning to lose hold. Louis had heard such voices before, though not for many years. And he was quickly over the little shock, for while it was unexpected to hear this voice up here, it was not unimaginable. A tractor will sometimes overturn on a slope and pin a farm-hand under it; an early-morning poacher can have an accident with his gun – those acacia branches at gaps . . .

Where had the voice come from? Close by. Could it be within the spinney?

'Where are you?'

'Thirst,' said the voice again. It was no more than a croak; it was very near, certainly not in the spinney. Its owner had heard the step, or perhaps the breathing. Was it in the ditch? Louis ran a few steps and saw that a rocky hummock hid a dip: a man lay there, face down. It struck Louis immediately that it was not a farmhand, nor a poacher, for the man was wearing town clothes. And at that instant Louis realized that there was something much more peculiar still about this man. He had spoken in Russian.

Louis was so accustomed to hearing Russian that it had not struck him at all. Was it not his daily bread to hear the voices and put them into French without the slightest break in con-tinuity? The silky voice of Mr Tsara, the permanent delegate; the coarser, chesty burr of Mr Volapkhin, the Minister – though this voice had been like neither. Not that he had any *opinion* about it – who would or could, from a single word half gasped half yelped?

Louis ran the last steps, stumbled on a root, caught himself, went on his knees beside the figure that lay stretched with its face on its forearms. What a Russian was doing in the Doubs valley on a lonely rocky ridge did not bother him. After all, what was he doing there himself? And perhaps in a subconscious link-age of these scraps of idea as well as in excitement he spoke Russian himself. He was not only an interpreter as well as a translator – he had fought for two years on the Russian front.

24

'Where does it hurt?' And the voice, immediately, sounded frightened.

'Who are you? Where do you come from?'

'It doesn't matter,' kindly. He realized then and switched into French. 'Where does it hurt?'

'Did you know?'

'What? That you were here? No.'

'What are you doing?' with sudden ferocity. 'What do you want, here?'

Must be a bit delirious. But what could have happened to him?

'Just walking. Looking for flowers, a bit. Let me help you. Can you turn? Is it your leg?'

'No,' fiercely. 'Don't touch me. You can't help me. Go away.'

It was an *order*, thought Louis.

'That's all right, all right,' patiently. 'You need help, a doctor probably. I can fetch help and get you moved since you can't walk.'

The man laughed, a horrid cackle that really frightened Louis.

'I don't want any doctor.' There was such a long pause that Louis, kneeling there with his mouth open, thought the man had fainted. 'Go on – get away,' faintly. 'You can't help. Get out, pushti, look for flowers somewhere else.'

'You are thirsty,' slowly, in Russian. 'You want water. I can get you that. There isn't any on this hillside but at the bottom of the field I've a bottle. It'll take me fifteen, twenty minutes to go down and get back. Just be patient that long.'

'Are you Russian?'

'A bit.' What importance had that?

'Did you follow me? Did you know?'

'Know what?'

'You're a fool,' muttered the voice. 'Dead fool. Get your water. If you live that long.'

Delirious for sure, but what could be wrong with him? – whatever it was a sip of water could hardly hurt him. The neat, expensive town suit was draggled and wet; the man might have been there hours. If Louis got the farmer and the farmer got a doctor, and they could get the farmer's deux-chevaux up this slope . . . but first, water.

He was back in hardly more than ten minutes, panting, carrying the bottle of Vittel. He wrenched the cap off and knelt again – the man did not seem to have moved.

'I'll turn you over – can you sit up?'

'Don't touch me – give it here.' He moved with a sudden violent energy, his face turned away from Louis, shielding it with his uppermost arm from the sky – or from view? He reached out clumsily with his lower arm that lay awkward under his body. The hand was a mess of dirt and dried blood, looking more like a dirty claw than a hand. Perhaps he had been climbing – he might have fallen off rocks on to one of those filthy slopes of scree. But he was on *top* of a ridge. Louis placed the bottle upright on the grass inside the claw's grasp. The arm curled and cringed to hide the face; the claw scrabbled, knocked the bottle over, got it upright again, tilted it, spilling water over the elbow that hid the jaw, got the neck to the mouth; the man drank frantically, heaving and writhing his whole body, making sucking slobbering noises. When he stopped the bottle was two-thirds empty. The claw let it go, or perhaps just dropped it. Louis bent hurriedly to save what was left; there was blood around the mouth of the bottle. The head writhed back into the old position between the two upper arms. Both sleeves were smeared thick with blood and mucus. The man had a bad facial injury.

'Thank you,' the man said with more texture in the monotone voice since drinking. 'You're a pushti, but thank you.' There was a pause, again. 'Do you want a *reward*?' There was a jeer in the word, not an amiable mockery but a bitter ferocious joke. Louis was reminded of a time he had been with a Resistance group, that had caught a man suspected of having given another, larger group away to the occupiers.

'We only suspect,' a voice in his memory was saying, in this very tone. 'We don't *know*. So we'll just crop your ears into points.'

They had, with a razor.

'I have a reward,' suddenly from the ground, from the man who might, too, have been carved by a razor. 'But it's no good

26

to me; I'll soon be dead. A pity to lose it. I will make you a present – in return for the water. It's not far – and it's worth having, oh yes. You will see from me how much people find it worth having. From me – by me.' The chuckle was as sinister a sound as Louis had ever heard. This was not delirium; there was a nasty sort of consequence about it. The voice died away; Louis, kneeling holding the bottle, did nothing: he didn't know what to do.

'I wonder whether they went,' said the voice suddenly, talking to something deep in the man's interior where resolve still burned.

'Did you see anything on your way up here, pushti? Anyone, any person? Anything at all out of the way? Bar me.' There was another of those horrible laughs.

'No. The animals were all quiet too, so there is nobody about.'

'Were they indeed? That's very good to know. And you see nothing now?'

Louis looked, with more care than he had before. A pheasant walked out of the spinney twenty metres away, strutting in immense self-admiration. Two rabbits had come out for elevenses; the rooks were still gossiping in the same tea-party voices.

'There's nobody.'

'You can see this little wood, can't you?' Peculiar question. How could anyone fail to see it? – it was at least a hundred metres long, probably fifty deep, extremely dense. 'You could hunt for something a long time in there – something small. But if I was to tell you . . . it would be easy. True or not?

'You like flowers, pushti? I'll make you a present of a flower you won't find the like of in a hurry. You like flowers, I guess you can recognize a quince-tree. A wild one, a crab. There might be several. This one has a mark on the trunk. Dig down in the roots of that and you'll find a quince. Green – hard – not good to eat. . . .' It trailed off into another of those diabolical chuckles. 'Look after it well.'

'Why tell me?' lamely. He could make little sense of this quince chat. The man had something on his mind, that was plain. He had hidden something, probably stolen, and he was telling Louis where to find it – but why?

It was an irritation – and Louis recognized the familiar tug telling him he was becoming *involved*. That didn't do, he thought indignantly. He detested getting involved, in anything. He had his trowel, of course; his little stainless-steel one he used to lift plant roots.

Curiosity rebelled against the involved feelings, but he was not at all inclined to give in to it. What was it under the quince-tree? Was it responsible for bringing this man into this piteous – pitiable – state? Why was he a Russian? Who were 'any other people' that might have been around but weren't? Louis had had dealings with the Gestapo in his day – the fine days of his youth. That seemed ridiculous enough. There was nothing to get unduly *alarmed* about, was there?

What did alarm him – duly – was a wood-pigeon, that fire-siren of the countryside. He was planted there on one knee stupidly, day-dreaming about the past, when he had been called a terrorist and the Gestapo had called itself, prudishly, 'counter-terrorist measures', when the pigeon made him jump, and he felt suddenly he had to look round. A man was standing there behind him, smiling at him, and pointing a pistol at him. The pistol was a flat, snub, ungainly Browning type, looking about seven-sixty-five calibre. The man was not very tall, not fat either but one might perhaps say chubby; he had a bald forehead in front of dark bushy hair, and wore knickerbockers, and a loden cape. One would have said some-one like Louis – perhaps a German Louis to judge by the knickerbockers. Anyway a country-loving type, perhaps a bird-watcher – his binoculars were still around his neck.

He had a placid mellow face with nothing disagreeable about it at first; the pistol seemed unnecessary. But as Louis looked he did not like the smile, and behind it, he thought, there was a flat bad look, the look of a man who treads on spiders, snails, and all small inoffensive animals.

If Louis had not been living in a past where he had done exciting things, and certainly if he had not had supple skiing muscles, he would in a second from then have been a squashed spider. The man had waited for him to turn round and get a sickening realization, first, of what was coming to him. He had not wanted Louis never to know what hit him. He enjoyed waiting for knowledge to dawn, and that was why he smiled. If the man had not had this revolting instinct of sadism it would all have gone perfectly smoothly, but Louis had a reaction that belonged, properly, to a Louis who had been dead for twenty years, barring a possible day or two each year, the Dresden days as he called them, that he hated, dreaded.

A skier who falls with his skis crossed rolls on his back and twists; powerful muscles in his stomach and the back of his neck form a fulcrum that flips his body and brings him on to one hand with his skis straightened and his feet under him. Louis did this, not very neatly but the result was adequate. One hand on the ground; the other held a bottle. The bottle left the hand and settled on the chubby man's smile. The shot went off but winged upwards among larks. The chubby man jack-knived with surprise replacing satisfaction and Louis, in a frog crouch but jumping out of it off excellent quadriceps muscles, took him by the throat. The small harmless animal had become a scorpion.

Feeling thoroughly vicious Louis kicked the chubby man's feet from under him, banged the balding head on the grass, got hold of the right wrist, doubled it in, drove a knee into a stomach that was really too thick to stop all this happening, grabbed the pistol and used it to punch two holes – neat in front, less neat at the back – into the bald forehead. He got up with a tight throat. Most of what water was left had spilt but there was a mouthful still. He drank half of what there was without bothering about the trace of blood on the bottle and stood injecting air into himself.

The Russian – if he was a Russian – did not seem to have moved at all. He lay there incurious with his head on his forearms still. As though three shots from a medium calibre pistol interested him no more than a street-urchin picking its nose. Not anything one bothered *looking* at.

Louis felt suddenly sick of all this.

He bent down, took hold roughly of a damp, neatly tailored dark-blue worsted shoulder, and rolled the man straight over on his back. The man's face was unrecognizable as a face and there were no eyes left. There might have been an expression of fear, of horror, or of torment, but there was now no way of telling it.

Louis lost his balance and sat on the grass. 'God,' he said, and slowly got up again, trying to pull himself together.

'There was a man,' stupidly. 'Looked like a German, with knickerbockers. Ears stuck out. Going bald – he had a gun – I've shot him – know anyone like that?'

The man with no face was making no further effort to hide it, or turn, or bury himself in the short, pleasant-smelling grass of the hillsides in the Jura.

'Ah,' he said very calmly. 'He was there, after all. Never trust birds. He is a German. Was: I am, I was. I would have been. And you shot him, did you? I should like to have *seen* that.'

Louis had nothing to say to this.

'Is there any water left?'

'A very little. I threw the bottle at him; it spilt.'

'You've got the pistol, though.'

'I've got to get a doctor for you.'

'No.' It came out again in Russian, sharp. 'No doctors, no idiocies. Give me the bottle where I can reach it. Let me drink. The moment my mouth touches the water shoot me in the temple.'

Louis thought for some time and then did – no, it was a Louis he had forgotten existed – what he had been told. There didn't seem much a doctor could do for either man, and there wasn't a rabbit or a pheasant left within a square kilometre anyway, so the noise hardly mattered either.

He put the pistol in his pocket, without really knowing why. A municipal ambulance . . . a municipal form – didn't the Americans call it a Dead-on-Arrival? – a municipal grave-digger. . . . With a lot of hard work he got them both into the most ragged part of the ditch under the overgrown brambles, which scratched his arms and face. There was not a lot to show when he got back. Four copper jackets sprung on the grass – he tossed them in the spinney, and sent the empty blood-dabbled mineral water bottle to join them. In a few hours the uneven turf would not even show trampling. There was nothing left, was there, to mark the passage of souls and feet?

Was there? Something that reflected light was there gleaming at him by a tooth of rock – not bright, but with a shine – something small, moulded, like a plastic toy. It was a plastic toy, a small microphone looking as though it had been sold in a toyshop: 'The Young Radio Mechanic' in black on the lid of a red cardboard box. From it a thin, fragile plastic cable led back towards the spinney and disappeared in a bush where there would be hazelnuts some time. A metre from this bush was a hole at ground level in the tough, tangled stalks – made by the badger, perhaps. Louis made his shoulders small; the chubby man had got in all right. The stalks, moist and sappy with spring, did not rustle: the chubby man had made no noise either, coming out.

Inside was a nest made with a plastic-sprayed cotton poncho, effectively damp-proof. The chubby man had been warmly dressed in *sensible* clothes for crawling in hedgerows, and had not been greatly discommoded. He had not been able to see very well but that had not worried him; he had heard every whisper. His listening set was just like an ordinary transistor radio which, carried, attracts no attention whatever. He was quite well supplied too, with a large-scale map, bread and blood sausage, two big bottles of dark Munich beer, and three apples. He might have other things in his pockets but Louis was not going to look. It was even distasteful to be on his knees in the nest where the man had lain; he sat on his heels and his eye rested on a spot in the undergrowth, ten-seconds'-crawling away. Trunk buried under rubbish, branches crooked and untidy as they always are, wild sprays quarrelling with a spindly apology for a christmas-tree – a messy, sterile little bastard of a quince. Why not? These spinneys are full of everything imaginable. Louis wriggled his ten seconds' worth with a kind of self-contempt and scraped with his hand at the dead leaves. The trunk was covered in greenish mould but – no, that had not been made by any animal.

Louis lay flat on his back and stared up towards a very small patch of sky like someone looking for a *sign*. People who do this do not generally get one, but he did. Hanging above his head on a spiky twig, at hardly more than arm's length, a ring – he reached and got it – a cheap ring of thin brass with poor quality silvering that had worn off most of the surface. A cheap ring with cheap ideas: it was shaped into a skull and had once had bits of red glass stuck in the eye-sockets; a vulgar, trashy thing such as one no longer sees, even in Germany. Louis laughed and felt in his pocket for the little botanical trowel: the man had not been sure of finding his hiding-place for the mark might have become obliterated and that would have been frustrating. Louis started excavating vaguely in the leaf-mould. It would not be deep. He had intended to hurry off quick, since the chubby man might have friends – no, people like that did not have friends; say associates – but he had now forgotten this. The hider presumably had not brought a spade, nor, probably, a handy modern little tool like his own. He would have dug with a knife-blade and his hands.

It was surprisingly deep, though: about thirty centimetres; but the ground was not hard, being half touchwood and leaf-mould. It was a bundle of rotted, shredded stuff that had once been coarse brown wool, perhaps a piece of army blanket. Small bright centipedes had since made it their own. Inside this was a mildewy roll of some kind of oilskin. It was tied up like a rolled loin of bacon with rotted string which he broke without effort. Inside was a very dirty army shirt that looked as if it had come straight off a very dirty, probably lousy soldier. And inside that was a ragged piece, discoloured, abased, hacked into a rough square, of what once had been fine, heavy, plum-coloured silk velvet. A hard square thing was wrapped in the velvet.

It was a silver box, baroque eighteenth century, elaborate and decorative but with the essential simplicity that made it a thing of beauty. It had oval medallions of brightly painted enamel: fruit, flowers and butterflies, tiny and brilliant. It was a thing that had no exceptional value, but whose delicacy and femininity pulls the childish dirty hand of a looting soldier. It was big enough to hold a Breguet watch, thought Louis. It seems exaggerated, but people have taken this much trouble to hide Breguet watches, and have even killed for them. The tiny watchmaker's hinges opened easily and Louis saw that he had been conventional again. Bedded on a scrap of the same plum-coloured velvet was a very large diamond. He looked at it for some thirty seconds without moving, then put it back in the box, wound the box again in the velvet, thrust it into his inner pocket, thrust the wrappings into the hole he had dug, pushed back earth and centipedes, strewed and patted to make it natural, and wormed back the way he had come.

Strange: the chubby man had spent, probably, several hours in ambush, a carefully constructed ambush, to discover the hiding-place of a fantastic treasure, that had been a metre or so away from his dirty feet the whole while and was now in Louis' old jacket, a thing that had cost seven thousand eight hundred *ancient* francs four years ago and now held no more than mild interest for the rag-and-bone man. He did not know how the diamond had come to an obscure spinney in the Jura foothills, but he thought he knew where it had come from: it should, moreover, be quite easy to find out.

He reeled in the microphone cable and stopped at the entrance to look carefully: there was nothing to see. He got up, wiped his hands on the sides of his trousers, and met nobody on his way downhill. His bike was not hidden, but would cause no comment. The farmer, and a few other people, used the path between the hedges daily, but he did not think anyone would be going to the top of the field for some time. The farmer had no particular interest in the spinney at this time of year, nor would other people, he thought. It led nowhere particular, it wasn't the mushroom season, there weren't any lilies-of-the-valley here – if there were it was too early for them – and the weather was unstable.

Someone would appear sooner or later. The chubby man had counted on that. He had tortured the Russian, who had not spoken, and had left him there as a staked-out bait, thinking presumably that the Russian, maddened by pain and fogged by delirium, would talk to himself – or might even let his secret drop if anyone did happen along. The ironic thing was that when the anyone – Louis, damn it – happened along the Russian had not let his secret fall out of weakness or fever. He had done it on purpose, heaven knew why. What had gone on in the blinded head; what fiercely black joke had lodged there? Had he known that the chubby man had stayed there in hiding?

Louis had not up to now been frightened because he had not had time but now, back on his bicycle, he was frightened. The chubby man had very likely pals as nasty as he was. They would find the two bodies without difficulty, and they would draw conclusions. The farmer might pick that very day to stroll up there. . . . The shots would not have carried from the top of the field, but anyone might have seen his bicycle, might even have had the curiosity to read the little identity plaque on the frame. . . . Louis pedalled down the lane with his skin crawling. The farmer would go straight to the police, and Louis did not care for that idea at all. The lane seemed unusually full of people, and they all seemed to stare curiously at him. An evident countryman, it was true, in patched overalls and rubber boots, towing a decrepit trailer behind a ratty bike: an obvious farmer's wife with a tanned wrinkled face. But who was the smiling man in the black 404? What was he doing in the lane?

He told himself not to be a fool: he forbade himself to stop in the village for a marc he wanted badly: he repeated all the way home that it was the vet come to castrate a calf or something. The silver box was large and uncomfortable; it all added up to evil presage. Ghosts from a past he had resolutely buried had arisen, gibbering, rattling chains and winding sheets, all the classical ghost properties. For he felt pretty sure.

To make sure, directly he got home, he locked the silver box in his bureau, and ran straight out again on foot. The information he wanted should be easy to find in a book; he went over the bridge to the old town.

It was the kind of bookseller whose shop is full of stuff nobody buys. Coffee-table books on Byzantine Mosaics, Giotto and Dürer at a hundred and forty francs the throw, travel books more expensive than going there to see for yourself, the *Golden Age of Landscape Gardening*, simplistic, giving you the idea you could do it yourself after half an hour's study. But he found what he was looking for inside a minute: he was not surprised; he had known he would – it was *ordained*.

Yes, here was Dresden, peeled like an onion for him skin by skin. Back at home he lit a cigarette feverishly. Great fire of 1491, definitive form of schloss 1550, Sophienkirche 1660 – he turned pages, got to kings – Moritz, Christian the First – still nothing. Artists – better; this was firmer ground. Now he could even recall the town, it grew vivid before him, forgotten names clicked into places and buildings rose up like the phoenix. Nosseni, the Brühl Terrace, Poppelmann, when were we going to get to the Zwinger? Yes, here at last – the Treasure Rooms, the 'Grünes Gewölbe', that was it surely. He read on feverish – seven rooms, Leplat, Court Goldsmith Dinglinger . . . Ivory Room, 'Hofhalt des Grossmoguls', 'Bath of Diana', Kändler . . . no. Expectation and excitement tailed off; there was nothing after all. But it had to be, it must be, he told himself.

He realized then that this was an art book. The writer was not interested in things not made by man. The eccentricities of Augustus the Strong, who swopped a regiment of dragoons for a pair of porcelain vases, delighted him, but the famous collection of jewels was of little interest. Not even the Dresden Green, all forty carats of it. He had not even thought it worth mentioning.

But it existed. Every visitor to Dresden had seen it, and Louis too – had he not spent the most precious months of his life in Dresden? Was it not in a sense his treasure, his forty carats, his Dresden Green? He had said to Fabienne, one day, jokingly: 'You are my green diamond – the most precious thing in Europe.' And he had it in his bureau drawer!

It had not been removed. Who would ever conquer Dresden, jewel at the heart of the Thousand Year Reich? Who would ever bomb it? And bombing had not destroyed a diamond.

It had been lost. The story ran that the Russians had looted it. Perhaps what he had found bore that out. It had been a German army shirt – he should know! But why should not a Russian wear a German shirt? Better than his own maybe, if indeed he had any. . . . It was of no consequence. It was of no consequence either that one of the world's most extraordinary treasures, a thing worth staggering sums, should have come to him. What should he do with it? Sell it? The thing was not worth a penny. All the diamonds in the world were not worth one of the people that had died. And on the night of February in nineteen forty-five when the city of Dresden, architectural jewel of Europe, had been wiped out, more than a hundred thousand people had been wiped out with it. A hundred and twenty thousand, the official figure was, he believed. Official figure indeed! Double it! Even if one accepted the famous

35

official figure, it was enough. It had been the great holocaust of the war. More victims – civilian victims – than the fire-bombing of Tokyo. More than Hiroshima! He knew the dreary little tale by heart; there was no need to go to a book for it. Facts, nothing but facts. Dresden had been destroyed. Buildings, people, treasures. Among the people had been his wife and his three-year-old son. Nothing had survived that rain of fire except the Dresden Green Diamond.

He could not stay still; he was distracted out of all self-control. In a sort of delirium he ran to the bureau, put the silver box in his pocket, rushed out.

Of course going down the endless stone stairs calmed him. He had regained self-possession by the time he reached the bottom. He had even regained automatic, meaningless gestures like stopping in front of his post-box. Not that anyone ever wrote him letters. Typewritten envelopes, municipal bumf, the Percepteur des Impôts, the Mairie, the Sécurité Sociale. Today too there was one, a typewritten envelope. Some circular – no, the paper was of too good a quality! What did he care? He thrust it in his pocket; it would wait.

He walked along the road to a café, the quiet over-furnished kind that would calm his fever. He wanted marc but this was not the place. Potato schnapps more than likely! – he ordered a cognac and sat at a table. It was too much trouble to talk, to think.

It was possible, perhaps, to justify the bombing of Tokyo. Even Hiroshima had, it was said, shortened the war. But Dresden was an act of wantonness, of wickedness. Hitler had ordered Rotterdam to be bombed, Paris burnt – did that excuse it? Massacred the Jews – did that alter it? Dresden had never been bombed; not only was it far away from bombers' bases, but there was nothing there, no military installations, no industrial complexes, no great strategic marshalling point of men or material. Nothing that made a difference to the War Effort. The old Saxon capital on the Elbe; lying in the garden of Germany, in cornland and vineyard; famous as a centre of beauty. That was why he had sent Fabienne there. One still ate, there, one was quiet, but it was not only safe, it was beautiful, and that had been important too, in '44. Towns of

36

Strauss operas, of Weber and Wagner, of the huge rich orchestra with twelve horns, the most harmonious, the most exquisite in its homogeneity, in Europe. Town of the Vermeer Procuress and the Raphael Madonna. Town of the Zwinger, the Albertinum, the Frauenkirche.

What was it they had wanted to destroy? The statue to Weber, or the packed mass of refugees? Had anyone known just how many people there were in Dresden? As many as Eichmann's trains had carried to Auschwitz? The bombers had made as efficient, as neat, as not-messy a job of killing as the most punctilious German could wish for.

Louis knew all the excuses, the lame and feeble explanations. The Germans, so had declared a pathological little maniac of a general, could always patch up and mend, when specific targets were damaged. But it would take them months to restore the services and labour forces of a whole community.

That was what you called putting it in a nutshell! The services and labour forces of a whole community – there was a phrase . . .

In February, nineteen forty-five, it had been decided that the community of Dresden might win the war for Germany. And with perfect visibility and no opposition, the community had been destroyed and the destroyers first handsomely praised and then decorated. It had later – quite a while later – been admitted that 'there might have been some over-bombing'.

There were more reasons. Always there are such good reasons. There was a threatening situation: V twos, and schnorkel submarines, coming into action. And Dresden was full of both, naturally? Well no, not exactly, but you see it was felt desirable to strike a discouraging blow at Germany. That was a very good adjective, was it not? They had certainly *discouraged* everybody.

And then of course the Prime Minister – or had it been the Pope? – had wished to have targets in Eastern Germany attacked. He hadn't wished the Russians to become discouraged.

And naturally, Bomber Command had long wished to *reach*

out into Eastern Germany, and they could now do so without incurring *heavy loss*. Dresden was ideal for that. Bomber Command, doubtless feeling that Augustus the Strong, in his good city between 1694 and 1733, had also caused heavy loss. Very well, he would now be made to regret it.

It was a piece of strategic bombing. If you want to know, tactics is shooting at a soldier in a different uniform, but strategy is dropping a bomb on the eighteenth century.

Governments were all the same, naturally. The English had been discouraged by the Americans thinking it immoral for people to have colonies. The Americans, poor chaps, had been discouraged by the Russians not behaving like gentlemen about Berlin. The French, discouraged by everybody, were now being discouraging to everybody right back – enjoying it, what was more. As for Germans, nothing ever discourages them, not even their own history.

Louis knew what he was talking about. He had been as discouraged by governments as most people.

Louis Schweitzer. Born in Alsace in 1918, he had been registered as Ludwig, and baptized as Louis. Accomplished his military service in France. Remobilized in '39. Entered the Resistance in '40, arrested in '42, deported to a camp.

His father, Frédéric Schweitzer, had been born in Alsace too, under the German occupation. He had crossed over in '14 to volunteer – had fought with the French army till '17. He had come back without his right arm, to say that it would not be long now.

The grandfather, Marc Schweitzer, had fought at Belfort in '70, with Denfert-Rochereau. He had opted in '71 for French nationality, but he was a stubborn old man, and instead of going with the settlers to Algeria he had gone back to Alsace to be beastly to the Germans.

Louis, applying for a post under French administration after the war, had needed a certificate of French nationality for the dossier. It had been refused. He had been born in German-ruled Alsace. His father had never applied for the 'certificat de réintégration de plein droit' made legally necessary after '18. He had no right arm to sign it with, if indeed he had ever heard of it. Louis, sighing, applied to the mayor of the community where he was born for this famous certificate with the fine name, and was told indulgently that it did not arise. Had not his grandfather opted for French nationality in 1871?

Louis told the *authorities* that nobody had asked him for any certificate the day he entered the French army, or on the day he got married, or on the day he got a Resistance decoration. They were unmoved. He discovered other people later in the same boat. He even heard of a general, and a most distinguished one, who had fought through *both* wars, was loaded with medals and citations, and wasn't French either. . . . He had got into the paper for it. He wasn't worried. He was a general with a pension. But Louis had been ground fine by the millstones of bureaucracy.

He needed *some* nationality: he didn't much care what. He had gone to the Germans – he knew how to manage them! They had maintained of course that he was French, but they were floored by the legality of an embarrassing decision of Adolf's, made when he was Head of the German State. Anybody, he had said, wherever he comes from, who volunteers for the Waffen SS, shall have the right to receive on demand the *privilege* of German nationality. Louis, arrested on suspicion of Resistance activity, and deported to Neuengausen, had – to save his skin, and Fabienne! – volunteered for the Russian front. And to make it really good had insisted, with an impudence characteristic of him in those days, on being sent to a Waffen SS unit. He had done pretty well there too. Had got out with several wounds and a handful of medals. He had got his German nationality – as though he cared! His sins had always been against 'le bon ordre'. Just like the mayor who against regulations had put a homeless family with ten children into a municipal lodging that had already been *allotted*. Sanctions had been taken – the mayor was no longer mayor. When it came to being *discouraging* . . .

What was he to do with the worthless treasure of Augustus the Strong that fortune had bestowed upon him with such *amusing* and ironic courtesy? He had killed two men to get it. He was a murderer. On which thought he got up and went home blindly, without looking right or left, or noticing one single thing or person upon his passage.

Friday Afternoon

It decidedly would not do to go to the police. He was not only the copybook patsy for the unexplainable presence of two dead bodies but he was in possession of the Dresden Green. He was perfectly aware that despite his resistance decorations, despite his present utter respectability, there existed some question marks on a dossier buried in the cellars of the préfecture. Louis had turned up in the Jura in the autumn of 1944, wearing a German uniform. With medals from the Russian front. Small wonder that a local partisan group, a decidedly communist organization, had viewed him with suspicion. Even the highly successful delivery of five of the area Sicherheitsdienst group, trousers round their ankles, had increased rather than allayed this suspicion, despite a clear and provable record of resistance activity up to 1942. What exactly *had* he been doing in Germany between '42 and '44? How was it that he had avoided death in Neuengausen? If Louis turned up wearing two dead men in his buttonhole, one Russian and the other German, and loot from Dresden in his pocket, there was no knowing quite what might happen. There were people who had said that Louis was no more than a fellow more adept than most at changing sides at the right moment.

He took the silver box out of his pocket and tossed it on the bureau. With it came the letter he had picked out of his postbox an hour or so ago. It fluttered to the floor and he picked it up mechanically; it was only then that he noticed that there was neither stamp nor postmark on the envelope. Municipal and government offices spread, besides, their names, addresses, and frequently futile functions all over their envelopes. Whereas this was a plain, bare white envelope. Name and address typed. No more. It still could be a circular, of course. The way to find out was to open it. It astonished him that he should need resolution to do anything so simple. The diamond had changed him already. Inside the envelope was a sheet of white paper, the same good plain quality as the envelope had been, holding a half-page of formally spaced, properly composed typing, neatly paragraphed.

'Monsieur Schweitzer,

'I have reason to believe that you have come into possession of an object whose considerable worth you have not failed to notice. This object is the property of the German nation, which I am charged to protect. Failure to return this object to those responsible for its safe custody would have grave and painful consequences. To publicize the circumstances in which you gained possession of this object would be most unwise and I must seriously dissuade you from such a course. Your loss would be irrevocable.

'The action I propose is simple, discreet, and advantageous. Please be so good as to place the object in question in the same depository in which you found this letter. You will notice, the next time that you pass, that the object has been restored to its legal owners, and has been replaced by a sum I judge to be fit compensation for your cooperative discretion and the mental anguish you have undergone. Five thousand francs.

'I have no wish to involve you in explanations with the judicial authorities, nor, you will agree, is it in your interest to involve yourself.

'That you may be convinced beyond doubt both of my confidence and my good faith you will now find, as you place the object in the spot named, that half the sum named has already been deposited for your convenience. The sum of two thousand five hundred francs is in clean bills of one hundred francs, enclosed in a plain envelope, and I assure you that they are neither stolen nor counterfeit. Upon your return a similar envelope will be awaiting you.

'I have the honour to remain, dear Mr Schweitzer,

'Your obedient servant

'Squiggle'

Under the squiggle, in a magnificent German phrase, was a heavy embossed stamp that said 'The Committee for Recovery of Works of Art, Property of the German Nation'.

Louis burst out laughing. It was extraordinary to recover his sensations, his thoughts, his opinions, his instincts, of twenty years before, but that, he realized, was what had once again happened. The click – and he started to laugh. The impudence of them – and he had been frightened!

As a boy, like every boy, he had read Dumas. Now a passage that had been one of his favourites slid back into his memory, that in which Fouquet, the presumed all-powerful Surintendant of Finances, is warned that Colbert is about to attack him and that this enmity is dangerous.

'Such men are like meteors,' says the speaker, in a mysterious, sinister manner, 'only known when they strike.' Fouquet is amused. A meteor! Oh, oh, how dramatic! 'Corbleu,' says Fouquet pleasantly. 'We confront the meteor.'

Louis knew immediately that he too was going to confront this meteor. Germans were only Germans. He had dealt with them before. Naturally he needed to think a little. He wished to know where the concierge was, he needed to rethink himself a little into the skin of the old, the forgotten Louis, but he would, oh yes he would. They did not know who he was!

They were competent, evidently, as well as rapid. They had wasted no time in learning – from the name and address on his bicycle identity plaque; it could be nothing else – quite a lot about him, to judge by the letter. Age, job, general characteristics, probable behaviour. A middle-aged, clerical, timid person. Intelligent enough – there had not been a lot of menace, and it had been neatly coated with chocolate. That would have surprised them – he had after all *killed* the chubby man – but they would have concluded that their chubby pal had been clumsy, negligent and over-confident, whereas really, of course, he had simply been over-nasty!

There were a lot of things they did not know. They did not, for example, know that he was not afraid. He had just considered the possibility of being shot in the street or otherwise attacked with violence. Not that they would – yet! But they could not know that he did not give a damn. He had no candy-coloured hopes from life. He was more worried about what he should do than about what they might do.

They wouldn't try any melodramatic stuff like running him over in the street. It might attract the attention of the police, who would be indifferent to the recovery of German Works of Art. Of course if they did, thought Louis acidly, the most it would cause would be annoyance. There was no one to feel sorrow for his death. Annoyance to his colleagues, who would have to contribute for a wreath – and delegate a victim to carry it! Annoyance to Mr Mestli, the head of Administration at the Europahaus for translations, a pleasant fellow who loved little charts and graphs made in four-colour ballpoint, and who would be aggrieved. To the concierge, who would have to tidy the flat, arrange for the junk-dealer, show to prospective tenants, train the chosen lamb in her fussy dustbin routine. She liked him: he never made the stairs dirty, made no noises, paid his bills promptly, neither caused nor uttered complaints, and never had boring people disturbing her by inquiring after him and then moaning because there was no lift! Never, that is to say, till now, possibly . . .

He had nobody. No-bo-dy. Splendid. It was an advantage. They could not possibly know how little he had to lose.

Nor did they know his past. They knew nothing about Dresden, about Fabienne. They did not know that he disliked East Germans, who had left the ruins of Dresden just lying there. If it had been Poles now, who had against all economic sense insisted obstinately on building Warsaw stone for stone up again exactly as it had been before, he would, very likely, have given the diamond back with no hesitation.

They would try to kidnap him, as they had the Russian. That would not be as easy as it sounded; he was expecting it. No no, this fellow who had written the letter might be able and capable of thinking up clever things but he, Louis, was also able.

Was it the letter, or was it the possession of the diamond, that had so reinflated his vanity?

Louis finished smoking his cigarette and began to pack a holiday suitcase. He didn't quite know what he intended to do but he intended to keep his diamond. He put on his working suit and his raincoat; he did not pack much – spare trousers and underclothes. The diamond he tucked into a pair of socks. There was still room in the case when he had finished, and he tarew in a few more things, the type one always thinks one will want, which one never uses at all, and curses on the journey for making the case needlessly heavy. Like the pistol he had taken from the chubby man. What on earth did he think he was going to do with that? Or the book about Dresden.

He put the silver box in his raincoat pocket and leaned over the balcony. Nobody was in the courtyard below. He hadn't expected there would be; getting into the house was something that needed careful preparation, which they had no time for. He sent the case down on the rope-lift and jumped down the stairs feeling his eyes clear, not watery, not bloodshot! Pottering about in the hallway was the concierge.

'Ah, Madame Hagenbeck.'

'Oh it's you. What, off on a holiday?'

'Probably not more than a fortnight,' airily. 'Keep any post, will you? I'll give you my key: I've locked the flat.'

'All right. Have a pleasant time. Looks like we might get some more sun, now,' amiably enough.

'I'll call a taxi on the phone if I may.'

With satisfaction he saw that she was going to mop the hall-way, polish the knocker, the bell-pushes, the lids of letter-boxes! His timing had been good: that should give him a good start. He left his own letter-box alone.

'Europahaus,' he told the driver, glancing round as he got into the taxi, with the jauntiness of someone who has got rid of the heroin and feels his conscience quiet. Yes, there was a little dark-blue Simca with two inhabitants that appeared to be taking an interest. He gave the concierge the little wave one has for Tante Mathilde after a stay, affection for her swelling as one leaves her on the step.

At the side entrance of the Peace Palace he left his case with the doorkeeper, a fat man who was a stickler for observances: it would be quite safe there. He wondered whether the two clowns with their Simca had followed him; he had seen nothing from the taxi. He didn't feel worried.

There was no session this morning, and tourists were wandering about admiring the bronze busts of Kennedy, Robert Schumann, and the heroic Comrade Chairman Matusjek. He walked along to the office where Mr Mestli would certainly be busy with his little charts.

'Why, hallo, Louis, good afternoon. But we've nothing on today; what brings you here?'

'I just stopped by to say I'd have to ask you to do without me for a little while.'

'What's the matter then? No family troubles, I hope?' He knew perfectly well that Louis had no family.

'More a kind of family business. I need to have my hands free for some few days.'

'Well now, Louis, that's all very well. Delighted to oblige you at any ordinary time, of course, but you've forgotten the Oder-Neisse debate, haven't you? I could see what I can do at the end of next week.' The idiot was already fussing with his chart.

'No, now: my business won't wait, alas.'

'Hum. That would have to come under the heading of emergency leave, wouldn't it, Louis, now? I can't let you have that, as you know, without written justification, can I now? I'd have the Under Secretary after me.'

'Very well, I'm ill,' irritably. 'Since apparently you want me to be ill, I've acute nervous fatigue, and when Mr Tsara is speaking I'm liable to lose the thread altogether – and then we'd have to tell the Under Secretary that you insisted on my staying – and *he'd* have to explain to Mr Tsara, which he won't like at all.'

'Now now, Louis,' conciliatory, 'no need to bother the Under Secretary, and no need to make a drama as though you were being oppressed. The point is that without you we'll be short-handed and then Mr Tsara – '

'Have I ever asked for an exception? Have I ever failed you? Don't I have the right to expect a request to be granted without this damned shilly-shally?'

'Oh it's too bad,' said Mr Mestli, which was his way of saying 'merde'. He made a furious annotation in green ball-point. 'Just as I was confident of getting through the week without a panic.' At that moment the telephone rang. He arranged his features – it might be the Under Secretary – but listening he relaxed unctuous lips back into cross petulance and pushed the standard across the desk.

'Some agitated female wanting you.'

'You don't think I *invented* the need for a break, do you?' in a disagreeable voice. He had a sense of foreboding. The phone quacked at him.

'Oh, Mr Schweitzer, I didn't know where else to try and find you. It's good that you're there – at least, I *hope* it's good.' The concierge's voice was ominously excited, and had a sniffy, censorious tone. 'The police are here and what they may want with you I do not know, but I thought it my duty to try and call you, nobody can say I'm not above board, and it's my duty of course to tell them you're there, and I'm sure I hope you've no cause to dread their coming, Mr Schweitzer, leaving as suddenly as you did. They've a search-warrant, and they insisted on my opening your letter-box as well as the flat, and I stood there of course and they behaved quite properly but why have they searched your flat so minutely is what I feel I have a right to know, Mr Schweitzer, considering my responsibilities – '

He cut into it; it was too shrill. Mr Mestli's eyebrows were gathered into an elaborate arch of amused query.

'No cause for concern, Madame Hagenbeck. You simply tell them I'm here. I haven't run away. And you need have no worries; it's not anything that would interest the newspapers.' This was malicious of him; she had certainly had happy thoughts of finding herself the vedette of the boulevard press. 'Concierge Vital Link in Great Dope Shake-up: Key Witness Speaks Out.'

'Well, I'm certainly glad to hear you say so: you know I'd never dream of imagining you doing something wrong.'

'Quite. And now you can feel perfectly happy. I've no doubt they'll warn you to be discreet, so I won't need to repeat that, will I?'

'Oh no no – but I'm glad there's no trouble.'

'None whatever. Thank you for ringing.'

He put the phone down with as much gentle steadiness as he could command. Mr Mestli was shiny and swollen with expectancy.

'Did I really hear the woman say police?'

'You did. My concierge. Don't worry; they're not after me. I told you I needed a free hand.' Fellow beamed, toad that he was.

'*I see.* Well, I can be discreet too. And as for the leave, since the police need your assistance, we'll say no more about it, shall we? I'll manage somehow.'

'Good of you.' He turned abruptly, hoping his knees would

carry him across the room, and closed the door with exaggerated softness so as not to wake any sleeping babies. He had underestimated these people; they had certainly lost no time. They now knew that he was in this building with the Dresden Green diamond; they would probably not have notions of playing policeman here, but they would also know that he could stay in the building a limited length of time.

From the lavatory window he could survey the frontage, and needed no binoculars to see the blue Simca. As he watched it was joined by an unostentatious dusty black Mercedes, containing three men, which made five. They had a conference; it was too far to distinguish any features and the most he could say was spring overcoats and businessmen's hats like anyone else.

Well. . . . He had still resources, of course. Bluff was always the best way with Germans. Much better to have no papers at all than false papers. He could walk straight up to them, extremely stiff and pompous, and inform them in ringing tones that he knew nothing about German works of art, and cared less, and he had felt it his duty to hand the whole thing over to the Under Secretary – or even the Secretary . . . that would stop their gallop for a few hours, and during that time he could probably shake them off. That damned suitcase was a nuisance; he wished he hadn't brought it, now.

All his vanity had ebbed away, and he felt very old. Talking about 'shaking them off' – where was he going to go? Dresden didn't exist any more. How foolish he had been. Bathing in a rosy memory of past exploits – but those days were absolutely prehistoric. He was aged nearly fifty, and was proposing to play hide-and-seek with a crowd that was probably laughing its head off at his preposterous tiny manoeuvres. Success – over-easy – with the chubby man had given him false confidence by recalling the happy time when he had scoured across Europe like a Tartar, with his star. Had he not had Fabienne?

In the tightest spots he had been in he had never thought he would not get out again. Even in France, in forty-two, when he had been put in the local police cells to await the arrival of the area Gestapo commandant – and he had known that it hung on a pretty thin thread. . . . The baby had been four, five months old? Fabienne had wheeled the go-cart along the dank street behind the police-barrack exercise yard, talking to the baby in an exaggeratedly clear voice. He had had a cell on that side – the star! – and had answered with his uproarious loud laugh that she called his shocking laugh. That was the best message he could send, and would startle these owls into the bargain. . . . She had moved on, to avoid any suspicions of contacts, and had strolled back along the rank alley twenty minutes later, and had started to sing. Her voice was not big, but gained strength to pierce the slimy brickwork to where he was lying on a bare concrete shelf with his jacket folded under him for a pillow, hands behind his head, wishing he had a cigarette. At home when Fabienne sang it was, quite likely, 'I want to marry the butcher's boy, the butcher's boy for me' or one of the terribly gooey songs of the thirties that she enjoyed: 'Twas on the Isle of Capri that I met ha-ar' or even 'Red Sails in the Sunset'; and it was typical of Fabienne that here she should have chosen to sing Cherubino's song. In Italian: Italians were allies; nobody could complain about that, could they? And an *Austrian* composer. 'Voi che sapete . . . ' He had known. He had got out. He would always get out, till the February night in Dresden.

This diamond was a paltry thing. Why had he resolved to keep it, when everything else had been melted into ash? Or was there some fragment of Fabienne somewhere still, that had crystallized in the fire? Was not a diamond carbon? She was carbon. He could trust her: if she turned into a diamond it would be a forty-carat green one.

Louis sat in the room that was used by the translators as their standby room, very like the 'Final Lounge' at an airport, waiting for one's flight to be called. It was a large room with a boarding school look given it by little lockers where the women kept their knitting and the men crosswords and paperback copies of *War and Peace*, or *Splendeurs et misères des courtisans*. The centre of the room had the airport, or rather the provincial-hotel, touch: uncomfortable armchairs arranged round glass-topped tables, and ashtrays with vermouth advertisements. There were two writing tables with official Peace Palace paper and envelopes, a beige Ministry-of-Works carpet, and some approved M-o-W pictures, and on one wall the big clock and the electronic 'scoreboard' that summoned them and told what was going on in the Chamber. It was part of a kind of suite kept for translators, with an austere canteen on one side – alcoholic drinks not provided – and garde-robes and wash-rooms on the other. Most translators belonged to little cliques, with their own shop, private jokes, recognition signals, a per-petual revolving card game or a syndicate for betting the race-horse 'tiercé'. Louis didn't.

At the moment, there was no sitting, and nobody to interrupt his meditation, so that he looked up almost with indignation when somebody came in. It could have been worse! It was Madame Wisniewski, a dumpy, inelegant soul on the Polish section. At least, Louis told himself, she was a lone one; not a sunny chatterer who would ask him whatever was he doing here. What after all was she doing here? She had no curiosity, and after a glance and her habitual little bow 'good afternoon, Mr Schweitzer', she went over and got out her library books, evidently off to change them. He was opposite, and since he had nothing to do watched with a vague interest: her cupboard was tidy – most of them overflowed with rubbish directly the door opened, and a few were perfect apothecary's shops where one could be sure of getting aspirin, cough-remedy, keep-awake pills and even sophisticated things like de-sensitizing sprays – translators were a neurotic crowd, much given to itches, tickles, nervous allergies, and comparing illnesses. Wisniewski was one of the few obstinate, abominably healthy ones who didn't even have occupational hazards like laryngitis.

Louis quite liked her. She was dowdy in a sympathetic way, and she was kind. She never complained at late duty, and would always fill in for someone pretending laryngitis – for a girl or a concert. She never gave Mr Mestli occasion to use his india-rubber on the charts. Louis had never really looked at her. Now he did. She wasn't anything to write home to mother about. Legs a bit solid – would have been quite nice had she worn higher, more frivolous shoes. Figure a bit hippy, more comfortable than graceful. Top half tolerable, neck clean, straight ash-blonde hair that might have been pretty but lacked lustre, lifted off the neck and pinned up with combs in a pretty, unself-conscious style, that of someone who never reads fashion magazines.

Her back was to Louis, but he knew she had good teeth, the wrong shade of lipstick, nose on the snub side, rather coarse skin, and over-small eyes, colour of the North Sea on a winter day, below eyebrows that had never been plucked. She was about forty, he supposed; he had heard vaguely she was a widow. She was quite bright – had a sworn-interpreter's job with the Poles as well as doing Sim. Tran. But she had struck him always as a sensible woman. Still, he was surprised to hear his own voice.

'Madame Wisniewski.' Urh, he cleared his throat; it had come out a bit false. She turned round. 'I beg your pardon.'

'Why?' Politeness, calmness, goodness.

'Are you in a hurry?' awkwardly.

'Not a bit. I was only on the way to the library. I've loads of time.' Her French was good – professional. Her voice soft and clear – well, that was professional too. There was a sort of old-fashioned simplicity about her. She did not try to be complicated to make herself interesting.

'Really – I would like to ask your advice about something.'

Worse than ever. What had possessed him? But no titter, no archness – 'Oh I always give good advice.' She simply sat down, put her books on the odious glass-topped table, set her handbag on her lap, changed her mind and put it on the floor, listened. Neither suprised nor bothered.

'Something extremely disconcerting has happened – would you like a cigarette?'

'I don't smoke; thank you though.'

Louis found himself telling her what had happened since that morning. The wall clock, whirring round, took a quarter of an hour: she hadn't moved or interrupted.

'It's obviously no good at all suggesting the police.'

'They wouldn't believe me, I'm afraid. They give me no trouble, since I'm a quiet person and interfere with nobody. But if I came to them with this tale they'd look up my past, which was a bit stormy. They'd find I had been regarded with suspicion once on political grounds, and that I had once been mixed up with these people in the east. I feel sure they'd regard me as more guilty than anything else. I have to try and defend myself on my own.'

'Yes, I see. On your own is asking rather a lot. There wouldn't be any harm, would there, I mean in anyway making use of them, as far as one could? I mean in getting out of here,' with a comic, serious innocence. Louis felt pleased, suddenly. This dowdy Polish woman was an ally, the first he had met.

'I know what you mean, I know Gérard – that's the thick one with the dark moustache. He's a nice fellow; I'm quite friendly with him. I don't know any of the others much – I didn't notice who was on today.'

'It's Necky,' she said. 'That's what I call him. He looks forbidding – but he's nice, really.'

He knew who she meant, an elderly depressed policeman with an awkward bony body and a habit of carrying his head on one side, as though he had a rheumaticky shoulder.

'I know him of course. I've never spoken to him though.'

'He's sort of gruff. I've spoken to him though, quite often. It seems to me the urgent thing is getting out of here. I mean you can't just stay, with five of them hanging about. And that pretending to be police – they might even try to get *in*. Even if they don't care it's dismal sitting here, and sort of hopeless.'

'Yes. I got Mestli to give me a fortnight off.'

She brightened. 'Oh, that's good. You don't have to come running back. I'm not on till Monday,' she added thoughtfully. He wondered what that had to do with it.

'I think Necky would help us.' Us, indeed. . . . 'You've got a case, you said.'

'Yes, in the doorkeeper's little place. I told my concierge I was going on a holiday. I had to come and see Mestli. I thought I had an hour at least but they let no grass grow.'

'No,' seriously. 'Where were you making for? I mean to shake them off, evidently, but where?'

'The station, I suppose. I have plenty of money. I hadn't thought it out. I need somewhere to consider in peace just what I ought to do with this thing.'

'But you have friends, or relatives, someone you feel you can trust – where you could stay?'

Louis felt foolish again.

'I'm afraid I haven't.'

She thought, without looking at him, without not-looking at him: just thinking. She would always stop to think it out, even in the middle of the street. Even if it was only a question of some knitting wool, a good bargain, marked down because slightly faded, she wouldn't just run in and buy it. She would stop first to think it out carefully, not letting herself be chatted up.

She got up, unlocked her cupboard, and put the library books back.

'I can do that any time.' She picked up the handbag and tucked it under her arm. 'I'm going to go and have a word with Necky.'

Louis just sat there impotent. When she came back twenty minutes later he was still sitting, feeling stunned, not knowing what to think, thinking of nothing, or perhaps like an animal pretty low on the biological scale. Like an oyster perhaps, which presumably thinks of closing its shell to avoid getting eaten. She was carrying his suitcase, but he just went on not-thinking, not asking how she had got it from the concierge.

'I think it will be quite easy,' she said. 'I've spoken to Necky, and I've been round to the back, the kitchen entrance. There's a van there that takes kitchen refuse; they turn it into manure or something. The driver is a nice man; he'll give us a lift.'

'A lift,' feebly. 'What, and no questions asked?'

'I didn't give any explanation, and he didn't ask for any,' simply.

'I told Necky I didn't like the look of those men. He'd seen them – they weren't doing anything to draw his attention, of course; just hanging about. But he'll go and be officious, tell them they're parked wrong, anything he can think of to be annoying. Just to harass them and distract them for a while. He'll be amused. He's bored stiff. I knew he was nice. Two of them are floating round the building among the tourists, but they can't get in here of course.'

'I'll just get on the first train,' he said. 'You've been very kind; I don't know how to thank you. My brain got sort of anchylosed, somehow.'

'What good is the first train? Or the last, come to that?' Her voice was not really tart, or impatient, but conveyed clearly that he was being *silly*. 'As for where to go – ' She stopped and began suddenly to blush in a schoolgirlish way. 'I was going to ask you to come with me. Perhaps you'd rather not?'

'Of course not – I mean' – 'wildly – that's very kind, but it might involve you in all sorts of trouble: I mean – '

'Come on quick,' she said sharply. 'That van won't wait for ever.'

He grabbed the case and followed her. He didn't even know where the kitchen was, had never been in this part of the building, but she seemed to know everything. She showed him where to push the case on a small freight lift that brought stuff up to the canteen, led the way down a spiral staircase, and at the bottom just ran away. He tried to keep up, puffing with the case, took the wrong turn into some scullery where a cleaning woman in a dirty white overall was gossiping with two grannies peeling carrots, backed out confused, and finally arrived at a back entrance, in a yard full of dustbins. An Estafette van stood parked and she was talking to a young man in overalls.

'Quick quick,' she said. The young man gave a push to the sliding door at the side and Louis scrambled in confusedly. 'The first to the right, you know, past the old fishmarket, and you come out the far end on the Louis Pasteur, more or less opposite the abattoir.' Her voice was meticulous, almost fussy: it was important not to lose time and more still not to lose the way. She hopped in on top of him and he scrambled up clumsily to let her sit on the upturned suitcase: he perched on a dustbin, which was fairly clean as far as one could judge in the gloom, though there was a pungent, penetrating smell.

He could follow the first couple of turns and the red light on the boulevard, after that he lost sense of direction or where he was. Once the van had to brake and two dustbins at the back clashed unmusically; he was shot forward into her arms and she sniggered unself-consciously.

'Stinks a bit, doesn't it? Still, I've had worse rides. He was very *kind*.'

That was what mattered most. All the same, it was a relief even after ten minutes to tumble out on the pavement, blinking after darkness.

Yes; it was one of those streets in the old town, narrow and dingy, which he did not recognize but could place from her directions – fishmarket, Quai Pasteur. It wasn't a fishmarket any longer, but a gloomy little square with a dreary classical church on one side and a garage on the other. They were about a hundred metres down the street, between a café and a scruffy épicerie with wilted carrots and dubious fruit.

'That was kind of you,' she was saying. 'You saved us an endless amount of trouble.'

'Pleasure, 'dame, nothing to thank for. No no, 'dame, what for?'

'Don't be silly, only something for a drink.'

'Thank you, 'dame, 'sieur, bye-bye.'

'If anybody *should* ask you whether you gave anyone a lift . . . '

'Don't worry – never even saw you. Let others mind theirs – know how to mind mine.'

'Good-bye and thank you again.'

The Estafette accelerated, avoided a large lorry neatly, and shot out on to the quay.

'That's that,' she said firmly, brushing a little dust off her skirt. 'Do come in anyhow. You can decide then what you want. That boy won't tell anyone: nobody knows you're here. He's the salt of the earth.' The old-fashioned biblical phrase did not sound odd in her mouth; it was her style, in a way. 'I'm afraid we're on the second floor; sorry, they don't have lifts in these houses.' What was she apologizing for? Louis followed still in his daze.

'Sit down. No, give me your coat first.' She took off her own.

'Excuse me a moment.' She went out through a sliding door in the wall, opposite the window: it was an old-fashioned 'en suite' room. He sat on a sofa and tried to collect his wits.

Polish, he supposed, the way things were arranged – linoleum on the floor, very highly polished: just the way one still saw in Alsace and up towards the Belgian border; housewives walking about with special felt soles under their shoes, called 'skates', so as not to mark the polish. Furniture French-traditional, also over-polished, the ornate kind one sees in junk-shops where dealers refer to it as 'Henri Deux'. The chairs were ugly, with ornate carved arms; solid though, and sittable. There was a Madonna on a shelf with a little lamp in front of her, a small radio and a vase of flowers stood on the buffet, and there were lace curtains over the window with a finger-plant on a bamboo stand between them. Provincial primness, but the room smelt fresh and aired, and was welcoming.

'Now.' She was back, in a tweed skirt and a jumper that was hand knitted, not extremely well. 'Are you perhaps hungry?'

'Not, truly, not a bit, thank you.'

'Well, we'll see about that later. But shall I put the kettle on?'

She opened the door back into the tiny kitchen, the way they had come in. 'Coffee, perhaps? I've nothing to drink, I'm afraid, but I could always get something.'

'No, I'd like coffee.' Poles – like Germans perhaps, loving tremendous pots of coffee at all hours. None of these horrible little espresso things, no, but good strong coffee in big comfortable cups with flowers on them. The mill whirred, the old gas-stove roared, and there came the clank of the filter put on the pot; Louis felt better. She hovered slightly in the doorway.

'I don't know whether you want to go anywhere; the doings is here opposite.'

He did want, and to wash grimy hands where sweat had dried. The little hallway between kitchen and bathroom was full of brooms and shoes; the bathroom itself was so small that the problem had been solved by one of those baths that tilt up out of the way behind a plastic curtain. He turned the tap on the wash-basin; gas popped up in the kitchen geyser and he picked up the soap gratefully. The kettle was boiling when he came back; she had shut the door into the living-room to be tactful, so he turned the flame down and with his own housewife style gave the filter its first dose of water.

'Would you like a biscuit?' pouring out the coffee – quite right he had been; big cups with field flowers painted on them.

'No thanks.'

'But smoke, please. I like the smell. I'll get you an ashtray; I hide them to discourage my son – he's twelve and he smokes on the sly every now and again.' She was not much accustomed to being hostess, he could see, and talked too much to cover her slight embarrassment. Whatever Polish women could not do they could make coffee, thought Louis, and whatever they economized on it wasn't this either; Louis knew good coffee when he smelt it.

'Lovely coffee.'

'Oh I am glad. It's an extravagance I allow myself. I'm sorry about this flat; it must seem awfully poky and tatty but there are only two of us, I haven't a husband you see, and it's hard to get anywhere much unless you can pay a fortune. This is a beastly room really, looking out over that depressing yard, but it gets more sun, and the other overlooks the street, which is noisy, so I have that as my bedroom because the noise is less at night of course.' Why on earth did she have to tell him all this? 'It's a pity only to have two rooms but there are plenty of people who haven't even that so I think about them when I get fed up – or try to.'

She drank her coffee, and put the cup down with a determined face. When this woman meets difficulties, thought Louis, she doesn't try to dodge; she looks things in the eye.

'I'm sure you'll be thinking "tiresome meddlesome woman", but I can't help thinking you are in a good deal of danger. These are quite unscrupulous people – one only has to look, I mean, what they did to that man. Even if they have some right – I mean formal, legal right – what is it one calls it, a title, isn't it? – to this thing, they forfeit it by the way they behave, surely. One thing strikes me and that is that you mustn't allow yourself to be bullied into submission. One can't compound with people like that either. The idea of taking money – what they mean is that they offer you money to keep quiet about that Russian, to forget about him, isn't it? There can't be any honest idea of paying you for the thing, which isn't yours after all. That's what makes it quite clear to my mind. You're the sort of custodian of this thing. You mustn't *compromise*.'

'I've no intention of doing so, but I'm not in an awfully strong position. Thanks to your quick thinking I have a sort of breathing space. I need time really, to think out what to do with the thing, because it's not easy to know, exactly.'

She opened her lips with an expression of vivacity, as though

56

to make some spontaneous protest, but thought better of it, and sat still, staring at the window with a stubborn look, that made her face seem heavier than it was. The face is a bit too blunt anyway to have been pretty, thought Louis vaguely, and of course giving her jaw that mutinous expression just exaggerates the lumpy look she has.

He was feeling tired now – reaction to tension. The day's been a rough one, he thought ruefully – not over yet, either. Could they – they were professionals – have thought of that van driver? Would they still be hanging about outside the Peace Palace? – hardly that soppy. They would have sniffed about, asked a lot of harmless-seeming questions. They would know quickly that he was no longer in the building, that the case was no longer with the concierge – would they find out that she, and not he, had taken it? Even if not, had they noticed her presence in the building, where no other translators were working that day? What might they conclude? He could count on them to miss little! And they wouldn't remain inactive . . .

He would have to warn her; she had not realized that her impetuous action might recoil in a way not likely to be pleasant. Telling her that . . . he wished he didn't feel so woolly. She was pouring out another cup of coffee. He had better get out of here quick – and he mustn't let her know where he was going: it might be a piece of information she would come to rue having.

'You've helped me a lot, Madame Wisniewski. I mustn't presume on you any longer, though. I'll have to be moving.' They were quite near the station here, he thought. That was fortunate. A taxi might be traced but he could walk it in ten minutes.

She frowned. 'You can't think of going to the station.' Damn it, as though he had spoken his thoughts aloud. 'That would be very foolish. Why, it's the first place they'd think of watching.'

In a numb way he realized this to be true. He had been absurdly slow – he should have gone there at once instead of coming up here, and now he had missed the opportunity: the little Simca would have been dispatched. Too slow! – and just for a cup of coffee. He was furious with himself, and unreasonably furious with this annoying woman who had made him waste time. Weakness – coming up for a chat as though he were at a tea-party. Once again, he was alarmed at his own lack of reflex. Too old for these games. All because he hadn't shifted into a higher gear – they would get him now: bye-bye Louis, bye-bye Ludwig. Fabienne had had a pet name. Louki – Lucky Luciano Schweitzer!

The second cup of coffee tasted bitter. Why, they were very likely outside the door right now, and he'd better not go to the window to look, either! Her bedroom window too, ha. Old maid – very likely she would make a face at the idea even of his going into it! But don't worry, Sis, I'm not going to ask – they'll have an eye screwed to that window-frame. Her voice, quiet and low, suddenly cut through his hot, tense nerves.

'I've no doubt at all – the best thing, indeed the only sensible thing – is for you to stay here. I was going to say for the night – I should have said a couple of days. I know it's not awfully comfortable; I'll do my best about that. I'll do some shopping; there's plenty of time. You can think, then. I might be able to go to the police and tell them something. It might be best to give them the thing even – at least they can keep it safe, and stop this gang business.'

'But I can't stay *here*,' Louis said in a voice he wanted to sound decisive. Instead he only sounded horrified, and of course she promptly misunderstood, the silly woman.

'Oh yes,' almost snappily. 'I've no doubt the pious old women would be much shocked at the idea – a single woman putting up a man in her apartment, especially only two rooms. Absolute rubbish – what do they know about life? They think it's easy – I know it's damn difficult.' The emphasis in her words was comic. 'I tell myself so every day,' earnestly. 'I'd write it down if I had a calendar or something. It's a difficult job being a human being. Very hard – the hardest; just being human. I don't care a rap. You're safe here at least.'

He jumped to his feet in a sort of rage.

'But it isn't safe – not for you. These people are dangerous, and they're sure to have found out you took my case from the concierge. They won't have any trouble inventing some excuse for finding out who you are and where you live.'

She looked at him then as though astonished at his naïveté.

'Do I really look so foolish? – I suppose I must – I'm sure I must. Well I am, probably, but really I thought of that. We got used to the Gestapo – I was a student in Poland – oh I don't mean we had any proper underground or anything, but we had meetings to inform ourselves – we weren't so stupid as to believe all the official things told us, we used to listen to the clandestine radio and plan to try and make some kind of resistance later – and when afterwards we were all deported to labour camps we got very cunning – I'm not *that* stupid,' quite indignantly.

'You mean you told the concierge some story?' stupidly.

'I mean he doesn't even know,' she answered with some impatience. 'He was outside talking to Necky, so I took it without him seeing, and I said quite casually to chase those horrible people away, and I said quite casually then to the concierge that you'd taken your case and gone off on holiday. They'll both keep quiet. I know he's a silly old fusspot there in his glass cage generating importance with his telephone and that way he has of thinking the building belongs to him, but he's all right. I know he'll be discreet because of just that – I mean that act of "everything is confidential". He didn't even know what I was talking to Necky about.'

Louis must have looked his surprise at all this intricate manoeuvring because she blushed again.

'I only wanted to let you know that I really do understand.'

'I'm sorry,' awkward.

'Just don't worry. You need some breathing space: you can tell me what you think tomorrow. Oh – here's Carlos.' Shuffle and bump, translated as a boy taking off his boots, in the little hallway.

He was a boy of about twelve, with her stocky look and brown hair that was darker than hers. Round serious face with no particular resemblance at all, but perhaps something of the look of stubbornness she had had a while back. Louis knew nothing whatever about how children behaved but he did think it pleasant that the boy went straight to his mother to give her a kiss affectionately.

'Hallo darling. I'll get you your goûter; I haven't made it yet. We've been drinking coffee; want some, or would you rather cocoa? Now show your manners; this is Mr – well, never mind his name, but he's an old friend from Poland. He's in quite a difficult situation but I'll tell you something about that in a minute.'

'I'm Louis,' smiling; he rather liked the look of this boy. He held his hand out. The boy took the hand, after making a little formal bow. 'I'm Carlos,' a bit sheepish under his mother's severe eye. 'Bonjour monsieur; did you have a good journey?'

'Reads better than it lives,' said Louis grinning; the woman had done that cleverly.

'I'd like coffee, mum, that is if you have any.'

'I have and I detest being called mum. I'll get you some. I'm going to ask you, though, to do your homework in the other room, I'm afraid, because Louis is extremely tired. You leave us in peace; we'll leave you in peace.'

The boy made a face. 'I hate that gloomy room. Light's no good either.'

'I know but that's the way it is. You can take the reading lamp from in here if you want.'

'O.K. then,' reaching for the biscuit Louis had not eaten.

'It would be more polite to wait till you're offered that. No, take it; nobody wants a biscuit with a bite out. You can have another too because I've no bananas. Now think, Carlos; er – Louis – has got here under difficulties and for reasons you can guess doesn't feel particularly safe yet. You don't need that explained. He hasn't even any right to be in France officially, and till he gets it, which might take time, the law says he is supposed to be kept in prison. So he's going to stay here with us till things are sorted out a little. I know I can rely on you to mention absolutely nothing and be extremely adult about things. I'll get your coffee. Would you like some more, Louis?'

He had to grin; she was a masterpiece in her way. Funny, this managing instinct, as though she had a need for responsibility.

'Thank you; no more for me.'

'Good for you,' said Carlos, mumbling rather round the biscuit. 'Are they after you?'

'I've reason to think they are,' said Louis ruefully. 'But I'm thinking up ways of giving them the slip.'

'Mad at you then,' with interest. 'They don't want to let it get out that you crossed over.'

'No, and neither do I, so don't broadcast the fact.'

'Carlos, don't be ridiculous,' from the kitchen.

'Ach mum, what do you know about it?'

'Rather more than snotnoses,' coming in. 'Don't be cheeky, and *don't* call me mum.'

'Sorry. But they'd not bother unless he was important. Don't worry, I won't let on. I know how to be discreet,' in a comic echo of his mother. He had spoken in Polish.

'But I don't know Polish,' said Louis in Russian, smiling a little.

'Oh, you're Russian – *sensas*.'

'A bit.' It startled him to recall that only that morning he had used that exact phrase, to the real Russian – who was now dead.

'No need to make a drama out of this, Carlos,' she said. 'Nobody knows he's here. They may know or think they know that he's somewhere in this town, so he won't be going out much; you can be useful there. Nobody knows about us; that's why he came here. I knew him slightly many years ago in Poland before you were born or thought of. This is not a game.'

'Of course not,' disgusted. 'Don't keep on, thinking I'm just a stupid kid. Can I put some more coffee in? You've made it too milky; you always do.'

'There isn't any more. Drink it and like it: if I have to tell you again not to be cheeky I shall become irritated. You'd better go now anyway and do your homework. What mark did you get for your composition?'

'Fourteen.'

'Oh Carlos, that's not sensational, is it?'

'I think it's not half bad,' going off. 'Roger only got an eleven.'

He pushed the sliding door, disappeared, came back again for the reading lamp, grinned at Louis conspiratorially, and went away again.

'Awful boy,' she said softly. 'No, he's nice, really.'

'I can see that.'

'I'm sorry I had to be familiar. But it's more convincing. You'd better call me Paule, too. You knew me after the war when I went back to the university.'

'I'm a bit old for that.'

'Well, I'm thirty-six.'

'Add ten more for me. When you were a student I was already retired.' He smiled, but he was thinking of Dresden. 'Sorry. It was smart of you. I accept. But how is it I knew where to find you?'

'Don't bother about that – he won't either. Just the idea that I knew you in the past, that's all that will stick in his head. And all that he'll need.'

'Fair enough.'

'That's the ticket' – another of her amusingly old-fashioned phrases. 'I'd stretch out if I were you, and get a bit of rest. That sofa's all right for going to sleep on – Carlos sleeps there. No, don't argue. His name is Charles really – he hates that. Says it's a sacristan's name. So he has become Carlos. Silly. Boys are silly.'

'I recall,' he said gravely.

'I'm just going to go out and do my shopping. Can I get you anything? Perhaps a book or something.'

'No thanks.' He was suddenly reminded of his flat, standing empty, of his books, his gramophone records, his cosy dull little life, his little suppers and the occasional visit to the house in the Avenue de Neuchâtel. Very remote. He tried to realize. It had probably been ransacked by the Germans. He tried to imagine the neat careful old-maidish rooms dishevelled – books standing on the floor, half open, pages bent and crumpled, spine in a painful v, undignified. Yes, he was very tired.

'I won't be much more than an hour, in any case. Less, probably.'

'No hurry.'

There was silence in the little flat. Carlos, doing his home-work next door, was extremely quiet. Louis smoked a cigarette, intending to think but not getting far with it. He took his shoes off and with relief put his feet up. Almost at once, without realizing he was so near it, he fell asleep.

The clock of the church at the top of the street chimed for six o'clock, clear in the stillness.

Friday Evening

He was woken by the stealthy movements of the boy putting his jacket on.

'Sorry. I hadn't wanted to disturb you.'

'Nothing to be sorry for. It was time I woke, that was all; you didn't make any noise. I dare say I was a bit tired, but no more than that.'

'I'm going out to see some chaps. Is there anything you want me to watch out for? If they are hunting about for you, it's as well to be prepared, I thought. I could keep my eyes open anyway. You know – anything seeming a bit unusual.' The air of earnestness tickled Louis.

'You start looking for things that might be unusual and you see one every thirty seconds, and it doesn't add up to a thing.' At the same time . . . he was not quite reassured by Paule Wisniewski's tale about the concierge. There were ways . . .

'There's one little thing – if you like.' Naturally, the boy did like; it was written all over him. And there were no sharper eyes than those of a twelve-year-old boy. 'You could keep an eye open for an auto that might be hanging about in what seemed an unnecessary way. There are two. One's a Mercedes, ordinary one-ninety, black, pretty dirty unless they've suddenly polished it. The other's a new-looking Simca thousand – blue France.'

'Plenty about, of both,' seriously – boy had been reading James Bond for sure. 'But I'd see, straight off. Reading the paper all casual with sunglasses on and the paper upside down.' He took a happy step sideways and backwards and twirled on his heel to the door, opened it swiftly, hit an imaginary person listening at it in the belly, disarmed him smartly, trod on his face, and said, 'I'll be back for supper all right; tell mum, would you?'

63

'Sure,' amused. He was a disappearing scientist, or what-ever it was that peopled the television serials. Engaging part to play – as long as there *weren't* any autos hanging about in the street. The boy would know, though. He had a temptation to look himself – it was nearly dark enough. But Paule would be back any minute; he had anyway a little delicacy – it was after all her bedroom. He lit another cigarette instead; the room was almost dark when he heard her come in.

'Sorry I took so long – I had quite a lot of provisioning.' She was panting a little from two flights with a loaded shopping bag and an extra bottle of mineral water. 'Everything seems quite ordinary, outside.' So she had looked, too. 'I don't believe there's the slightest risk, but it does no harm to make sure. So I didn't want anybody to guess I had an extra person – these shopkeepers in the quarter are incurable gossips of course. So I followed my usual pattern, which meant I had to go to several different shops, sometimes for the same thing.' She had never heard of James Bond, but she had thought it all out.

'I'm afraid you'll miss taking exercise, cramped up here.' She sounded quite bothered about that.

'I'll do physical jerks,' gaily.

'Yes,' seriously. 'It's important to keep supple. I'll open the window too; it's not a bad night and the evening air is good to breathe.' Tactfully put, he thought: what she meant was that the room stank from his sitting there in his socks smoking too much. She put the radio on, and there was amiably spine-less bright music with spineless bright chat in between, while she brought light and warmth into everything, shaking up cushions, brushing ash off the table, laying the table, putting pots on the stove, lighting it with a loud pop and a hollow roar – it was antiquated – like a far-away asthmatic aeroplane.

The meal was good, Polish in a comic way, he suspected: potato soup with fried onions and 'soldiers' of fried bread; marinated herring, tomato salad, Port Salut, apples, and mass-production Algerian white wine.

'I never thought of asking you,' worried. 'Would you have preferred beer?'

'No thanks; I hate beer.'

'We haven't a fridge, I'm afraid. I'm saving for one but it takes time. Carlos has a cunning arrangement whereby he gets the café next door to keep the wine cold for him. Awfully nice of them really since I never even go in there, but he has a pal at school, their son, the famous Roger: awful boy, drinks like a fish and I'm glad Carlos really only likes white wine.'

'Roger doesn't drink like a fish,' said Carlos through herring, 'he's just slightly given over to aperitifs.'

'Very expensive.'

'You don't think he *pays*, do you?' scathing.

'And very bad for him,' with emphatic disapproval.

The Polish soup was the real stuff, which sticks to you; Louis was surprised to find how hungry he was.

'Now he's going off to Roger to watch the beastly television serial,' she said resignedly: Carlos had shot off out of doors the moment supper was over. 'But he works very hard, and he even does the dishes when he comes back. It's only fair – I haven't got a television set or any of these things all boys seem to have now. A café is casual, too – I don't have to feel that he's constantly in other people's homes under their feet. I sometimes worry at his being out so late – he can sleep in my room, by the way, and then nobody will disturb you in here – have you ever noticed that no French children ever seem to get enough sleep?' To Louis' astonishment his eyes misted up and two tears got out of his screwed-up lids before he could control himself. She was horrified.

'Oh what have I said?'

'Nothing at all . . . truly nothing; I've no idea what can be the matter with me. Perhaps I have . . . I think I'm just getting old and dried out, and sometimes I have regrets . . . it's that damned diamond, I believe.'

'I don't think I understand.'

'No,' said Louis, recovering himself. 'There's no reason why you should – in fact it's impossible that you could. The diamond – I've no real proof even now but there's no doubt – comes from Dresden – it was part of a state treasure of the kings of Saxony. I have seen it there; I was certain before I got this ridiculous summons to hand it over.' Suddenly his wish to tell her, to confide – to *confess* – was too great for him. It was a perfectly egotistical feeling – she might have been a possible antidote, for poisons that had corroded him for twenty years.

'Do you have any taste at all for music?'

'I don't know anything much about music, I'm afraid.'

'It's of no consequence. The town you see – Dresden –' lingering on the word with affection; the affection with which one strokes an abscessed tooth – 'was very beautiful. It is set in wonderful countryside, and nothing changed in wartime. Some changes of course, and none for the better as you can imagine, but the countryside went on, and the opera went on, and the architecture was not altered – somebody who lived there told me that the place seemed to have nothing to do with the way people were thinking – and behaving – all over Europe – and that was in forty-three. I spent happy times there myself.

'You see – she was my wife. She had a child too. There came the sort of coincidence that one can never shake off. It was my birthday – I was twenty-seven – and the town was destroyed, and they were both killed. There must have been other birthdays – there were a hundred and thirty thousand killed; it was the worst air-raid, the biggest destruction, of the whole war. Hiroshima was smaller. I don't know' – savagely – 'whether the smoke over Dresden was like a mushroom; I was here, I was in France, or rather by that time we were in Germany, busy with Stuttgart. The city burned for seven days and nights, and I was glad. You see – I was happy that everything should go. It had, too. Nobody ever found out quite how many people had gone – it was full of refugees, you follow?'

She was sitting opposite with her elbows on her knees, her jaw on her palms, an ungraceful attitude. She said nothing.

'It's a long as well as a stupid story. And now this thing comes into my hands – the one thing out of all Dresden that could not be destroyed. It's no earthly good to me. I'm not going to give it back, though.'

'You see – just as I said. Not an easy job to be a human being.'

He had not listened.

'I've been wondering whether I wouldn't tempt them, lead them on, pretend I would give it them, let them see it even –

66

and throw it away, in the river perhaps. Somewhere they'd never find it again. Like the Rhinegold. They'd shoot me out of sheer rage, and I wouldn't care. What good is it? What good's my life? – not a scrap of worth to anyone.'

'Like the base Indian.'

'What?' He had no idea.

'He threw a pearl away richer than all his tribe – it's a man who kills his wife out of jealousy; I remember learning it at school.'

What was the woman talking about? Louis wished he had not come. He was like a drunk at a party, who vomits on the carpet, and has to be even more loud and brutal to conceal his shame. Polish nonsense – silly woman. His eye was caught by the Madonna with the little light burning under her. Typical Slav – superstitious, sentimental.

'You're a Catholic,' roughly. 'You go to church and everything. Eat fish on Fridays, and say prayers to the Madonna, and confess imaginary sins, and never look at a man.' She reddened unhappily.

'You're being hateful but I don't mind. I'm nowhere near as good as that. I've never been married.'

'Ah. You mean the boy's yours but you've never been married – so there was a time when you behaved like a human being,' nastily.

Her hands under her jaw had changed to miserable white-knuckled fists, and her face had filled with lines, but she did not move her position or her voice.

'You could say that, yes.'

'Well, behave like a bloody human now. You couldn't understand the things I've done – crimes, abject things, odious, cowardly, hatefully sly and smart – not if I were to spend all night telling. Suppose now I were to say to you I wanted your body, that I'd be damned if I would sleep here on this stinking sofa, that I insisted on sharing your bed. You'd throw me out, wouldn't you? And good luck to you: you'd be dead right. But thanks anyway, and I mean it, for the rest and the food. You and your base Indian – I know one too. Richard's himself again – you see, I'm not the person you'd want in the house, with either you or the boy.'

'Ssh. I hear him on the stairs.'

'Just what I meant. Ssh – not in front of the children, pah. A bomb doesn't stop in front of children, nor an auto, nor hunger . . .' He stopped. Her eyes were flashing with the first anger he had seen in her, and that relieved him. Carlos had come in.

'House is quiet,' the boy said. 'So's the street. Nothing peculiar anywhere.'

Louis had cooled; he still wanted to make some sarcastic comment on the innocent remark but stopped. Why drag the boy into it?

'Want me to do the supper things, mum? Sorry, mama.'

'Haven't you still exercises to do?'

'Silly old geography – I can do that in bed.'

'I'll do the supper things – you go and scrub yourself: it's quite late enough. You can sit and do your exercise here then. Please do me a favour and put the cap back on the toothpaste.'

'I'll think about it,' airily. 'Thanks for the dishes though. You sure? I'll dry for you.'

'It'll be quite enough if you clean the wash-basin after you, and please do that particularly well.'

'I'll be *scrupulous*,' comically. 'Here,' to Louis. 'Evening paper – I don't know if it's of any interest to you.'

'Thanks,' said Louis. He did not need to look, he knew there would be nothing about dead men or diamonds. He never read papers anyhow. He preferred a book – but the books there were here! The boy's school texts – abridged extracts from Victor Hugo, he should think. *Lettres de mon Moulin*. And so forth. He turned over pages listlessly – speech by foreign minister . . . anxiety of somebody faceless about continual industrial expansion . . . opening of swimming baths . . . auto accident, illustrated. Pah. More auto accidents, petty crimes and violences, suicides – *les faits divers !* . . . Pah. Next week's debate at the Peace Palace, good grief . . . parish-pump gossip, advertisements – washing-machines, brassières, floor-polish, sausage: all hitherto unheard-of, brand-new inventions offered to the public for the very first time, and out of pure philanthropy, natch . . . *Petites Annonces*, situations offered, flats wanted – oh well: there would soon be a top-floor apartment free in the Avenue du Jura. The boy came back in pyjamas with his hair sticking up. Paule, an economical woman, bought them too big and turned up sleeves and trousers. They ended up, probably, with the sleeves cut off to patch the knees. However, these were just at the in-between stage and one noticed nothing. 'What do you read?' Louis asked. The soft clash of dishes being dried came from the kitchen; pleasant, silver sound.

'Oh anything – everything.'

'And what are you reading now?'

'*Funeral Oration for Madame Henriette*.'

'That's at school.'

'Yes. And *Monte Cristo* – I've got to where Valentine's going to drink the poisoned lemonade. And Julien Green. And the *Battle of Dien Bien Phu*.'

'What, all together?' Louis was startled.

'Oh I pick them up and put them down again. I read quick. I've got to do this geography. I would have read tonight, but I thought you and mum probably wanted to be alone, so I stayed watching the telly with Roger. I don't usually – unless there's Catch.' Silence, Carlos seemingly absorbed in South American tropical forest. 'Do you have a gun?' suddenly. Louis nodded. 'Are you carrying it? May I see?' Wryly, Louis put his hand in his back pocket, hitched out the Browning that had been the chubby man's, and balanced it on his palm.

'Can I hold it?'

'No. It's loaded; you can't hold it.'

Paule came in.

'Make your bed, Carlos. Light out in fifteen minutes. It's a quarter past nine now.' Resigned, the boy propped his book upside-down and went to open a cupboard; there were bed-clothes folded and piled on the bottom shelf. 'You'll be more comfortable in the other room.' Louis did not look up, thinking she was talking to the boy. 'Louis – I was just saying I've switched the radiator on in the other room. I know it's rude to chase you this way, but Carlos needs the sleep.' He got up slightly astonished. On the inner side of the sliding door were curtains drawn across; some loose heavy jute material.

'I have to do a bit of tidying and general cleaning-up,' she went on in the same natural voice, 'and see that Carlos has his light out – I'll be with you in about a quarter of an hour.' She closed the door, leaving him still a bit astounded.

The room was as she had said, a dark, chilly room, facing east on to the gloomy street. Chintz curtains, conventional cream with a pattern of parrot tulips, were drawn across the window, which he went to look at: it was set slightly open on a hook and the wooden shutters were closed outside. The street had an evening stillness; mutterings came up, and scraping shufflings: an occasional auto motor roaring fast down to the quay, or an auto door banging.

Inside was bright and warming up – an electric oil radiator was chasing the chill. Simple furniture – a big old-fashioned wardrobe, a table writing-desk used, he could see, for putting the sewing machine on as well as for a dressing-table. A small looking-glass and a shelf of books hung above it. A cane armchair. A low table beside a bumpy-looking divan with bulbous gouty feet. And that was all. Behind another modest chintz curtain was the wash-basin, with a plastic bidet on a metal stand tidied neatly below it. Three clean towels on plastic rails, not very skilfully screwed in.

On the table an alarm-clock with a noisy tick. On the writing-desk two exercise books belonging to Carlos, a comb clean but with two teeth missing, and a box of water-colours; the brushes were standing upside down in a smeary mustard glass. He looked at the books. He might have known: moralizing novelists – Mauriac, Claudel, Bernanos, Péguy – a half smile – Romain Rolland; good heavens, did people still read him? Colette and Marcel Pagnol; now what were they doing in this company? A New Testament, Saint François de Sales, and a daily missal seemed unperturbed alongside. He picked up Pagnol – ah, *The Time of Secrets*, and sat in the cane armchair. Rather a wonderful book; it seemed scarcely a minute before Paule slipped in carrying his suitcase.

'I remembered to bring an ashtray,' putting it on the writing table. 'I'm going to have a bath – I hope you don't mind.' He hardly listened; it made no odds. She would be preparing him a lecture no doubt, but a lot he cared! It was sensible enough to wait till the boy was asleep. He quite agreed; why have a witness the more? But he had to get out, and he had to decide smartly, exactly where and how.

He opened the window further, and, with precaution, the blind a bit, enough to take a careful long look up and down. Nothing at all. That, on the top of the boy's assurance, which could probably be taken as very reliable, seemed reassuring. Anyway, the rest, and now the fresh air, was restoring his ability to think.

He could leave the town, sure – the railway station was not the only way out! He didn't think much of that; it left the whole problem up in the air. And it meant kissing goodbye to a comfortable life: a comfortable routine, with a little visit to Marie-Claire every now and again; an unexacting job, pretty well paid, a tidy handy flat. No, here he got value for his money, a thing increasingly rare in these days. He could go a lot further, and fare a lot worse. No, he had to stay in the town and find, somehow, a permanent solution – within a few days.

There was nowhere he knew of that would be really safe. Hotels – they could check them all, easily, any time they had a mind to. He had no friends. But why all this talk of hiding? The intelligent thing was surely not to hide, but to go home, calmly, sailing in without a worry. And then stare them down, with effrontery, damning their infernal impertinence. That was surely the way to handle it. It had been absurd, as well as a great mistake, to get into such a panic, storming out of the house, running about, simply showing them how impressed by them he was and how frightened: very bad tactics . . .

He had been disturbed to find himself of a sudden the centre of a melodrama. That was natural enough, he supposed. To the person like him, who stays at home, does nothing, takes great pains to stay alive and keep healthy, grow middle-aged and grey gracefully while still able to ski, everything is a melodrama, even crossing the road. One is never far from it in life.

It hadn't even disconcerted him to find the diamond. One reads stranger things in the *faits divers* column daily. The fact is, though, that these things happen to other people. It occurred to him that one acquired such a tolerance to excitement from the drug of the press, so high has the excitement-threshold become, that one reads these things without ever saying 'suppose it had been me'. And when a man with a gun walks in at one's own door one is *surprised*. A great mistake, thought Louis. *Vivere in pericolo* should be our daily motto.

He would go home. A step of that kind, particularly *after* the ignominious running away crouched quaking on a dustbin, would put them off their stroke.

He was interrupted in thought by the return of the woman. She had on a quilted nylon peignoir, washed to fraying point and worn to tatty comfort. Her hair was brushed out; she carried with her a warm not unpleasant smell of bathroom; of steam, toothpaste and cheap soap. It was the signal for him to push off; he stood up.

'Talk in a normal tone,' she said. 'Carlos is asleep and he sleeps very soundly. The curtains deaden voices, anyhow.'

'I don't want to make any noise though,' he said. 'If you'd just tell me where you hung my coat – I don't want to put the light on.'

'Your coat? What can you want with your coat?' Unfeigned astonishment, certainly. 'This bed, I'm afraid, is not designed for two people, but I hope you'll be able to sleep well.' He stared at her.

'You wanted to sleep in my bed,' still as though to a child. She was rummaging at the back of the deep shelves in the wardrobe. 'Do you like one pillow or two?' The lack of colour in the voice irritated him.

'No no: now that the boy is asleep I must be off. But thank you very much indeed for all your hospitality. I feel a great deal better – able now to cope.' She turned with the pillow in her hand to scrutinize him.

'What nonsense you are talking. You aren't only tired, you know; you've been badly upset and shocked as well as put under a continuous nervous strain on top of that. I know it sounds terribly conventional but you'll feel altogether new after you've had a good night. And you'll see things altogether differently into the bargain.' She switched on the little lamp, plumped the pillows up, climbed into bed, arranged herself sitting upright, and made herself immobile, with closed eyes and hands folded loosely in front of her. Louis stared. He did not want to break the silence; he could not be sure that she was not saying *prayers*. Damned woman was capable of anything!

It only dumbfounded him the more when she opened her eyes, gave him a broad innocent smile in a face that from looking young had suddenly become that of a very young girl, scarcely more than a child, hesitated a moment, and with a brusque movement unbuttoned the peignoir and pulled it off upwards, letting him see that she had nothing on under it. Louis stared. He didn't know what to do; like most men who do not know what to do he rubbed his jaw, which made a consoling scratchy noise, as though to reassure him that he was a man after all. Her breasts were small, well shaped, and slightly fallen: it was not terribly glamorous, hm, compared to the ingenious sophistications of – just to take the example he was most familiar with – Marie-Claire's girls. Paradoxically – from reading the *faits divers* one learns how unaccountable people are – he found that he desired this faded housewife of thirty-six a great deal more than he had ever coveted the lithe, shiny, elastic body of the luscious Christiane – a woman who spent more on her hair than this one did on clothes – and more on clothes than Paule Wisniewski did on food!

The smile was being maintained with an effort: she put her knees up and with a schoolgirl gesture clasped her arms round them to hide her breasts: the eyes dropped. Louis got up, his leg muscles feeling tight and heavy. He walked lumpishly over to the wardrobe and fumbled about till he found another pillow.

'I like two' – a lot of importance that had!

He undressed with a lot of weight, letting his shoes fall as though they were lead, feeling her eyes on his back, studying all this with curiosity – men undressing were plainly a novelty. . . . In bed she turned to him and held her arms out maternally. But she would not have been Paule if she had been able to keep her mouth shut. She had thought out another problem!

'One thing,' in a small pale voice that added strongly to the schoolgirl impression. 'Please don't ask – I mean I hate all pills and mechanisms very much. And please stay inside me. I'm sorry.'

'Don't talk,' more roughly than he meant. But she could not help it. She wanted to say something now that would show affection.

'Louki,' she said softly. It had been an expression of Fabienne's. Surely he had not told her that . . .

Saturday Morning

He had a vague memory of the bell of the alarm-clock going off, but he was far too sleepy, warm, and comfortable to care. The bed was not crowded either; he stretched earthily but was too sleepy to draw conclusions. There was a feeling of peace. What a sentimental notion, a tiny corner of his mind told him; he paid no heed to it. Physical contentment – you were extremely tired and you have slept very well. Even if a bed is narrow . . .

The corner of mind was growing larger; it reminded him unexpectedly that it was twenty years – twenty years! – since he had slept the whole night through in a bed with somebody, exactly as though she were your wife. He refused to think about this, turned over with a groan of luxury and buried his nose in the pillow. A very good smell of woman. Possessing the whole bed was wonderful; he dozed off again deliberately. It was like a very good hard dark chocolate, with cognac, and a whole fresh cherry inside. You must not *bite* at it; you must close your mouth round it and stay absolutely immobile while it *melts*. Louis had a vague notion that Brillat-Savarin or someone had said that this was what you should do with ortolans. Alas, Louis had never eaten an ortolan. But this was, he was convinced, very much the same.

When he woke again there was a smell of coffee, and a small mousy noise in the stillness. A woman's noise, that of tidying-up-the-room-next-door while the men are still out from underfoot. He opened an eye and saw a fine delicate streak of sunlight that was illuminating the dingy street and had pierced a hinge, leaving its minute magic trace on the curtain. It would only last a few minutes before the angle cut it off, but he had woken in those minutes. A very good omen. No, it was more than that. His semi-conscious mind had been right after all; it was peace.

A rumbling sound as gentle as that which tells you, standing on the deserted platform at a dead hour, that a tube train is coming at last, together with a slight current of air, meant that she was opening the door with exaggerated caution. It was so still in the apartment that it must be late; the boy had certainly gone to school. He opened the eye again cautiously and caught her putting something back on the bookshelf. A missal, and she had her coat on – the woman had been to church! Did she do that every day, or was it just because of . . . ?

She took off the coat, back to him still, and hung it up; the cupboard door creaked and the hanger made a scuttering noise on the rail. She glanced around fearfully but he had the eye shut in time. Her figure, from behind, was young, soft, blurred by a woolly jumper and a tweedy skirt. He would give her some fresh ideas! With a movement quite as rapid as that of throwing a half-empty bottle of Vittel in the face of the chubby man, yesterday (but he had forgotten all about it), he flew out of bed and caught her in a 'grip of steel'. He turned her round, and pushed her smartly so that she stumbled and had to lean forward with her hands on the bed to save herself falling, which was the whole idea but she had not known that. But no no, it was not brutality. Louis realized that it was nothing but a gesture of affection. She gave a gasp of being taken by surprise, but directly she realized the meaning of all this nonsense she gave what sounded like a giggle, though he could not tell whether it was a sound of amusement or of protest.

'You,' putting a hairpin in her mouth. 'I don't seem to have to ask whether you've slept well; good morning. The coffee's filtering – why don't you have a bath, or a shower if you like?' It was quite difficult to get her balance back; she looked, besides, extremely ridiculous, thought Louis. But no. It was not a wish to humiliate, nor to be sadistic, though it is easy to think that a woman pushed over with her skirt round her neck is there to be beaten or treated with ignominy. No; he was warm and happy clear through. Sunshine, peace, affection – strange.

She pulled up her knickers in an awkward sort of way, caught his eye and gave a guilty grin. Now, he thought, she is going to shoo me out and go and sit on that iniquitous plastic bidet. Exactly like Christiane – except that hers of course was ivory porcelain with rosebuds. The notion infuriated him. He didn't want anything like Christiane. He wanted Fabienne, with whom nothing that concerned making love, either before or after, had ever been in the least slimy. Last night – and this morning – disgusted him neither to think about nor to write about. He remembered the letters he had written to Fabienne, grinning at the thought of enlivening, perhaps, a military censor's day. They had not, though, been in the least obscene. The funny thing was that he felt as though Paule was no different.

'Come on and we'll both have a quick shower,' happily. She looked startled – horrified too.

'You don't want to make love *again*, do you?' Exactly as though he had put two of the expensive chocolates in his mouth at one go. The horror was at abominable greed, and he burst out laughing.

'No. Just to wash. But I want to be near you.'

She understood at once. And so did he! That was it; it was only now that he realized it. As well as wanting to look at her, to study her with no clothes on, to discover her – indeed much more-than, not just as-well-as, – he wished to have her close to him. A sensation so unexpected, so recovered, fished up out of deep water, that he stopped laughing. A warm sharp shock struck him, of memory, from days before Dresden. It warmed his stomach, like the coffee he could smell. Prickling damp came in his eyes, exactly as though the coffee-mill had been fed with raw onions, and he had to splash the shower-head into his face so that she would not notice. Infernally unexpected.

He felt – but yes – like the ordinary, everyday Louis, wheeling his bike out of the courtyard into the Avenue du Jura, through the dingy tiled passage and past the horrible little notice about rent pinned to Madame Hasenpfeffer's – whatever her name was – door.

Down the step at the front, across the pavement, swinging his leg over, exactly as he did and would do every day, wondering what restaurant to pick for lunch. And discovering to his horror that somebody had fitted the motor from a Ferrari sports-auto to the back of his bike. Even in bottom gear he had almost overrun the traffic-light at the corner before his bemused foot found the brake and stood on it. Ridiculous.

But it was so. The green Dresden diamond was a talisman, and he was shaving, and she was pouring out the coffee, and he possessed Djinns, all-powerful.

He studied her while he slid the razor up and down, cocking his jaw, trying her out from different angles with a deliberate, slow, *rude* look. She saw and blushed enormously, now in a welter of confusion, pretending to be looking out of the window, embarrassed to the stage where she had to pretend to be worried about a place on the cretonne curtain, where the hem had come loose and a few threads were fraying. Preposterous. Perhaps last night in bed she had been awkward, and this morning pushed across the bed she had been tactful, but just now, standing under the shower where there was certainly not room enough for two people, she had been laughing and spontaneous. And now, dressed up and arranged with her dowdy clothes and her hair pinned up in a way that was un-modish but graceful, becoming, and even curiously elegant – and fortified into the bargain behind her coffee-pot – she was hot and scarlet with shamed embarrassment. Would she seize her prayer-book and run straight back to church?

I am astonishingly alive, thought Louis; four eyes, four ears. She had brought fresh bread on her way back and he was eating quantities of it with butter and sharp quetsch jam – Louis Schweitzer, who never touched jam! – he was even dipping it into his coffee-bowl and loving it . . .

Fabienne had been used to do that, and he had snapped at her for it. *Unladylike* – how young he had been! There had been so few times to sit with Fabienne over breakfast – fewer still with big bowls of strong coffee. Polish coffee – he was being disloyal, he told himself severely; Fabienne had come from the high Alps down near Val d'Isère – it was she who had taught him to ski – and her coffee had been quite as good as anything Polish.

He saw her vividly. She had never faded in his mind; Fabienne was not a woman to fade. She was blurred, some-times, the sharp shimmering outlines withdrawn and veiled – even the Alps did that sometimes! But he could never lose the tiny crescent-moon line at the corners of her mouth, nor the modelling of her forehead, so massive and so delicate, nor the angle at which she tucked flowers into her unexpectedly fair hair – and so few women are able to put flowers in their hair without becoming at once absurdly precious. Her hair had been a very clear light brown, seeming pale and rather dull at first – dull-boring, not dull-dirty! No, he had not lost the feel and smell of that hair, nor the contours of her face when she put glasses on – her eyesight had been bad – nor the balance and texture of her singing voice that was like her hair, a clear pale soprano, thin, but true.

He saw her walking. Very tall and elastic, with the longest legs he had ever known in any woman. The carriage of her body had been the most vivid, striking, instantly seized thing about her. He saw Fabienne pregnant, still in France, at a time when he was away nearly all the time. She had worked as a barmaid in a café-restaurant in Grenoble, and had told him later laughing how many of the men had wistfully offered to marry her, gallantly, thinking her husband killed, to give her baby a father, every one of them had said.

'Being pregnant is most successful. I was extremely good-looking.'

Nerves, anxiety, hardship, hunger had made her face too fine, too bony, before the end, but she had never lost that readiness, that quickness to accept all that life might send, that total generosity of her spirit.

He had not been good enough for her. She had never known about his poltrooneries – only about his confidence in the *star*. He had boasted of his cheek, of the way he had shouted 'Imbecile cretin' at the police commandant, of the icy voice he had found to say 'The Reichsführer will be exceedingly *displeased*' to the head of the Gestapo in south-western France (they weren't going to ring up and *ask*, which had saved him at the brink of a firing-squad). He had been able to write, openly, to her instead of getting the bullet in the back of the neck later in Germany, to tell her that he had gone to the Russian front, and not as fodder either, not among the *malgré eux* of France that had been thrown out there to die. No no – the star – he was sent to conquer, in a Waffen SS unit, and not one made up of renegade Alsaciens either. Fabienne had laughed and laughed – his biggest triumph had been getting her out of France and to Dresden, after he was granted leave, as a hero! Wounded four times, with a first-class Cross and the one that spoke a language to every soldier that had seen Russia – the one you only got for over eleven hand-to-hand combats. He had become a shining light, that got pointed out to recruits, and when things began to go badly they had dug up and revived his file, the one in which he had spouted about his *special knowledge*, the one with his phrase about the 'encirclement of Switzerland' in it that he had been sure would fetch them. He had been detached, and sent to Chambéry to join the local SD unit. He hadn't liked that at all – a bigger risk than any he had taken in Russia, for if ever one was marked down for a bullet in the back. . . . In a nastier colder sweat than he had ever known he had managed to catch that SD quartet and hand it over, lock, stock and a still very venomous barrel, to the French who had not been caught in the Vercors – a communist of course; Louis had suppressed his Russian decorations! He remembered that cold sweat, for he got it still, on the left side, creeping across his shrinking ribs, when he heard the melodies that Fabienne had most loved – 'Porgi amor', Suzanne's 'De vieni' in the velvet night air under the chestnut trees – and 'Voi che sapete' . . . of course . . .

Fabienne was still in Dresden, safest place in all Germany, with the child. He had worked out the whole plan for her getting out, how she should get to Nürnberg, and thence to Stuttgart, and how to meet there the Americans, or the French, whichever got there first.

He had not boasted to Fabienne of all he had done. She would have laughed, yes, but she was too honest a person. . . . She had never known. The February night in Dresden had caught up with her, a day or two before she was due to go, with all her papers in order . . . he came back with a start; more Polish coffee was being poured in his bowl. Paule was carefully paying no heed to his reverie.

Yalta had ruined him, just as it had everyone else. Roosevelt trusted Russians, and loathed the French. . . . He didn't even know whether there was a cemetery in Dresden. Where had they put the half million who had accompanied Fabienne underground?

'I'm sorry,' he said to Paule.

'It's all right,' hastily. 'I am free all day. I was thinking about dinner. I was going to go to the Europahaus too, to get my library books. Perhaps Necky will be on duty. He might have noticed something. He would know whether there's been any hanging around, or efforts to root for information. Do you want me to see your concierge? Or get anything for you from your flat?'

'No no. They'll have eyes everywhere. I'll probably end up going to the flat myself – I can think of no better way of getting to grips. I have to do it frontally.' Yes yes; the encirclement of Switzerland.

'What are you going to do with the thing, though?' she asked abruptly. 'You won't let them have it, under any circumstances, but you're not going to try and keep it yourself? Are you?'

'I don't know.'

'Why don't you give it to the French government? They'd keep it safe, in the vaults of the Louvre, or somewhere.'

'They would, yes. They'd take it, and put it in the vaults of the Louvre, and no human eye would ever again behold it. They'd never admit they'd got it.' She was looking puzzled.

'Look – they want no trouble, either with the Russians or the East Germans. They don't want anyone to lose face. They're all realists, you see.'

'Realists,' said Paule scornfully. 'I hate realists. Opportunists, you mean. Who does the thing really belong to?'

'It was part of the crown treasure of the Kings of Saxony.'

'So it belongs to the people.'

'You think it would help them?'

'But the government is the people. I mean I know all about the shortcomings,' flushing now in an uprush of her honest manner, her stubbornness over anything she would see as principle – not just a personal thing, like a sin of the flesh. 'I mean the government over there in Saxony must be extremely bad, but is it really much worse than some of the specimens we see over on our side? A bit like ours in Poland perhaps

– under the thumb of the Russians is the chief drawback.'

'What are you trying to tell me?'

'Suppose you just went to them – you could do it through those nignogs they have here at the delegation – and just gave them the thing, honestly. Saying here, this is yours, use it for the people. Then they would feel perhaps that people here were genuinely on their side. What I feel is all wrong is the drawing back of our skirts all the time, as though they were *dirty*.' She was well wound up.

'I'm afraid you're being naïve.'

'That's what people always say. Is it so *bad*?'

'Look. To start with there wasn't even any idealism about getting that delegation over here. It was partly to stop the stupid hypocrisy of pretending they don't exist, true. But it was self-aggrandizement too. You know the line our lot go on – we are the only ones with any real sense. Nobody wants idealism. If anybody made an individual move instead of working out meaningless joint communiqués there'd be a panic. It would upset the West Germans – that would never do. The others are just as suspicious – if one gave the thing back as you suggest they'd wonder what the catch was. They know the jets and the bomb aren't for any Russians – they know it's for them. They know neither the Poles nor we will ever give way on the Oder-Neisse.'

She was crying. 'I know,' she said. 'I know. But if you at least gave it them, they'd disown this pack of gangsters, these murderers. It all sounds so starry-eyed – but if nobody ever attempted any kind of individual action then indeed we're lost.'

Louis lit another cigarette. How was he to make her understand? That delegations had nothing to do with governments, and still less with activities like the committee for recovering Works of Art.

'You've noticed the Kafka atmosphere where we work.'

'The what?'

'Oh that's not important – Czech writer, not much good, thought highly of because he's good at the facelessness of bureaucracy. People in his books spend their lives wandering around mysterious huge buildings full of corridors, where people bustle about with papers all day, where nothing ever gets done, where everything is meaningless, where there's no answer to anything. Lends his name to the dream worlds – helplessness, unreality, incomprehension, doubletalk.' Her face showed a sense of fun – he had wondered whether she was able to make jokes.

'The préfecture, you mean, or the tax-office – where they look human – make human faces and talk in human voices but where it all comes out Chinese.' Her laugh was innocent. 'But the Europahaus is not that bad. They talk nonsense, of course, but they do try.'

'Try,' annoyed. 'Lot of use that is. They don't even understand each other. Haven't you seen that we are parasites, that translations are just one more layer of opacity and stupidity? In Vienna in 1814 the negotiators were educated, intelligent men, who all spoke French, who understood each other, respected each other – there weren't any translators. What are our delegates? Suspicious peasants, can't even talk their own language, have no notion of history. All we hear is banalities, uttered by mediocrities listening to their own voices. Self-importance and dishonest bonhomie. Trash.' And she surprised him very much by getting in a rage.

'I don't agree a bit. Senseless quibbling a lot, yes, naturally, but I think a lot of them are simple honest men, and if they don't seem very educated always that's because the world's got a lot more complicated and fragmented since eighteen fourteen: the comparison's ridiculous.' Ridiculous, he thought – good word for spitting contemptuously in a Polish furious way. 'All the more reason to be simple, to cut through speeches and translations. Does one need to be well-read in history, or philosophy? Jeanne d'Arc couldn't read or write.'

Louis smiled. 'Is that what we need?'

'You find me childish and absurd, but yes, I think we do,' tartly bumping a coffee-cup on top of another.

'Don't be mad at me because we disagree – that's like delegates.'

She smiled, and surprised him by kissing him suddenly while pretending to gather crumbs together.

'It's your problem. You have to decide. I haven't any right to confuse you with my ludicrous ideas.'

'I don't approve of everything I do,' he said, smiling sideways. 'You do things you don't approve of either. Sleeping with me for instance.'

And she blushed of course again, richly. He felt affection for those tremendous blushes of hers.

'I won't be long away. I always walk – I like the fresh air.'

'I'll hold the fort,' lazily, comfortably.

The flat felt still and empty with her gone, and Louis was restless. He got out the silver box, and sat for a minute looking at the diamond before putting it away. He laughed suddenly; he would give it to her to take care of! He put the silver box on her table in the bedroom; he found a scatter of hairpins there. He covered the diamond with a crumpled Kleenex tissue and put the hairpins in on top.

He had nothing to do. He cast about for a book, but thank you, not in the mood for Paule's moralists. Last night's evening paper – not a stimulating thought. He switched the radio on – no short wave, and the medium band was filled with drool, vitamins for the housewife pottering with her duster. He went to his suitcase with a vague notion of finding something there to settle his restless thoughts, and came across the book on Dresden that he had put in, he still wondered why. Well – bite on it. What harm could it do him now? It might disinfect his ideas, cleanse and tighten his slack flabby microbes of thought – astringent, a squeeze of lemon juice. Pure lemon juice will kill a typhoid germ, he told himself.

He opened the book vaguely, anywhere, and found himself gazing at the façade of the opera. It hadn't been bad! A scrap vulgar, a scrap overweight, a scrap grandiose, not quite the purity of the best Dresden buildings. And look at that marvellous little balcony above the heavy portal with the proud monogram: 'A', presumably standing for Augustus – no, not vainglorious, quite justified. He turned the page – there was the inside, heavy perhaps, but what a texture; the smell of every first night there ever was. The opera was the People's Palace – right that it should be grandiose. Compare it with the architecture of modern people's palaces – with the Europahaus, for instance. Louis snorted with laughter. His remarks about the Congress of Vienna had been disingenuous perhaps – had thrown no dust in Paule's eyes besides, but he would certainly like to abolish all speeches and translations together, and have one performance of 'Fidelio' every month instead. He would gladly take a part as a prisoner.

He was turning the idea around with a wry amusement when a slight noise in the silence made him start and the book slid off his knees. The 'front door' on the landing being closed gently – Paule back already?

'You were quick,' he said amiably.

'I'm always quick,' answered a voice, equally amiable. His muscles went rigid: it was the voice of a man.

'Good morning, Mr Schweitzer.' Not only amiable; a gentle voice, even – the word used in its sense of mild, delicate, perhaps well-bred. The man had come through the doorway from the tiny hallway and was standing there with an agreeable smile on his face.

'Don't bother to get up. Perhaps you will allow me to sit down instead.' Louis had himself under control by now, telling himself ruefully that once again he had underestimated these people.

'I do realize,' the man sat elegantly, disposed himself, crossed his knees comfortably – 'that I owe you an explanation. It occurred to me that the best way of giving it was to find a quiet spot for a peaceful talk. No no,' he held up an unhurried hand at Louis, who was tensing himself as though 'gathering for a spring', 'I have no companions and it is not in my purpose to menace you, nor to engender any act of violence – you have please to take my word for that. Give me at least the opportunity to wave my olive branch.'

'But I suppose the acolytes are at the street door.'

'No no,' again, smiling faintly. 'Quite alone, an emissary of peace and nothing else.'

'Then why don't I jump on you and wring your neck?'

The smile broadened at this entertaining fantasy.

'But you are far too reasonable a person to do anything so foolish, Mr Schweitzer; I have had time to discover that. Consider the situation. I do not for a moment hold your action of yesterday against you, nor do I nurse vengeful projects in retribution. You felt yourself threatened, and you reacted to the

84

threat, which is as a brave man should. Come, it was a *reasonable* act. Courageous and reasonable, and directly I knew of it I felt that I had been over-hasty and that I had made a mistake. You have only fortified my judgement by your subsequent actions. Very properly you took yourself off, out of harm's way,' the smile was ironic, 'and found a corner where you could think things over in peace. You made no scandal, you ran to no policemen, you took pains to enjoin discretion on your colleagues and your concierge – no, I have nothing but admiration for the way you have behaved, and on that account my ambition was no more than to come and introduce myself.

'It was rude of me, certainly, to penetrate in this rather stealthy fashion into your retreat, but I had to inspire your confidence. I should like to ask Madame Wisniewski to forgive me, but she will not be back for quite some time: I feel sure that after her errands she will think about her housekeeping, and whether to buy a cabbage or a cauliflower.' The smile had a knowing tinge; he was in no doubt about the errands!

'We have time before us. Of course, if you would rather, we can go on talking in a public place – a café, a restaurant? – perhaps it would reassure you? – name any place you wish and you will find that I will follow meekly. No? – it has no consequence – merely to demonstrate that there is no trap or plot. May I put my hat on this table?' For he was still holding it, a neat, modish little hat, of lightweight supple felt, dark chocolate brown. He made himself comfortable, unbuttoning his raincoat and spreading it out so as not to sit creases into it. He fussed slightly with the cushion of Paule's solid, shabby armchair before everything was arranged just so.

It is a sort of key, thought Louis. He stayed still and stared as though attempting to sum the man up, and the man seemed to realize this, sitting there still and perfectly at ease, supporting the examination with the continued patient mildness. Yes, felt Louis; the hat is a key, the first, for all this man's appearance and bearing is in harmony with it.

He was a slight, medium-height, graceful personage of indeterminate age, with slender wrists and fine tapering hands; he wore no rings, nor any other jewellery. His suit was expensive, looking cut-in-Paris, and his shirt and shoes were certainly handmade, and his tie was silk, a discreet greenish thing that matched the lisle socks. He had a handsome, determined, intelligent face with a high forehead made higher still by hair that had begun to ebb – faded fair hair, the colour of Paule's! An aquiline nose below alert, amused blue eyes. The clothes sat on him beautifully without an awkward or uncertain thread; the shoes were sober black leather – not a man to wear suède shoes, nor things with eccentric forms, or little punched patterns! Louis felt he looked somehow not quite *provincial* enough for his job. Too well-dressed, too mannered, and a voice sounding as though trained in a bureau of the Quai d'Orsay.

'Well,' at last, with that ambassadorial smile, 'you begin to feel fewer misgivings? Perhaps you wish to question me? – it is your right and I wish to give you satisfaction. You see, Mr Schweitzer, I have taken the trouble – since you kindly afforded me the time – to learn that you are a man out of the common: you have intelligence, and energy, and ability – you lack perhaps ambition, but that is neither here nor there. A mistake, really, but there, that is your business – but come now, let us leave personalities behind: let us come to the facts and examine them: that will benefit us both much more than remaining wary of each other. And let us not be afraid to speak our mind – I certainly do not despise the social conventions of the western world, but we must not neglect our duties to society purely out of a polite wish to spare one another's feelings.'

'I doubt,' said Louis, 'whether you could give me any explanation that would satisfy me, without sounding false, hypocritical – certainly completely cynical.' It came out in a sort of growl, and sounded boorish beside that mannered voice. Louis cleared his throat, searching for the key to his professional voice, the one he used for Mr Tsara, the chief Russian delegate, a man of great charm and wit – one of the few able to make the owls of the Europahaus laugh.

'It would be a step forward if you would allow me to try.'

Charm – but the smile round the sensitive mouth was fine, susceptible to nuance – he had to yield, at least to meet the man on the ground he had chosen – what could one lose by civility?

'One begins with one's name, generally,' he said. 'And one's function, in any matter of importance. One's credentials, put it.' He took his cigarettes out of his jacket. The pistol he had taken from the chubby man was in his back trouser pocket, not easy to reach sitting down – but it was not, perhaps, the right moment for pistols.

'Arnim Taillefer is my name, my function that of adjunct curator of state museums, credentials – I fear I have no diplomatic status. The People's Democratic Republic has no servants officially accredited to the occidental governments. Whether that is regrettable or not is not my affair, though it would lighten my task often if there were diplomatic missions – at this moment, for instance, since an embassy in Paris could identify me readily – but have no distrust; I am what I seem.'

'Being a curator of state museums – the duties include putting people's eyes out, in the Democratic Republic?'

The smile faded, but the easy unembarrassed manner did not change.

'I quite agree that that was detestable – the man responsible would have received exemplary punishment. That he did not receive it was your fault, my dear Monsieur Schweitzer, for you killed him, for which I congratulate you heartily – I should have done the same myself. I did not know that the man was mentally unbalanced, nor that his aberrations would take the form of brute sadism. Infinitely regrettable – one of the main motives for my coming to offer you my excuses.'

'You employed the man – you gave him instructions. If he overstepped those instructions the fault is yours – you should know how to keep people within bounds.'

'A delicate point. Mankind is fallible. I was deceived in the man, and the man betrayed me. Tools do occasionally betray one, and when that happens one discards them. I must, as well, emphasize a point unknown to you. The man – not the man I have described as a clumsy and in this case treacherous tool – was not such a man as you are. He was a debased and brutal person, alive to nothing but his personal gain; he had a record of robbery and of violence; he was a deserter from the armed forces of the Soviet Union and was actively searched for by the police forces of other countries – including your own. You need not be concerned at the thought of those bodies, my dear Mr Schweitzer. When they are found, the police will accept the thesis of a settlement of accounts.

'Where I allowed myself to be even more gravely misled – I really must apologize – was upon my realization that this creature had given you his confidence. The point caused me to act over-hastily, no doubt, and without proper consideration towards you. It seemed to me that you were an accomplice of that person – perhaps a criminal. Do you understand?'

'Yes.'

'I was wrong, but you will see that the thought was natural, and, I hope, forgivable.'

'What I do not understand is this talk of confidence. The man, I take it, possessed some secret. You think that I share it. Why?'

The smile was broad and tolerant; the elegant hands spread apologetically.

'My dear Mr Schweitzer. Why leave your comfortable flat in such a hurry? Why tell your concierge you had left on a holiday – such a sudden holiday? Why not go on a holiday? Why leave the Europahaus in so unconventional – and so furtive – a manner? Why this sudden warm friendship with the admirable Madame Wisniewski?'

I was indeed an awful fool, thought Louis, hoping his face did not betray his thoughts. After all I knew perfectly well, and always have known, that the way to treat Germans is to scream at them in tones of outrage.

'I am not a fool. I had found myself dealing with a crude gangster who tried to kill me. Your letter gave me no evidence that I was not dealing with people just as nasty as he was. I may be brave but I try to be prudent. I appreciate your coming to offer your excuses, but I cannot help you. The man may have had all the criminal instincts you lend him – he's not here to state the contrary – but I know nothing about it. He gave me no confidence. I can't even pretend to know what you're talking about.'

Monsieur Taillefer laughed, jovially, with unforced merriment.

'Oh really, really,' in reproof, a chiding kindness. 'My tool was there to learn the whereabouts of an article of value. He overstepped his instructions. He then thought that he would listen to conversations that might prove useful – no, no, come, please, the significance of that microphone does not escape me, any more than it escaped you. He would quite certainly not have come out of hiding had he not thought that you possessed valuable information. He may even have thought that you should not be allowed to carry your knowledge further.' A suave thoughtfulness, thought Louis.

'It rather looks,' said Taillefer regretfully, 'as though that man had decided to use his knowledge for his own, unworthy ends, and to suppress yours. Fortunately you are a resourceful man, Mr Schweitzer. Fortunately, perhaps, too, so am I. I had not given my tool an unlimited confidence. I had an eye upon him.'

'It was you, in the lane – in a black 404?' suddenly.

'It was,' with gravity. 'Do please now explain to me – how did it come about that the Russian should have confided to you the hiding-place of his loot?'

'The man was dying and delirious,' in a hard bitter voice. 'He spoke to me – he could not *see* me, you know – in his own tongue, instinctively. By a coincidence I understand that tongue, and without thought I answered him in it. He asked for water. I gave it him. While I was helping him drink I looked around and saw your *tool*, standing there pointing a gun at me.'

'Then it was you that shot the Russian,' with a peculiar smile; 'I wonder why?'

'He asked me to,' simply.

'I see.'

'He was grateful for the water. He felt, perhaps, that I was a compatriot, dimly, and that he could ask me that favour. Between Russians. I know something of their mentality. He gave me no confidence.'

'I, too,' and the smile was now *appetizing*, 'know something of Russians. He did.'

'I can only maintain to you that he did not.'

'You have dropped your book,' said Taillefer pleasantly. 'Well, well, Dresden as it was. That is very encouraging, Mr

Schweitzer; we are further along than I thought. Not only do you know the whereabouts of this treasure – you know what it is. Or are you a student of architecture? That would be too great a coincidence, would it not? You know what it is that you have found, and where it comes from.'

Feeling a deep sense of betrayal, Louis said nothing.

'You will have no hesitation in recognizing that it forms part of the property of the German State. You will have, I am sure, equally no hesitation in confiding it to my keeping, as the official under the German State responsible for its safe-keeping. I am pleased that you found it – it was well hidden.'

'Who said I'd found anything?'

'You would not have resisted the temptation to look.'

'Not so fast.' Louis spoke slowly, searching for ways of re-treating without showing how utterly his defence had been pierced. 'Not so fast. I can't take a responsibility like that. Good, I know what this object is. I have been learning about it, as you so skilfully saw. It's part of the ancient crown treasury of Saxony. Its ownership is by no means proved. Even assuming that it is the property of a German state museum, and assuming that you are even what you say you are, a responsible museum official, you had a man killed to get hold of this object. Maybe others, I do not know. You sent me a threatening letter, you invaded my house, you ransacked my belongings, posing as an officer of the French state police apparatus. You try to explain that by saying you took me for a criminal or a criminal's accomplice – all right, perhaps that's reasonable, if it's true, but it doesn't exactly fill me with sympathy for you. You lack scruples, and that makes me the more scrupulous. Why shouldn't the French government decide this matter, since I have been thinking of giving them any odd items or scraps of knowledge I might have? You may have no embassy in Paris, but if you are what you say you are you can find means of negotiating with Monsieur Malraux – and satisfy him!'

There was a pause. Taillefer seemed to be turning this notion over, dispassionately.

'I do not doubt that means could be found to do as you suggest. I am not convinced that you will find it as good a notion, after a little reflection, as it might appear at first thought. It might even entangle you in unforeseen and trouble-some consequences. The French government, as you rightly observe, would proceed with great caution. And very *slowly*. It would certainly wish to satisfy itself as to how, and under what circumstances, the object came into your possession.'

'My possession?'

'How you acquired your knowledge, if you prefer. It would compromise you – and me too, I do not take the trouble to deny it. I suspect, though, that the thought has already occurred to you. Or you would hardly have waited twenty-four hours be-fore going to the police. The opportunity was not lacking, but you preferred to avoid the resultant complications and for do-ing so I can only congratulate you – I repeat it – on your wisdom. What concerns me is that you have undoubtedly suffered indignities and harassments as a result of an inter-vention that was clumsy and uninspired on my part. Now I recall that my offer to you was the kind of sum governments generally offer to the finders of treasure-trove – paltry, really. I am empowered, however, to use sums at my disposal for com-pensations. I should like to make a really generous settlement – and that to include Madame Wisniewski, who has kindly acted with what she thought of as loyalty towards you. You need feel no resentment at my inability to set a price on your purity of motive. Put it simply that my government feels strong grati-tude for your help. Fifty thousand francs – an investment, put it. It can be kept discreet, to avoid the attention of the percep-teur – another busybody French official,' with a charming smile. 'But there – I have intruded upon you quite long enough, and you may feel embarrassed at the suddenness of all this? You need a little time to settle your mind, and to rear-range the domestic circumstances I ruffled so clumsily. Please feel free to consult Madame Wisniewski's admirable judge-ment. Shall I perhaps say that I will contact you – at your flat? – or wherever you please – after reflection? Let us say after forty-eight hours. I must go now and put an end to this – irruption. Good morning, Herr Schweitzer.'

He picked up his hat, made a deep respectful bow, and had slipped through the doorway before Louis had thought of any-thing to say. The Dresden book lay on the table; he leafed it through idly, wondering what Fabienne would have said. What would she have expected of him? What would she have waited for?

What would Paule expect, come to that? She was part of this – she would benefit – or suffer – from his decision. It struck him suddenly that there was not all that much difference. What Paule would expect, could be simply enough defined as an action Fabienne would have recognized.

Louis went back into the living-room, and noticed that the room reeked of cigarette smoke and stale air. All that from me, he thought, and I had a bath this morning, too. From the exquisite Monsieur Taillefer as well, of course – and he probably has a bath four times a day. Uppercrust personage. This room – opening the window furiously – stinks of corruption. He heard the door to the landing bang open, and wondered if it were more cultural gentlemen come to restore him, but it was only Paule with her cauliflower, her hands too full to shut the door any other way but with a kick.

Part Two

Saturday Midday

The day had clouded over after a promising start, and the
dirty grey sky had closed in tightly over the town. The
atmosphere even by the open window was close and breathless.
A thin greasy drizzle was threatening to fall, and had already
fallen a couple of times for a half-hearted ten minutes, before
taking itself off to brood over someone else's rooftop a half
kilometre further.

'I'm sorry' – Paule was shaking out her damp headscarf –
'I've been rather a long time.'

'Le métier d'homme est difficile.'

'Yes, I tell myself so daily. I would like to have it printed on
a calendar – one of those tear-off ones that have little mottoes
for each day. "Being a man is a hard job." Tear off and repeat,
three hundred and sixty-five times.' It was amusing from a
woman not ordinarily imaginative.

'Nobody would buy it – one must have perky, optimist
notions – Beaumarchais, or Marivaux.'

'Sorry I was so long,' she said again. 'Saturday is always
bad. I had a chore too that took me a little while.'

'What was that?'

'Nothing of any importance' – she was blushing again;
woman had been up to something! 'Everybody seemed quite
as usual at the Europahaus – they've been sniffing about all
right, and I've a notion they've been on at Mr Mestli, but I
didn't want to draw attention to myself by seeming curious. I
don't think they can have got very far.'

Mr Mestli! Louis might have known it.

'Further than you think,' Louis smiled at her, to be reassuring, 'I had a visitor while you were away.'

'You didn't! You mean one of them? – but of course you do;
it couldn't have been anyone else.'

'Walked in at the door – as easy as you did yourself this minute.'

'Oh!' – aghast. 'I hadn't locked it since you were here anyhow. It's only a tinpot lock of course, but I have nothing valuable.' You have, he thought, but you don't know it. 'Anyone can get in the house of course; there isn't even a proper concierge.'

'Anyone did. Though anyone is not quite the right word. A sort of ambassador.' The play on the word amused him in a childish way. 'Could even be a real ambassador – you know, living in a palace in the sixteenth *arrondissement*. Very polite.'

'What did he say?' breathless.

'Offered me fifty thousand francs. And a present for you.'

'A slimy bribe. Really these people are despicable.'

'Perhaps. There were no real threats. I'm supposed to *think about it*. They may be despicable but they're rather formidable, you know. They won't give up, and we see that they're not shaken off easily. I'm afraid we were a bit optimistic, my dear, with our little tricks. These people are properly organized. Must have gone through that fool Mestli like a dose of salts.'

'I'm sure it wasn't the concierge. Or the van driver,' stoutly.

'It doesn't matter. Highly trained, competent technicians. Real professionals.'

'But who are they?'

'Germans – most of them – probably. Hard to say whether they've any real government connexion. The delegates, for instance, certainly wouldn't even know they exist.'

'Do they know where the thing is?'

'They can't be sure I've got it, or even know where it is. Nobody could possibly have seen me, inside that spinney.'

'Are they *spies*?' asked Paule, in a voice of disgust and horror more than fear. She might have been asking about scorpions.

'Very likely, in a deliberately confused way. They have a solid front – in fact it's genuine; it's their real business all right. As we now know.'

'You mean this art committee nonsense is real?'

'It's real enough; there's no reason why it shouldn't be. One of the striking things about art is that it's movable – even portable. It never loses its value – in fact it gains in value, quicker than almost anything else. Very handy to run away with, or hide against a rainy day.

'Also it always takes the fancy of invaders. Barbarians imagine that they civilize themselves by stealing it. Very true, often: think of Napoleon, who stole immense quantities. So did all his generals; if it didn't civilize people like Augereau that's only because nothing could.

'What's more in times of war and revolution people run about with it – squirrel it away and forget where it was put. People in want sell it cheap. After the Revolution the English all stuffed their houses chocker with furniture from the big houses here – bought for sixpence. Not only dukes – jumped-up fellows wanting to acquire ancestors. In the last war, to protect things from the tides of invasion – first the Germans and then the Americans, all great *acquirers* – whole museums full were dismantled in a hurry, not even properly catalogued, and stuffed away in odd corners. Records were burned, devoted curators got killed; people forgot where it had all been put. Fantastic things turned up in saltmines and the basements of obscure sous-préfectures. Half of it never got back home. All the countries have these gangs of experts toddling about hunting for it, and it still goes on, because nobody is quite sure what was destroyed, or what got shipped to Russia – or to William Randolph Hearst. A lot's been found, but there's a lot of art,' acidly. 'The big museums have twenty times as much as they can find space ever to show or even look after properly. Places like the Louvre have cellars twenty kilometres long so stuffed with mouldy art they don't know themselves what they've got. Just the other day the Comédie found a completely unknown manuscript of Marivaux in the cellar – been there unsuspected for two hundred years. Someone else came up with a lost Bach cantata.'

Paule was listening dazedly to this flood, but obediently not interrupting. She had never heard of William Randolph Hearst!

'No – it's natural enough that these people should exist.

Dresden was plundered by the Russians. Nobody knows what disappeared. Our Mr Taillefer – or whatever he may call himself – is very keen to follow up any clues. Offers money for them, what's more.'

Paule was quick to puncture this *respectable* occupation.

'They aren't all art experts,' she said scathingly.

'No, they aren't. There are people there good at capturing or beating up or killing people, as well as at following up things, and people, that try to give them the slip.'

'And was this man who came a sort of boss?'

'According to himself. I dare say – lot of intelligence and ability there. I don't know what to do about him. A man capable of killing – is that a man who will ever understand anything about art?'

'And now they know where you are.'

'Yes – no point in staying hiding here now – I can go out, walk about, stroll in the sun, sit in the park. I don't like your being involved – we must make it plain that this has nothing to do with you at all. Separate you from the whole business – they'll leave you alone, then. Whatever happens – to me – you must keep perfectly silent. If you tried to stir up trouble for them they're likely to become extremely nasty, and you are very vulnerable. I think I'm going to go back to my own flat – not much they can do there.'

'No?' scornfully. 'They terrorized your concierge without effort. They could walk you out at the point of a gun and nobody would utter a peep.'

'And here? What would you do? Scream?'

'Yes. I would open the window and shriek, that they weren't police at all, that they were gangsters, Germans. They wouldn't dare shoot or make a noise.'

'I'm not anxious to put it to the test,' said Louis dryly.

'Neither am I.' She stopped, then said in a small voice, 'I am a great coward. But I'm not frightened of being shot. My fear is of being drowned or strangled, of not being able to breathe. I'm more frightened of an anaesthetic than I would be of a surgeon.'

'I'm frightened of everything,' said Louis sourly. 'Nice for them if they heard that.'

Suddenly he leaped up and across the room, to the old-fashioned armchair, covered in rubbed faded velveteen, where Mr Taillefer had sat, his legs elegantly crossed. He lifted the cushion, and plunged his hand into the tight dusty chink between the back and the seat. He wriggled his hand with difficulty; suddenly he made a face. Paule had her mouth open; she started moving her jaw, preparatory to saying 'What on earth are you doing?' but stopped at the face. With some trouble he was extracting a flat plastic box, like a small pocket-edition book in shape. She began to say 'What on earth is that?' but his gargoyle expression with a finger to his lip suppressed her. Quietly he tiptoed out to the kitchen and laid it on the floor, then came softly back.

'But – what is it?' she whispered anxiously. 'Is it a bomb?'

'No,' smiling despite himself. 'Not a bomb. Tell me, though, when is the dustbin emptied?'

'It was this morning – no, yesterday morning. Not till Monday.'

'Pity. Can't just chuck it in the street.' He thought for a little then tiptoed back. After hunting for a moment in the kitchen he found a polythene bucket, which he filled three quarters full with water. Carefully he immersed the plastic box and left it lying there at the bottom.

'Oh it *is* a bomb,' whispered Paule, really terrified now.

'No,' he said in a normal voice, and grinned to reassure her. 'Truly – that will muffle it enough, I reckon. Distort it anyway – won't stop it carrying noises but just indistinct grumbles, I think. It's a radio sender – tiny transistor thing, battery powered. A transmitter. It would repeat anything we said – would be very handy for them, might save a lot of trouble. Lucky we've said nothing, I think, to give them any conclusive information. Just as well, though, the idea struck me.'

'I've heard of concealed microphones. But I always thought they had to have wires.'

'Ha,' said Louis, 'so did I. Don't think I'm an expert on this subject. You know Monsieur Marie?'

'Of course. You mean the little man who looks after our machines at work? – nice little man but he talks so technically I can't understand a word. He insists on telling one and all about it each time there's something on the blink.'

'Exactly. He does that with everybody. Not that I was the least interested, but he was telling me only a month ago that this microphone lark with wires is absolutely stone-age. The thing now is that gadget there, no wires or anything, looks quite innocuous, weighs hardly anything, takes up scarcely any space. You walk in and leave it on a bookshelf, or scotch tape it behind a picture or something. For no reason it came into my head of a sudden. But my friend didn't have the chance to walk around the room. That chair was the only possible place – even there you'd never have found it unless you were looking.'

'How fortunate that you did think of it.' Paule was much impressed with his cleverness. Louis was rather cheered up by it himself, a very masculine sentiment to have.

'At least we can talk,' he said. 'I would like a drink.'

'Oh dear. I haven't anything in the house till Carlos comes in and brings us a bottle from Roger's. I'll pop out.'

'No. I'll pop out. Can't do any harm. They may watch me, and write it all in a little book, but they won't do anything. I'm supposed to have forty-eight hours anyway. For reflection.'

He went down the stairs whistling, strolled along the street, stopped at the épicerie and went in for a bottle of porto. As he was paying and the old woman was looking for the next customer, a familiar ironic voice said, 'A packet of salted peanuts if you please,' a delicate hand laid exactly one franc twenty-five on the counter, and Louis turned. Monsieur Taillefer smiled in a friendly way and raised his hat.

'Good appetite,' he said – just the way any man buying peanuts will say to any other man he meets buying port, at midday.

Louis strolled exaggeratedly back to Paule's house with his bottle. This time he did not whistle; it seemed too schoolboyish. A peculiar thing, he thought climbing the stairs. I was not frightened – or not really frightened. Now, though, I am. I have become extremely frightened.

It was not, though, because he was consistently finding these people more determined, more skilful, more tricky than he had imagined. Why was it?

He understood when he opened the door and saw Paule sitting there waiting for him. It was really extremely simple. He had been feeling affection for her – he was beginning to love her.

She had changed while he was out – and made a big effort to be less dowdy. She had put her vegetables on, taken off her apron, and changed into a frock. Greenish, linen – rather a pretty shade. Almond-green, he decided. Her hair was tidied; she was wearing lipstick too; she was even wearing pearl earrings! She looked young, pretty, sympathetic. One would say she was enjoying herself, but perhaps it is just courage, thought Louis, unwrapping the port bottle.

'What kind of glass do you need?'

'Two – you're going to have some too.'

'I don't think I've ever had any – will I like it?'

'Yes.'

He had understood, quite suddenly, instinctively. The way he had *guessed* that Monsieur Taillefer had craftily left a little machine to listen to them. Talking, dressing, undressing, going to bed, making love – bastard. She loved him. There were no wine-glasses the right size so he took two ordinary ones.

'That's a great deal – what a pretty colour.'

'The world's best medicine,' happily. 'Doctor Sandeman's Cure-All, only thirteen francs the kick.'

'It's extraordinarily good,' in great surprise.

'Of course it's good. All the things I get are good.'

She burst out laughing. 'Leaving the diamond on my dressing-table like that . . .'

'If they come in and search the place they'll make a thorough job. Luckily they can't be absolutely sure I really do have it. If they come they'll likely pick it up first go, and they might, just, miss it altogether. I have to think of something better.'

'Just don't think of it for the moment,' said Paule earnestly.

The door banged noisily, which meant no suave and silent-footed gangsters, but Carlos.

'Hi, ma. Eh, what's come over you to be glam all of a sudden?'

'It's extremely rude – as you very well know – to make personal comments. You might perhaps say good morning to Louis: that would be more to the point.'

'Good morning,' grinning, not squashed at all.

'Good morning. Got your Latin declensions right?'

'Only that old ablative absolute. Caesar was a bore, wasn't he? – I mean think of being a general, and scouring round Gaul conquering tribes, and still sitting down to write a diary every evening – sort of thing Americans do. What's that, port? Port! – ma drinking port!' Lunatic cackle of vulgar laughter, at which Paule was extremely indignant.

'And don't think for a single second that I'm going to put up with that' – when really cross the Polish accent became stronger. 'You can just leave the room at once and I don't want to see you again before dinner is ready.' Obediently enough the boy went off into the other room, without any answering back either, and once there could be heard singing what sounded an unsuitable song to show he was undefeated.

'Awful boy.' She was suppressing a desire to laugh, but felt it her duty to say it.

'No, not an awful boy,' said Louis decisively. 'The good ones are like that. Not a dull boy, not a stupid boy.'

'I hope I don't become drunk. Anyway I must go and put the cutlets on.' She went out to the kitchen, where she upset the salt and muttered reproaches at herself in Polish: very likely she was a bit drunk. Louis sat feeling very likely he was drunk himself. Why else was he so lighthearted? And where had he got his decision from about Carlos? – what did he know about it? But have no fear; Doctor is here. . . . The door to the bedroom reopened cautiously.

'I say, what's this paperweight thing? Some sort of crystal by the look of it – never seen it that colour before.'

'Just a souvenir I brought your mother from Poland. It looks like that there. Polish crystal – traces of copper mineral in the ground.'

The boy was perfectly satisfied with this morsel of science.

'Can I have some port?'

'Why not?' comfortably; Louis was feeling at peace with all the world and would have been as hospitable with Monsieur Taillefer. However the kitchen door was not properly closed.

'Carlos!'

'Oh now, mum, don't fuss now please. I've often had port with Roger.'

'The things you and that horrible boy get up to – sometimes I'm glad I *don't* know. And don't call me mum,' ended Paule, rather weakly.

'Have you got your gun?' wheedled Carlos, who had sensed at once that Louis was in an easy-going mood. 'Do you carry it all the time?'

'I have been. Now that I think of it, there's no point in that at all. It's extremely uncomfortable anyway. I'd better find somewhere to keep it.' The sizzle of the cutlets quietened as Paule turned the gas down and reappeared to finish her port.

'Carlos was looking at the crystal paperweight,' said Louis casually, shoving the pistol into his suitcase.

'He's no business fidgeting with my things. I don't think I want to leave it there anyhow – I'm putting it in the drawer here,' in a loud voice for Louis' benefit, 'and I hope you know by now that I won't have you messing in my drawer under any pretext.' It gave Louis an idea, not a very brilliant one, but something to make the odds a little longer, possibly. . .

Suppose a man was searching the flat, and opened Paule's drawer – the silver box caught the eye at once and neither hair-pins nor a Kleenex would provide much safeguard. The only way of dealing with that was to put something else in the drawer that provided a distraction to the eye. The pistol, for instance. Men were not so unlike boys! Suppose Carlos opened that drawer and saw the pistol lying there. He would have no eyes for anything else, least of all a little silver box – some woman's toy. . . . He went back to his suitcase.

'Since, as your mother remarks, you are not allowed in this drawer it might be a good place to keep this.'

'You certainly don't have to fear my touching it,' said Paule, eyeing the beastly thing with distrust.

'Can I just hold it a second?' begged Carlos nicely. 'With you there it couldn't do any harm. And if I've seen it I won't be tempted to open the drawer, you see.'

'Very well,' said Louis, entertained by this logic. 'Certainly if you learn to handle a thing like this properly there's less risk of any accident.'

Paule gave a resigned glance, decided not to be a fussy mum any longer, and went back into the kitchen where she had work to do, where she would not have to look, and where, probably, she ran less risk of being shot. Which was also perfectly good logic when you came to look at it.

'You hold it like this. You do not, under any circumstances, put your finger on the trigger. You keep your finger outside the trigger-guard – flat against the side. Like that, yes.'

'But the catch is on so there's no danger.'

'The catch is on but there *is* danger,' corrected Louis. 'First, the catch slips off very easily – look. Second, the catch might not be on and one doesn't always stop to look. Keep your finger away and learn to do it always, automatically. This is the most uncertain, unreliable, dangerous weapon there is. Never never touch the trigger of a pistol.'

> 'Never never let your gun
> Pointed be at anyone.
> That it may unloaded be
> Matters not a scrap to me.

'Roger's father taught him that before he allowed him to hold the carbine.'

'Quite so, but that's a rifle, a pistol is even worse. Not only do you not point, you do not touch. Anyway, besides everything I've said, this is only one make. Sometimes the catch is in another place – or even worse, in the same place but going the exact opposite way, so that you'd tell yourself the catch was on and it would be off. Now that'll do. Put it in the drawer. Formal interdiction, once from your mother and once again from me.'

'Dinner, everyone,' said Paule, putting her head round the door now that she judged it was safe to do so.

Sunday

Louis woke up feeling bleary, and reached for his watch. Paule was out of bed, but had left the shutters closed, so that the light would not wake him. Eight o'clock; he thought about going to sleep again but decided against it – Paule would be back from church and making coffee, and would bring him some: he hated coffee in bed. One fell asleep and woke again to find it cold, and when one did drink it one was so bleary that one spilt half on the pillow, which was squalid.

An even better reason was that he felt squalid. He had gone for a walk in the dark of the evening, with the transistor radio under his arm, meaning to chuck it in the river. But dark or not, there had been an eye. Taillefer? – he couldn't tell: probably not in *person*. He had not chucked it in the river, for they might conclude it was the diamond. And he might then, quite easily, finish in the river himself. He had not got very far, had he, in his thoughts about what to do with the infernal thing? The walk in the cool dark evening air had been supposed to sharpen his wits, and it hadn't: it had if anything confused them further. In the end he had stopped in the marketplace where there were dustbins full of rotten oranges and yellowed cabbage-leaves. He had opened one and laid the radio gently on top of stuff that simply would not do for selling on Monday, hoping that it would sweeten them a bit to have it back. Taillefer might even be amused – if Louis had understood him at all he would hold no grudge at having been caught out. He might even be pleased to discover that Louis was not that stupid. Had he not praised Louis' intelligence? Was it not *intelligence* that was supposed to dictate the right answer? And the right answer, surely, was to give the diamond back to Taillefer on Monday morning, and go to work at the Europahaus as usual, forgetting all about it. . . . A sober little walk to work, with Madame Wisniewski for company.

He had, instead, sent Carlos out for a bottle of vino. He had come back with the best Roger's father could recommend, a really solid bottle of red, guaranteed genuine Beaujolais, and Louis had drunk the whole bottle. . . . He had not been too sleepy to make love, but he had fallen asleep virtually on top of poor Paule, and very likely he snored, and generally behaved in an abject fashion. He felt humiliated and dirty.

There was also an extremely disagreeable taste in his mouth, reminding him he had not cleaned his teeth. He lurched out to the bathroom. Paule was lying in wait in the kitchen with the water boiling, but he did not look at her, and she was too tactful perhaps – she was learning – to say anything.

He spent some time scrubbing in corners, lengthy and meticulous. The teeth are not too bad, he told himself. Show a lot of work and a good deal of odd bits of metal – shell splinters! – but at bottom, when you got down to it, all his. He didn't feel all that encouraged by this discovery. Like Notre Dame or wherever, he thought vaguely. Carcassonne, wasn't it? – yes, and Pierrefonds – all these places Viollet-le-Duc restored. The same, and not the same. He found himself thinking about these stones, that in their time had been pillaged and broken in wars and riots, by furious humans, with the fires and cannonballs said humans had thought up to remove all obstacles to their passion for destruction.

Quite old fashioned all that; things have changed. Fewer people nowadays get their teeth broken for them by some chap with brass knuckles and a grievance – and there is quite an outcry when it does happen. Nobody, feeling, let's say, aggressive about being out of work, would knock bits off Notre Dame nowadays. Our age is more *gentle*. More apt at concealing hypocrisy behind soapy words, more scared of the sight of blood – after all, poison is less messy. Only in our age are we regaled by people complaining of the odious brutality of boxing, and the passer by, glancing up at Notre Dame, tells himself with satisfaction that in our day things are cared for. It looks so reassuringly normal – a little black, but that can't be helped. Progress has been made, has it not, since the vandalism of the nineteenth century, pulling Fontainebleau to pieces after deciding it was old fashioned, or selling Marly and Anet to speculators?

In fact we are very *virtuous*, and a rosy glow takes possession of every tourist staring at the vast hideous elephant in the Place de l'Étoile being scrubbed back to the appearance of a monstrous ice-cream tart by the lily fingers of the twentieth century. How clean we are. Housemaids, dusting. The tourist does not notice that all these holy old stones are not only black but have been eaten, very much in the way sun eats snow.

Nobody notices snow. It falls, and is pretty, and then it is kicked and shovelled and trampled – a kind of modernized carving – and is no longer pretty, and nobody looks at it any more. The heaps freeze quite often into compact masses that seem as permanent as stone, being as solid, as resistant to the hand, but nobody is taken in because everybody knows how fragile and impermanent it is in reality and that a few weeks at most will sweep it all into oblivion. So that nobody is excited when after a day or so of sun and wind the packed carved surface is pocked and pitted – eaten – into a corruption of grey and yellow cavities like teeth. Not our teeth, which are plastic, but the teeth of an old Normandy peasant who has drunk three litres of rough cider a day for sixty years.

If the tourist looked at the carvings on, say, the elephant, he would have noticed, before the dentist came from Cultural Affairs, that all the faces and hands, all the shapely knees and elbows, all the swelling breasts and triumphal bottoms had been eaten – like snow, like teeth – back through their stone bones, through to their discoloured innards, by a twentieth-century leprosy, or syphilis of stone.

It is all like that, the stone, everywhere, in every town – the Gothic traceries crumbling cobwebs of foulness, the Renaissance columns bashed as though by armies of puritan image-breakers, the frescoes and bas-reliefs smeared away to dirty shadows – the good housemaid with her duster has become the housemaid who was disappointed in love, in 'The Light that Failed', who rubbed out the painter's masterpiece with turps.

We know vaguely, of course, that this is done by the famous acids of the air – vaguely we know that it is factory chimneys, auto exhausts, and so on, that turn our stone into dirty snow, just the way the rough cider on the breath erodes the teeth. Just one of those little prices we pay for our progress, like the fish floating belly up, like the oil on our beaches, like the lemons painted with diphenyl to discourage penicillin.

Louis looked at his face in the cheap distorting glass that hung on the wall of the tiny bathroom, and shrugged. If the century did that to stone what did it do to his skin, his lungs, his conscience, his inner fabrics? Corruption. . .

Sorry sir, said the waitress in the teashop, the pudding's *off*. We can do you a nice ice-cream though. Of course . . . no stone but plenty of nice ice-cream concrete. Tuberculosis is off, but we can do you a most sophisticated cancer – strawberry, chocolate, or pistachio?

A good thing, thought Louis, plodding back towards his heap of clothes, that Dresden had been bombed, probably. It would cost a socialist state much too much to go restoring all that stonework. Why, that money could be spent building a nice rocket, for an informed scientific glance at Pluto. No no, nothing to do with the underworld, old chap – you been reading myths or something? – no, you know – that dog on the movies.

Governments, thought Louis, staring at Paule who was tidying the living-room and not seeing her, no longer build. Can't afford it. Not with autoroutes the price they are. Price, you see; nobody understands price. It is an economic necessity that the farmer gets a sou for the amount of flour the housewife pays one franc fifty for, just as it is an economic necessity that the 'best craftsman' gets a putty medal and a limp handshake from a prefect while a pop singer gets a Ferrari to kill anybody that may have survived his last record, a pretty suit to wear over his sweaty underpants, and at least six weeks of absolute immortality.

He was shaken out of his contemplation by Carlos' eyes. The boy had followed him with his glance, through the bedroom door towards a rumpled bed hollowed by two people in the middle. Louis caught the eyes, which were thoughtful, and in shame shut the door in a hurry. The windows were still shut, and the shutters outside them, and the room reeked. Louis opened them hastily. Corruption here too. What sort of an object is a human being? He washes like mad, lives surrounded by bidets and toothbrushes, if German he even shaves his armpits and sprays himself with anti-sweat – and a lot of good may that do him. He still stinks.

Louis sat in a black mood, and did not even notice the door open, with the razor buzzing stupidly in his ear like a bumblebee going round and round the same flower wondering dimly whether there is any more honey. Paule kissed him gently above his ear; he flapped the lead of the razor irritably as though she had come to pester him.

'Give me your clothes and I'll wash them.' He snapped the razor off and only then realized that she smelt nice. She had gone out and bought perfume; a nice one too, something light and clean, with a suggestion of lemon about it, or was it mint, in the hot sunshine? Nothing clawky and sexy – the black mood fell off.

'Breakfast is ready,' she said. A Sunday breakfast, with toast because the bread was stale. Never had the coffee tasted so good, but Louis sat uncomfortably. Carlos had his eyes in his coffee-cup, into which he was dipping pieces of toast reflectively, and had nothing to say. Suppose he made some remark? – what answer should one make? Louis didn't know at all what one said to a teenage boy. He felt furtive and nasty, as though he had stolen a shabby purse from an old-age pensioner. He wanted to run out of the house. He broke a piece of toast awkwardly, and a lump fell in his cup. He fished it out again awkwardly and put it on his plate, where it sat sodden and beastly, oozing greasy coffee. With childish sullenness he pushed the plate away and felt for a cigarette. There was no ashtray.

'Give me that,' said Paule, reaching for the plate. 'And your cup – I'll rinse it and give you fresh hot coffee. And an ashtray.' She went out to the kitchen and in the dead silence he could hear the tap run and the clash of plate and cup in the sink.

'You're sleeping with Mama, aren't you?' said Carlos flatly, in a quiet, level voice.

He had to give *some* answer.

'Yes. But I love her, you see.'

'Could I have the butter?' in exactly the voice in which one does ask for the butter. Louis wanted to say something else, something *better*, but Paule came back in. The smell of perfume was just barely perceptible through the smell of very hot coffee.

'Now drink that.'

'Can I have some more too?' asked Carlos.

'Of course.'

'I'll get it.'

'No. Sunday. You don't need to work on a Sunday.' She went out again but came back before Louis had thought of anything to say.

'I'm going to the swimming-bath after church. If I see Michou he might be coming out this afternoon. Lousy day, though.'

Real Sunday weather, thought Louis, looking out of the window. It was raining steadily and every now and then the wind blew it in gusty curtains across the street. Women were coming back from early mass clutching hats, umbrellas held in front of them like anti-tank defences. The fathers of families were hunched inside turned-up coat-collars, trying to shield cardboard cake-boxes under their arm, nattering at the children not to step in the gutter in their sparkling Sunday shoes. I wish it were me, thought Louis. I would like to be out there too shepherding a little girl in a pleated skirt and a short braided jacket, with patent-leather slippers and little white cotton gloves. A bad-weather Sunday had always been the blank hole in his life. Work was the only answer, he had found long ago, and it had always been on Sundays that the most ambitious of his smyrna rugs had got done. And there was music – that never deserted one. But it had always seemed as though one was stumbling drearily along – the plodding marchers of the slow movement in Beethoven's third symphony.

'I suppose the idea of going to church wouldn't interest you at all, no?' asked Paule with embarrassment.

'May I?' stupidly.

'Not exactly a secret society,' laughing. Certainly she was not conscious of any strain. 'I would like that. Do you want to go as you are or make yourself resplendent?'

'I'll put on a suit.' He was anxious to do the job properly.

'Carlos, one job I'm afraid you do have to do and that is polish your shoes.'

'Give them to me,' said Louis. 'I have to do mine. You said yourself he shouldn't work on a Sunday.'

'It's only that he does have to work very hard during the week, and his school programme will get stiffer and stiffer, and I think Sunday ought to be really free,' hastily. 'I like him to go and enjoy himself. It's nicest when the gang has organized something between themselves.'

'Michou has an aeroplane we were going to try out. But I think there's too much wind.'

'Find me the shoe-polish.'

'And I'll start getting the dinner ready.'

'And I'm going to see whether Roger's going out.'

And there he was after all, thought Louis sardonically. Stepping carefully along the uneven pavement to avoid puddles, not wanting to get his beautiful shoes splashed. Paule, beside him, in a sedate bluish-green woollen suit under her coat, with a headscarf that had pictures of Gothic cathedrals on it. Carlos' progress was more erratic, a complex course that took him round lamp-posts and parked autos. He seemed perfectly lighthearted; Louis could not tell whether he was *upset* or not. And suppose he is – what am I supposed to be able to do about it? Go to confession with Paule?

He had not been to church since his childhood. Fabienne had gone occasionally, he never knew quite when nor why, for she did not talk about it, she just disappeared, and said briefly when questioned, 'I've been to church', and then changed the subject at once as though she were ashamed of it.

Things had changed for the better, he noticed. Less mumbo-jumbo, less obscure muttering. Prayers were said loudly, carefully, in full view, by a man who meant what he said, a small thin man with a pale military face and hair gone prematurely grey, a man Louis liked very much. The sermon was just as he remembered – a much older man with a beard who looked like Monsieur Fallières and had a flowery oratory belonging to a Third Republic politician that was boring and tiresome in the extreme. Carlos fidgeted with his feet, yawned, slept, stared about and finally got deeply interested in the floor; Paule, and the grey-haired young man, sat with an extraordinary controlled patience that impressed him. It went on for twenty-five terrible minutes of booming and high rhetorical wails while Louis crossed his arms grimly and wished he had not come.

But afterwards things changed subtly. The words amplified slightly by the microphone on the altar fluttered past him before dying away up in the vaulted roof in a soft sighing mutter, peeling off, it seemed to him, skins of boredom and distrust. The words were familiar, and he found he knew each phrase just before it was spoken, but for the first time in his experience they seemed more than just formulae: they burned in, with a quiet but intense – even ferocious – pain that changed slowly into an unwilling, unsure peace. Yes, he had been thinking of that moment in the third symphony when it seems that the stumbling, blinded footsteps will never reach anywhere – and now the other moments were coming to his mind one after the other – the huge hammer-blows in the first movement, the sudden little swirling undercurrents of melody filled with gaiety and hope, the full, calm sweep of faith and resolution – and the great climax of rock on which the big Atlantic waves break in a tower of spray ten metres high. . .

The moment in the funeral march too when the heavens open and the unbearable weight lifts. The moment at the end of the march when the whirl of the scherzo brings a thick rapid pulse of blood to the listener at the end of his forces. . .

Paule – she had been fornicating – did not go to communion, no. He realized that. He would have liked to take hold of her arm and say 'Come' – he felt miserable, shut out – yet he was part too of the great crowd plodding slowly forward in the march that Beethoven saw – halt and blind and paralytic, poor and wretched, the prisoners; all those in pain . . . *Seigneur je ne suis pas digne – dis seulement une parole – je serai guéri* . . .

It was during the communion too that in a restless turn of the head to shake off an oppression that was growing too much for him he saw, behind and a little to one side, observing him with an elegant, benevolent, faintly mocking eye, Monsieur Taillefer. In vain was he told to go in the peace of Christ, in vain did he echo faintly the reply '*Nous rendons grâce à Dieu*' – the peace that for a moment had reached him at the words '*Agneau de Dieu*' was lost. In vain did he remind himself that the end, too, was like the finale to the third symphony, a surge into the sunburst of fresh air and light, of an animated gaiety all around of greetings and conversation, the jump and whoop of children let off the leash, and the happy prospect of drinks, cake – first the buying of the cake according to the Sunday ritual, and later, after the roast meats, the equally ritual eating of that cake in a gluttony that is somehow not criminal, since it is a Sunday after all. All that was poisoned now. Although the clouds had parted, the wind had fallen, and a blinding April sun was streaming down on the brilliant wet pavements. Paule smiled at him happily.

'You go on,' he said. 'I'm going to buy cake. And have a drink. Go on ahead and put the dinner on and when I get back we'll have porto.'

'Very well. I must hurry anyway, or I'll never be ready in time. I shall be *expecting* you.'

He turned. Taillefer lifted his hat with a smile of greeting.

'Rather an unusual experience. But interesting, most interesting. These odd survivals always are.'

'Come and have a drink,' said Louis grimly.

'Be delighted to. Uncommonly agreeable of you to suggest it.'

'What would you like?'

'Porto?' with a hint of malice.

'Two Pernods,' said Louis firmly. He was determined to counterattack; damn it, he wasn't going to have this fellow like a kind of Mephistopheles grinning at him all day.

'Yes, interesting,' he began at once. 'Pity about the architecture of that church – not very like Dresden, is it?'

'No,' agreed Taillefer shortly. 'It is not. But in a palace of ignorance and superstition, does it matter?'

'You know,' said Louis, looking straight at him, 'you want me to help you. Assuming, as a hypothesis, that I could, I would like you to give me a good reason why I should. I would be a great deal more willing if, for instance, your people had rebuilt Dresden.'

Taillefer stirred the ice-blocks in his Pernod and studied the colour intently.

'You are among those who have a sentimental attachment to the past, I see. We do not share it. We have broken with the past; our eyes are turned resolutely to the future.'

'I hear that cliché daily, spouted out in a bellow from some cretin or other at the Europahaus. The future does not exist except in the fabric of the past. Your future is a sterility.'

'You misunderstand. The Dresden collections will be housed in buildings that the people will understand and appreciate. They will be enabled to see how the evil of the past is used to instruct them, in order that the crimes and follies of the régimes that have been swept away with all the other cobwebs can never be repeated. The lessons will always be under their eyes.'

'Don't give me that baby-talk,' said Louis angrily. 'You're an intelligent man and so am I. In another minute you will be telling me that all good, peace-loving Germans, all the really loyal Germans, all the Germans who did not believe in Hitler, are all gathered under your banner. Whereas the reactionaries and the aggressors are one and all banded together in the Federal Republic.'

'We do not wish to be reunited with the Federal Republic,' stiffly. 'We do not wish the old aggressive spirit of Prussian expansionism to reawake.'

Louis took a big drink.

'Now listen to me a second and be reasonable. Leave all the slogans aside a moment and listen. Two facts – first, the country was chopped in half to make it for ever impotent. Never again a threat to Poland, to Czechoslovakia, to Russia itself. Thesis supported by all the rest of us from Norway to Sicily – there isn't a man who would not be subconsciously afraid of what German industrial power might not do or be capable of. Fair enough?'

'If you have an argument, state it.'

'Fact two – partitioning a country for this purpose never works. They will go on having a yearning to rejoin. Your friends are all for the yearning of Vietnam and against the yearning of Germany, which makes the position ridiculous.'

'And to resolve this fundamental contradiction?' said Taillefer smiling faintly.

'Simple,' said Louis. 'You guarantee the inviolable nature of the Oder-Neisse. Never again Baltic nibbling, never again hungering about Poland. Stettin, Danzig, Königsberg, Posen, Breslau – inviolable and immovable. You simply restore the three lost provinces that are genuinely German – Thuringia, Saxony, Mecklenburg – and Brandenburg of course. At one sweep you remove all resentment that an artificial partition can only nourish. You remove all this revanchard lark. You make the whole of the so-called eastern sector a demilitarized zone. No German army, no atom weapons, no nothing.'

'How naïve,' laughing. 'Your reunited German nation, free

of all military burdens, possessing once more an unequalled energy and resources, would frighten all the corrupt and incompetent occident into creeping underground. You move the Bonn government into Berlin, and whether or not it possesses a tank or a plane, in a year it has total political and economic hegemony.'

'I don't see why. You maintain all the American, French and British bases on their present West-German soil. You stipulate that all costs are born by Germany alone – that takes care of the military burden angle. Economic hegemony? – you once allow the whole of Europe to unite and England balances the eastern provinces. The whole weeping sepsis ceases to exist.'

Taillefer finished his drink carefully, making sure that no delectable drop remained tucked behind the ice-blocks.

'You have listened too often to the song of Gaullist propaganda. Ancient nationalist myths. I am too good a German to be tempted by the prospect of a return to all you mention. I have watched the western half of Germany become more and more Americanized, more and more plastic to the manipulations of capitalists still existing like dinosaurs in a world too enfeebled to withstand them. It no longer tempts us, Herr Schweitzer, to be one with towns that now are German only in the sense that Minneapolis or Milwaukee are German. We have been given the chance to make a clean break from all that – we have been the first generation of a pioneer socialist state that shall belong to no one but the people. It is hard. We live on a frontier, tossed between warring interests. We have to build our house handicapped, mutilated, as a man tries to build a house who has only one arm and one leg. But we will do it. When we rebuild Dresden, and put back the reunited art collections, they shall not be the ransom of greed and oppression, given to museums by beer-barons trying to dodge their tax-commitments. And they shall not be housed in palaces every stone of which cost the blood of a thousand peasants. They shall be ours, as the country is ours. We do not want the fat bloated corpse of that American colony next door to us tied to our limbs. What has it to offer us? No. We are thin, we are poor, we are ragged – but we are pure. We will work while the bloated occident tears itself to rags for handfuls of paper money, and we with our little handful of gold coins earned honestly will dance upon its grave.'

He had become quite impassioned; he leaned forward across the café table and shook a finger at Louis. 'Another five years, my friend. The nineteenth century will go down then into its grave at last. Churchill is gone. Adenauer will soon go. De Gaulle, Franco, Salazar will follow. Socialist governments will stretch then from the Atlantic to the Urals – and then – you will all be begging on your knees to join us. You will ask our help in throwing the last American off the coast of Europe. Then you will turn to Dresden – for a model in helping you rebuild wrecked and ruined Paris after the Americans have bombed it.'

The finger aimed itself at Louis and stabbed the air. 'That diamond, my friend, is not part of the past as you imagine. It is one of the foundation stones of the clean future.' He got up and walked away rapidly; Louis sat gazing after him. It had clouded over again, and the cold northerly wind was whipping up more rain, which fell on him in the five minutes back to Paule's flat. He arrived chilled and stiffened. There was a smell of roast beef, and under the little Polish Madonna a new candle was burning. Why not an electric light? We are poor and we are pure, thought Louis acidly. In our industrial age a candle costs ten times what electricity would – but in our pride we maintain it, because it has life. A flame is the symbol of life and of hope, of the future and of a vow.

His arm felt stiff and half paralysed; all his old wounds were hurting him. Only the chill of rain and the bluster of the north-west wind. His trousers below the knee had an unpleasant moist feel and his modern capitalist raincoat had not given his neck any protection, so that damp had oozed inside his collar. Ah – why don't we wear the real raincoats, the old leather ones, hot and immensely heavy, with the collar that came to the ears, the skirt to the bottom of the calves – or the tops of your boots, it depended – and the built-in inner cuffs that kept the wrists dry and warm? They just make one look too East German, that's why. He walked heavily into the kitchen where Paule was peeling apples and pinned her against the table in a revanchist fashion.

'Oh Louis, your sleeve is damp; you must change that suit.'

'In a little while.'

'My dearest – the boy!'

'Gone to the swimming-baths.'

'Leave me please. I tell you he can come in at any second.'

He let her alone irritably and propped himself on the table.

'I feel old, worthless and sterile,' he said heavily. Paule was not having this.

'Exactly the feeling one gets when one is open to picking up a touch of grippe. You're shivering. Get out of that damp suit at once and I'll find the aspirin.'

'Listen,' she said, when he came back in corduroy trousers and the heaviest sweater he had – she was holding out three aspirins on the palm of her hand – 'he'll certainly be out all afternoon, and if you feel seedy you get into bed, and if you want I'll come in with you.'

He swallowed the aspirin obediently.

'Do you have any feelings about the Oder-Neisse line?' quite casually. He was astonished, because she went on fire at once, just as fiercely as Taillefer if in a different way.

'I don't care what you hear at the Europahaus,' brandishing the potato-peeler as though it were a sabre and her name Poniatowski. 'No German must ever be allowed to set a foot on the Baltic. Just let them come there for holidays! I tell you, you'd see them the way you do in Strasbourg, flaunting about pushing Poles off the pavements, every gesture meaning they think they own it. Never never never. And you won't find a Pole who doesn't feel the way I do. You were on the Russian front – where were you?'

'In the south. Caucasus.'

'In the spearhead. With tanks?'

'Yes.'

'In a Waffen SS unit?'

'Yes.'

'Then you never saw what happened afterwards. You were the point – but what of the weight of the body that deliberately sat on province after province like so many butterflies, stamping them into dust? You never saw that. There were Poles at first that were happy to see the Russians driven back from our border – but they learned – they learned.'

'But Russia's invaded Poland innumerable times. Surely they're as bad.'

She softened her voice, realizing she was shouting. 'Yes, poor Poland. Living between Germany and Russia for ever, throughout history – up to the end of the world. You cannot know what that means. You have never studied Polish history. You do not know what hope Poland always, for hundreds of years, has put in the West, in France and in England. Till Yalta. When we knew that the Americans would halt on the Elbe we knew it was finished, that we would never shake off Russia again. But we shook off Germany.' She spat the word.

Taillefer was right. He had been too naïve.

Neither the aspirin nor even the roast beef stopped him shivering. He knew that it was not grippe, despite Paule's fussing over the damp suit, but after Carlos had disappeared with a preoccupied face – it was too windy for Michou's aeroplane but they were going to a ski-class – he needed no persuading to go to bed. The bed was terribly cold and felt damp, but she undressed and got into it with him.

'Animal warmth is best,' she said in a very serious tone, as though she had found him on a glacier after three days' exposure. At least he was not gangrenous yet – despite the Dresden green diamond!

He had fallen asleep. The skin of Paule's breast and shoulder – animal warmth is best – was sticking to his own chest in a very sympathetic way. Just so does the salt cod stick to one's greedy fingers when fished out of its hot bath to be boned, just so is the lovely glutinous texture of an oxtail stew or a winter soup into which one has dropped a calf's foot. Louis got one arm out of the nest and fished for a cigarette; the lighter fired first time, adding a little material contentment to his peace. The arm had got its articulation back too; it neither creaked nor hurt. He laid it out along the top of the blanket, an attractive sensuous feel – cool air on one surface and rough warm wool on the other. Paule woke up – if she had been asleep; she might have just been lying quietly thinking. Men can never stop themselves falling asleep, exactly like a baby that has eaten in a satisfyingly greedy way and snores immediately with a wonderful sticky mouth, blowing milky bubbles. He was staring at the ceiling, but he could feel her eye – a wifely eye – on his face.

'He hates us.'

'Who?'

'Taillefer – pooh, that's not his name, he's not called Taillefer at all, it's a typical theatrical pseudonym. The shaper of iron, the hammerer, the swordsmith. In his hands you are to be made white-hot and wrought. He betrays himself by dropping people on the floor and then jumping on them. He stamped on that Russian – I'm certain of it. He had a glib explanation about the man I squashed; he was a criminal, psychotic, and so on. He himself was greatly shocked, would have abolished the fellow himself, was extremely grateful to me for doing so, and so on, all honey: I don't believe a word of it. He has forgiven nothing, neither the Russians nor the Germans, nobody. I wouldn't mind betting there's a bitter tale in his history somewhere, that the man has suffered torments. But he'll hurt us, be vicious to us, any chance he gets, and he's waiting for that chance – he must know now that the big play he made, the effort to be silky, the elaborate chatting-up, had no effect. Tomorrow he'll be plotting something nasty.'

She lay very still.

'Interesting man – why those sophisticated western clothes, that diplomat's manner? It's not a blind; it's at least half a wish, I imagine – a subconscious wish, maybe – to be like us, only better, more perfect. You can't tell, of course – you'd need to dig down deep. But I can't let him have the diamond, and I must do my best to stop him taking it. I must find some way of getting his eye away from here, and especially from you. Getting it away – I must make him believe it's somewhere else though, first. Otherwise the moment I come out of the house and he has reason to think it's in my pocket he'll simply jump me. Beat my brains out then, I shouldn't wonder, till he finds out. A prospect I've no desire to run to meet.'

'The police, darling – surely it's the best solution in the long run.'

'I'm only going to contemplate the police absolutely as a

very last resort. No, I'm going to go, tomorrow, to the flat. He'll allow me to do that, unhindered. And from there on I intend to lead him a dance.'

'He can't be absolutely certain you've got it.'

'No, not absolutely certain. But I know where it is – of that he's over ninety per cent certain. There's a doubt in his mind what I can have done with it. He doesn't underestimate me that much; he knows I've thought about the idea, and that I might have done something eccentric. He's following me everywhere to study me, to read my mind and my intentions. Did you know that he was just behind us in church this morning?'

'No!'

'You were busy saying your prayers, my dear. I wish that you weren't so deeply involved in this. He may decide that you're the weak point in my fortifications.'

'Am I?'

'Ask me and I'll tell you you're the strong point,' said Louis with feeling.

'I'm going to get out of bed. Carlos will be home before long. Shall I make you some coffee?' Good hot strong Polish coffee, a cure to all ills. Between that and port . . .

'Carlos knows that you sleep with me.'

'He does? How can you be sure?'

'He followed me with his eyes, this morning. I'd been to clean my teeth. I was a bit sleepy and stupid. The door was open and he was just so placed that he could see the bed had been slept in by two people.'

'I don't mind. He knew you were sleeping in this room. He saw that I didn't go to communion this morning. He must have drawn his own conclusions.'

'Even before that. At breakfast; he just asked me, straight out.'

'And what did you say?'

'Said yes, of course; what could I have said?'

'Exactly. Without explanation?'

'Without explanation.'

'That is best, so. One must not try to keep things from them – they always find out anyway, they have eyes like needles.

One must never never lie, and one must never explain. I've learned that. He's not a fool. He will know I have my reasons.'

'Hm.' He looked at her, and laughed. He wished to tell her how much he loved her, but the moment, perhaps, would have been badly chosen. It is so easy – too easy – to tell a woman how much you love her after spending two hours in bed with her. The only time it is easier – and sounds falser – is just after you have got into bed with her.

Monday Morning

Louis did not take more than ten minutes to pack his case. Paule said nothing – it would only make matters worse. If explanations were to be avoided with Carlos how much more so now. As for him, he had said too much already the day before. Explanations were birdlimed; touch them and you never again got rid of them. He did not know exactly what it was he was going to do, and Paule knew that he did not know, and he knew that she knew. . . . He walked up the street to the square, where there was a taxi rank, lounging along with a cigarette in his mouth, staring around insolently for the benefit of any henchmen that might be hanging about.

Paule stood on the pavement in front of the house. That afternoon, it was agreed, she should trot off to work at the Europahaus just as usual, just as though nothing had ever happened. Louis had hoped – was hoping – that Taillefer would reason after his own instincts, and would think that surely Louis would never be such a fool as to tell the woman actually where the diamond was, and as for giving it her . . .

She felt as though only by an extreme effort was she stopping herself vomiting on the pavement. She would have liked to kiss him. Sense, she told herself; I am a sensible woman, that is what he sees in me. He finds me a sensible woman, reliable, and that is what I have to be. She did not think he loved her. She had been a good bandage for his wounds, and that was what he needed. That, she had decided, was justifiable. Wisniewski rallies round with the first-aid box. He had told her that unless actually in the hands of the enemy she would hear from him by lunchtime. Roger's mother in the café next door would take a message . . .

The taxi was a streaky, tatty, patchy-black old Simca Ariane looking as though just back from the Gobi Desert; the driver went with it. All drivers look like their own taxis but this was copybook: a thickish roundish middle-aged man with a snub nose, not much dusty hair, a good deal of dusty stubble, and a very dirty suède windbreaker.

'Where to, chief?'

'Avenue du Jura.'

Despite middle age he turned out to be one of the stock-car boys, like those American juveniles who work off their aggressions bumping one another with ancient Plymouths on cinder tracks. He started in second, speeded up to seventy in disregard of various housewives wavering across the road with eyes fixed on sausage, made a right turn with a faint scream and a steely snap into third, wrenched straight, letting a DS filter from the right with the width of his nerve to spare, and attacked the one-way street leading to the Place De Lattre in top, Louis holding his breath in silent groans. Not only nerve, of course. New brake-linings and an exact understanding of the intimate guts and private mannerisms of his auto.

Very simple system. If it comes from the right pretend you're going to hit it: if it comes from the left disregard it. If it's in front pass it and if it's behind the hell with it. Only one system simpler, thought Louis with amusement overcoming slight terror; the old army slogan of salute-it-if-it-moves-and-whitewash-it-if-it-doesn't . . .

Through the Place, down the Rue des Alpes, over the bridge and round the big tree-lined circle of the Square de l'Université, which, being round, isn't a square, but never mind.

The way along the river, the Quai des Pêcheurs, flows in here, and a big right-hand-drive Humber that was flowing along it arrived suddenly in the circle, was disconcerted at three different streams of traffic all aimed at him, forgot that on-the-right means in-the-right, and made a sharp cut-in under the Simca's nose. In France this is called tail-of-fish and quite often leads to combatants having to be separated, and a little later a sentence, not always suspended, for Blows and Injuries.

The taxi-driver did not even curse. He had never hit anything yet and wasn't going to begin now. He could not stop since he was doing seventy; he could not swing out further to the right because there was not only a pavement but trees – they hurt – so he locked his wheels and got into the gutter. Tyres howled, everybody in the street looked round, the front right tyre, nipped by the pavement, should have banged like a cannon but didn't, and Louis, getting his nose out of the ashtray, breathed. Everything came to a stop, and the door of the Simca slammed meaningfully.

'If you want to kill me,' with horrid calm, 'why not take an axe?'

'I'm frightfully sorry.' It was an Englishman, harassed and mortified. 'I do realize I was in the wrong there. I'm most sincerely sorry – I was watching the turn ahead.'

'Not the turn you want to watch it's out of your sodomiting window . . . '

'I do apologize – what more can I say? By great good luck there's no damage done though, is there? Marvellous how you stopped.' At this moment, wanting to be dramatic, the right front tyre subsided with a small vulgar sound. Suddenly the butler fainted . . .

'Oh no?'

'I mean,' hastily, 'not the kind of damage the insurance will make a *thing* of.'

'Who'll give me a new tyre then?' Loudly. 'Reverend Mother – or you?'

'Oh I say. No call to be rude. Please – I'll be happy to compensate that.' And indeed the Englishman had his wallet in his hand, peeling out a hundred-franc note and held it out. The hand remained outstretched inexorably.

'That stop took a year's wear off the other three – just take a look at the rubber on the road.' Another hundred crossed the gap, watched with delight by forty bystanders and a calm policeman.

'That'll do,' said the policeman. 'If you hadn't been rolling too fast you'd not have burned them.'

'Well I like that . . . ' with a death-to-cows tendency in the voice – he had been getting on nicely. 'What about my pas-senger's injuries, then?' The policeman turned a disbelieving eye on Louis, who was now rather enjoying the situation. Was there something to be made out of this unexpected incident that might confuse Monsieur Taillefer? Even put him in a flap? Should he pretend to have a weak heart and gasp out a demand to be taken immediately to hospital? But he was too late, for the policeman was only concerned with unblocking the circulation.

'He hasn't any injuries. Gentleman's paid you. He was in the wrong but he's a tourist and he was just a bit more awkward than he need have been.' That disposed of the injuries, but was a bit too mild towards the aggressor.

'Papers!' sharply to the Englishman. He turned on the crowd now with assumed indignation. 'Circulez, allez, push off.'

Put upon, the driver turned to Louis.

'Have to pay me off, chief. Can't take you no further – got to change my fornicating tyre now.'

'I really *am* sorry,' said the Englishman to Louis. He was a tall man of sixty odd, with a splendid wave of silver hair and a rosy healthy face. 'Can I perhaps give you a lift to wherever you want to go? – that seems the least I can do for upsetting you?'

'Doctor eh?' interrupted the policeman, handing back the papers.

'Ought to know what happens when two autos make love in the roadway huh – oughtn't you?'

'Yes. Yes, indeed,' humbly.

Louis had had a second in which to get a flash of immense cunning. An Englishman and a doctor, plainly very respect-able, probably wealthy – he had been thrown the finest chance imaginable to worry Monsieur Taillefer, who would be totally disconcerted. He could confuse his trail and the diamond would no longer be sticking to him! For all Taillefer would know he had handed it to this doctor, with a pompous tale that might quite likely send the chap hurrying straight to the British Ambassador.

'Yes please,' he said. 'That would indeed be most kind.'

With a great indignant crash the lid of the Simca was flung open to get the spare wheel out. No offer was made to get Louis' case – he got it himself.

'Don't be all day there either,' said the policeman strolling off, somewhere midway between the two, so that it could apply equally.

'Are you all right?' inquired the Englishman anxiously.

'Sure I'm all right. Put my case on top if I may.'

'Let me help you.' Three dusty cases on the roof already. 'Urgh, up she goes.'

'Allez, circulez,' said the policeman suddenly behind them, an impatient voice. 'I make no further reproach since you are a stranger, but get out of it now; you're blocking half the road. Remember to be more careful too, or it'll be the cause of something much worse.'

'Sorry, sorry.' Flustered, the Englishman started his motor and turned right, which was the quickest way to get out of sight.

'Where was it you wanted to go? I don't know the town well, I'm afraid, but perhaps you can direct me.'

'Well I *was* going towards the Avenue du Jura.' He could perhaps invite the doctor for a drink or something. But still flustered, the man was not listening properly. He had been bawled out, he had had a shock, he was sitting on the wrong side of the auto, he was in an anxious agony about hypothetical traffic from the right, and most of all he was flustered by having been the centre of publicity. He wanted to soothe any ruffled feathers there still might be, and of what Louis said he only caught the last word.

'Jura? But of course. Anywhere you please and with the greatest of pleasure. We're headed for Switzerland actually so it won't be the least out of our way. Only too glad.'

Louis was sitting at the back, beside a young woman who paid him no attention in a faintly bored manner, as though she had been so disgusted by the little scene that she could not bring herself to acknowledge his existence.

'Look out, Dad, that light's going red.' The tone was irritable, the voice clear and very high, that of a young English woman from a well-off professional family who has had an

125

expensive education. The Humber braked hastily and a little auto behind them that had counted on shooting the amber light squealed and uttered an irritated toot. Louis glanced back – grey Simca thousand. No sign of a blue one, nor the black Mercedes, but he felt that Monsieur Taillefer could not be far away. He would have his motor racing, what's more.

Louis felt pleased with his flash of cunning. Here he was ensconced in a pompous auto going to Switzerland! And they would be over the frontier in a couple of hours too. Jura – it was splendidly vague; he could say he was going to Switzerland too and they would take it quite for granted. He had no passport but could cross on his identiy card. He had a slight twinge of anxiety for all this beauty of this notion – quite a time to go before they reached the Swiss border and he could come back and cook Taillefer's goose by telling him that the diamond was in a bank vault in Zürich! Suppose – Taillefer did not lack re-source – they got somehow held up or delayed on the road. He had to find some way of casting doubt still, of getting the diamond to stick to someone else. And immediately he had a second flash of cunning. In front the doctor and his wife – presumably; smallish darkish woman who had not spoken – were watching tensely for the light to go green. The daughter – she looked to be about twenty, pleasant-looking young woman despite the sulky expression – was studying a roadmap with concentration and had no eyes for him. He had noticed her handbag beside him, large solid affair bulging with pass-ports and postcards, English money, Swiss money, French money, traveller's cheques, Michelin guides and paper hankies. He had his handkerchief in his hand; with a quiet movement, not over-hasty, he tucked it into the outside pocket of the bag. The light went green and the Humber started with a lurch.

'Sorry,' said the doctor apologetically. 'Seem to be put out of my stride a little; nearly a nasty accident, though – really that driver was quite within his rights shouting at me – he stopped very cleverly too. I felt most ashamed of myself.'

'Well it's over now and nobody any the worse,' said the woman beside him comfortably. A soft, quiet voice, quite un-like the daughter's.

'Now what does a yellow light *alone* mean, when it *winks*?'

'Means a dangerous crossing – blind road,' said Louis politely. 'You're supposed to drive slow and keep a good lookout to your right.'

'Believe me, I *will*.'

'You want to keep a lookout on the left, Dad. Should be a signpost somewhere soon saying Pontarlier.'

'But perhaps this gentleman doesn't want to go to Pontarlier. I must excuse my rudeness; my name is Harvey, Malcolm Harvey, and this is my wife and beside you is my daughter Stephanie. Er – whereabouts suits you best? You will know this countryside much better than we do,' deprecating.

'Very happy to make your acquaintance. Very kind of you too; Pontarlier will suit me fine. If you keep going along this road inside two minutes there's a fork and you take the right-hand one.'

'Splendid. I say, are you quite sure you're all right?'

'Perfectly. When he braked my nose flew suddenly towards the seat in front but it was soft cushion.'

'I'm relieved to hear that – I would have blamed myself bitterly. I'm wondering about lunch. Was thinking of trying to get into Switzerland first, but there might be a good place this side. Perhaps this gentleman would accept being our guest. Stephanie, you might get the Michelin out and see if there's a good restaurant – in Pontarlier, perhaps.'

Louis could see little of the couple in front – straight fine silver hair; rough dark curly hair – but he had a good sideways view of the girl and could study her – without being caught at it. With Paule's movements and gestures so vivid in his mind he found himself making comparisons – amusing. This girl was as unlike as you could get, if you were just looking superficially, of course. They were about the same height, but that was just average for anybody. This girl was thicker, stronger built; her shoulders and knees were muscular, as though she were a powerful hockey-player. Her hands were larger, her voice louder – or was it just higher?

Dark curly hair like the mother's, a big mouth with, for his taste, too much brilliant scarlet lipstick, smoky blue-grey eyes under fine dark brows that were beautifully shaped – really splendid, those eyebrows – large but pretty ears. Something muscular too about her manner, which was careless and gruff; she had given a sort of casual nod when her father spoke her name, and was sitting turned away from him with her bottom stuck out, almost rudely. Quite a big bottom too. Pretty wasn't the right word. Handsome girl, a scrap lumpy perhaps but with good features that would not fear wind or rain. She would run fast and well. A sort of Atalanta, but if one dropped an apple she was probably too modern to waste time stooping for it.

'Doesn't seem to be anything much along this road,' she said, still studying the sacred book. 'Just the usual hotels – sounding rather wet to tell the truth.' They were out on the main road now, the big car spanking along powerfully.

'Pity,' said papa. 'I was hoping there'd be a star, or those red inverted commas. There's a lake or something, I thought; isn't there one of those famous ones there?'

'No no, Dad – you're thinking of Annecy – that's simply miles away, right over the other side of Geneva.'

'Oh is it? I suppose I'm mistaken then,' mildly.

They were speaking English; Louis understood well enough. He spoke it awkwardly, with effort, but followed it fairly easily; he was a translator, after all. Not that he followed the thread of speeches – too dull! This looking game was one he played often too, for he was given to it; in the translator's cabins one was cut off from the world by sound-proofing, and one could abolish any voice at the flick of a switch – very handy – but the glass barriers gave one a good view of much of the assembly.

'You're driving a little fast, dear,' said mamma. He had not made much of her, apart from the soft voice – did it possibly have a slightly Scottish sound – or maybe Welsh? – and the hair, but she did not seem much more than forty; it was certainly young for the man, who was certainly sixty odd.

The girl stooped and fumbled in her bag without looking, and Louis had a second's nervousness, but she came up with cigarettes. He produced a lighter in a hurry to stop her rummaging any further. 'Thanks,' off hand. Feminist, maybe? Student, he supposed. What of? – the game got interesting at this point. Sciences-Po, something faintly boring of that kind? Sociology, or psychology?

'You know this countryside well, Mr Er?' asked Harvey, either making polite conversation or with his mind still running on lunch.

'No, I'm afraid. I know it well within a short distance of the town but not beyond that much. Been in the mountains a few times, like anyone else.' The conversation was not going to be pursued, for Louis, glancing out of the rear window, could see a black Mercedes coming up at a speed far greater than theirs. His heart bumped and he watched with apprehensive fascination as it overhauled, swung out to pass, whizzed by and cut in and out again, slowing abruptly, winking lights, swaying just in front and weaving, forcing them to slow and finally to stop. They weren't going to reach Pontarlier either.

'Now what in the world is all this about now?' asked Harvey in a patient tone, setting his handbrake. Louis could have told him, but already the elegant silhouette of Monsieur Taillefer, in a different suit this morning but the same jaunty hat, was bearing down in a relaxed leisured way that Louis knew by now was habitual.

'Good morning. Sorry to force you to stop, but there are some inquiries I'm afraid must be made. Swiss Federal Fraud Squad,' he added negligently; Louis was delighted at this, illogically. Trust Taillefer!

'Do not be alarmed,' it went on urbanely. 'No criminal act is imputed to you – not that I know of – which is to say I hope there isn't. I admit that I have reason to believe that you may be harbouring, perhaps quite unwittingly, stolen property, and that you might be – again unwittingly, very likely – concerned in an attempt to convey contraband across the Federal frontier.'

'I never heard of such nonsense,' said Harvey in the formal voice of indignant outrage.

'The remark is irrelevant, I fear. I will let it pass.'

'But I am a British citizen, a well-known man if I may say so, a doctor, and I'm sure that I could get the Consul to vouch for my character.'

'I have no doubt of that,' perfectly civilly, 'but may I point out that such people as yourself are for the very reasons you state the favourite cover for any manoeuvre that people might wish to escape the eye of the Federal authorities?'

Harvey looked disconcerted but he stood his ground.

'Are you really suggesting that there is some collusion between myself and this gentleman riding with us? – since I cannot think of anything else you could be referring to.'

'We do certainly know this gentleman.' The charming smile – the teeth were white and even – turned upon Louis merrily. God rest you, gentlemen – let nothing you dismay. It was the flavour of merriment like peppermint in Louis' mouth that warned him with a chill feeling. A hint in it to him, not to act any comedies: he wondered whether he really *had* done something clever.

'Now look,' said Harvey sturdily. 'I've no doubt that you know your business and that you may think yourself quite justified in stopping us. I don't even say you're overstepping your duty, but I really must state quite categorically that what you say is absurd – I can prove it, what's more. We met this gentleman quite by accident – he did not ask to accompany us, nor try to attach himself in any way – the fact is that by a misadventure I caused the taxi he was riding in to break down. I felt the least I could do was not to hinder his passage and I offered naturally enough to give him a lift.' The expression sounded a bit like a tramp jerking this thumb. 'Set him on his way.'

Taillefer was positively beaming.

'His business is his own and I know nothing of it. And since we are on our way to Switzerland and by a lucky coincidence he was going to Pontarlier, er . . . ' The beam was saintly.

'He was not going to Pontarlier or anywhere else, my dear sir. He simply took advantage of the fact that you were.' It quelled Harvey, who politely tried not to look with reproach at Louis who had got him into this. That mixture of tact and embarrassment that makes well-brought-up people avert their eyes from anyone in difficulties with the police.

It was the girl Stephanie, strangely enough, who was not quelled, or satisfied either. Louis was to realize later that being twenty years old and perhaps a Sciences-Po student alters things. The matter would otherwise have been settled then and there.

'Now I don't believe a word of all this,' she said in a carrying hockey-field tone. 'Now please, Daddy – allow me to speak. You're much too easily put down. How do we know there's anything in this tale?' she asked Taillefer, aggressively. 'Where's your authority for just hijacking people on the road-side? You might be just a thief for all we know.'

Together with Taillefer's teeth flashed a little plastic folder containing cards. With anybody else, thought Louis, it would have been pure bluff, a driving licence, grey card and vignette carried by all France, but with Taillefer they would be good enough to allay suspicion in anybody except, possibly, a real policeman. The girl stayed stubborn. She had even got out of the car, and walked round to where she could read over Taillefer's shoulder.

'I don't see anything Swiss about these. Anyway, if you're Swiss what are you doing on the French side of the frontier?' It takes an English person to have this kind of courage, thought Louis with admiration.

Taillefer didn't like it either, he could see. He was irritated, and perhaps perplexed, at this toughness of opposition, accustomed as he was to virtually universal subservience before anything that smelt of officialdom. But he stayed silky.

'Mademoiselle will notice that government officials work in close liaison. I do not know what things are like in England. Here French authorities are happy to co-operate with the Swiss.'

'That's all very well, but we have no guarantee that this isn't just some smooth banditry. Those cards could be fake – I wasn't born yesterday. Anybody can display some bogus card.'

'Mademoiselle, you will permit me to say that nobody threatens you with banditry. I have emphasized at some pains that your connexion with this matter is probably coincidental – haphazard – but this is an enquiry.' The words were spat out. 'It is now my duty to warn you that if you seek to obstruct me you will stir up considerable trouble – to yourself.'

He thinks I've told them who and what he is, Louis realized. He'll be certain now that I've given them the bloody diamond. He felt relieved that he hadn't even got it on him, but bothered now about what was going to happen.

He had better keep quiet! He had planned, in case Taillefer brought off an interception before they reached Switzerland, to do just what the girl was now suggesting. Cry bandit. The Swiss Federal Fraud Squad is – a good phrase came to him, a good *English* phrase – all my eye and Betty Martin! But he wasn't going to say so now; he was going to keep mum. He was listening carefully to that voice. The man would not stop now – not for anything; and if there were four witnesses – that might be just too bad. For them. This girl could not possibly know that, but worse – much worse – Taillefer would never believe that he had not put her up to it.

'You'd better keep quiet, I think, Stephanie,' said her mother nervously. Harvey said nothing. He was watching carefully, as though he were in his consulting-room, arriving at a diagnosis.

'I am going to ask a formal question,' said Taillefer, and he really did look formidable. 'Has any one of you been given, or been asked to keep, for any reason however specious, a packet, possibly an article of clothing – indeed any object whatever?'

'Certainly not.' Harvey, extremely firm.

'I must verify in that case that no object has, unbeknown to you, been concealed, in your car or among your property. Be so kind as to come out.'

'Now just you wait a minute,' said the girl hotly. She swung round on Louis. 'You're suspiciously quiet, it seems to me. Here you are, accused of all sorts of things – I don't know what – and you don't utter a peep.' No, he did not. He knew he was being cowardly but he could not see where this might end. There was perhaps one rather mangy chance.

'It seems to me, Mademoiselle,' and he made his voice as quiet and patient as he could, 'that the simplest way of showing that this is all nonsense is to let the gentleman search. They can satisfy themselves that none of us is carrying any contraband – or anything that could interest the Federal Fraud Squad' – he hoped that didn't sound too sarcastic. 'In that case they would allow us all to continue an innocent journey. They have no possible grounds for refusing that. I apologize,' he added to Harvey, 'for this trouble, which seems to be caused by my being mistaken for somebody else.'

'Very well spoken, my dear Mr Schweitzer,' said Taillefer with his cutting smile. 'An impudent bluff, but bravely tried.

Most succinct. You will know that we wish to cause *pain* to nobody.

And that was a hint too plain to disregard. It meant that the girl had better keep her mouth shut! But she didn't . . .

'You may be all as meek as lambs and satisfied as so many sheep,' she shouted, 'but I'm damn well not. If there's any searching that has to be done let it be done at the British Consulate is what I say. We might see then just how much truth is in all this.'

'Mademoiselle protests too much. She wishes a scandal. She wishes a tedious and timewasting journey that will spoil her holiday. She is, besides, not the person to make decisions.'

'Well,' began Harvey hesitantly. 'I suppose there's no harm in your looking at the car, since I've certainly nothing to hide. I don't see why it can't be done at the frontier, since the customs people might legitimately insist on searching again there. If they're present everybody could satisfy themselves that I'm not a smuggler. I will certainly mention the matter to the Consulate at Berne – your attitude appears to me distinctly high-handed.'

'Your Consul would tell you that Switzerland has every right to take whatever steps an official thinks fit to suppress this traffic in articles of value – a traffic that damages Switzerland's national policies and international good name. If you will kindly allow me to pass – this has gone on too long.'

'Do what you like,' said the girl violently. 'You make a step towards that car, and I stand here and scream. I want to know what all the people passing think about this. 'And indeed there were plenty of autos passing continually. Not that any of the people in them had given more than a casual glance in passing. Familiar sight on any road. Doubtless one auto had scraped the other slightly, in overtaking perhaps; explanations, insurance cover-cards were being exchanged. Nobody seemed hurt.

Taillefer stepped back to where his hands would be unseen by passers. Whitish lines had appeared in his face.

'Very well, Mademoiselle, very well. Since you insist, a scandal you shall have. I regard you, personally, at least, with the utmost distrust. You are all under arrest and may be charged with obstructing justice.'

'But arrest on what ground?' said Harvey, aghast. ' You've no proof or even evidence that we're attempting to smuggle anything.'

Taillefer said nothing. The girl opened her mouth again but a pistol appeared – the same sort of pistol that was in Paule Wisniewski's table drawer. There was a startled movement.

'Get quietly into the car. The first who moves or speaks I will shoot in the arm. At the back.' His free hand made an abrupt gesture towards the black Mercedes, and three men got out. Here are the boys, thought Louis. Won't be sorry to take a look at them – assuming I live that long. He won't shoot at anybody – he thinks the diamond is under his hand. Even when he finds it's not here he won't shoot anybody – as long, at least, as it remains unfound. The girl's pushed him much further than he wanted to go. He's in an awkward spot now – so are we. Taillefer might be perfectly capable of setting a stage – thinking perhaps of Sir Jack Drummond and Gaston Dominici. Three bodies might easily be found in a lonely spot where they had stopped to picnic. And he, Louis, might be the one picked to be handed to the French police with overwhelming guilt presumptions set up. Nothing easier. It could be used to force him to talk. Was his imagination running too fast?

He and the girl were gestured towards the Mercedes – he in front beside the driver, a thin shrimp with ginger hair under his hat. Girl at the back beside Taillefer. The other two pairs assembled themselves in the same order in the Humber.

'Move.'

The convoys drove rapidly back towards the town. Louis had a moment of wondering whether to try to make the auto crash. A sharp jerk at the wheel, perhaps, on a bend? Police would come – real police, who would not be altogether happy about the activities of the Federal Fraud Squad. At the speed they were going, he might just succeed in killing the lot of them, himself first – he was in the most vulnerable corner of any auto. He did nothing.

The truth was, he knew, that he was too cowardly. He did not possess that kind of courage: he did not lack a certain moral force, but the idea of being crushed, blinded, broken, arteries cut by flying glass, bleeding to death – being trapped very possibly in a burning cage . . .

Strange. In Russia I never showed fear of anything. I have changed – into what? Still, I always did prefer to try and work round the back of resistance. Ah well . . . just have to make do with whatever I do possess.

The girl kept up a sullen silence; neither Taillefer nor the driver seemed to have anything that needed saying.

They were going back through the woods and ridges of the Jura – foothills. They had turned off the main road, and were working back across byways that Louis knew vaguely. He caught glimpses of signposts, and realized that they were skirting round the outer fringe of the town's building projects. Finally they turned on to a narrow rough road hardly more than a single-line track, winding among trees and undergrowth up on to one of the hills, or rather ridges. Along the slopes and hollows of this ridge some villas had been built, without disturbing the thick woodland. Not terribly large houses, but expensive, in a timbered, sham-rustic style, with swimming pools, for people that were very rich indeed.

Privacy was the keynote of these houses, and quiet; all viewing by the curious was cut off by the clever choice of natural contours and the thick shrubberies. Everyone had four hectares or more of woodland – to himself. Noisy guests could play the gramophone full power and push happily shrieking girls into the pool, and there would be no complaints. What else did one pay high prices for, in these days?

There was an underground garage with rolling doors, wide enough for three autos the size of a Mercedes. Spiral steps of pink concrete led up to somewhere near the kitchen. He could not see where the others were taken: Taillefer's voice, quiet and monotonous, could be heard saying, 'See that they are comfortable. Something to read, something to eat. Patience: this may take some time.'

He and the girl were taken up a wooden staircase, rustic, with a peasant-carved balustrade, into a sort of study. Bookshelves full of leather-bound editions, that were very likely not books at all; a television set, radiogram and drinks cupboards all combined in a bulky and vulgar piece of furniture. The window looked on to a tangle of laurels and firs that made a dark room even darker. Taillefer sat at a large ministerial writing-desk, polished walnut with brass binding, switched on an ornate brass table lamp with a purple silk shade, and put his fingertips together. The other man left the room and closed the door. It was warm – invisible central heating – though the day had turned grey and dour, with more rain threatening and a chilly wind.

'Food will be provided when we have settled this matter' – he had got his soft voice back with the putting of the gun back in his pocket. 'There is no objection to a drink, I think.' He got up and opened the cupboard. 'Mr Schweitzer – you are fond of port, I recall. So am I. And you, Mademoiselle?'

'No,' rudely.

'Would you care for anything else?'

'I don't drink anything you have. Anywhere else I drink everything.'

'What a pity.' He handed Louis the glass, took a sip of his own, and studied the girl. 'May I have your handbag, please?'

She stared in front of her, obstinately.

'Try and act in an adult way. It would be disagreeable to me to be forced to take it from you.' She threw it on the floor contemptuously. He took another small peaceable sip of port, bent, dodged the heel of a shoe that darted at his head, straightened up, and leaned negligently against the desk.

'You wish to make me angry. To tempt me into offering you violence. You compelled me to take you off the road at the point of a pistol. I exceed my powers, you tell yourself. When you are in a position to make complaints, you think, all this will add weight and substance to your grievances. Disabuse yourself. My powers are considerable; no complaints will be made. You have heard, possibly, of the existence of the so-called parallel police in France, whose activities have sometimes been brought into a certain melodramatic light by zealous journalists; their struggle with illegal organizations such as the Armée Secrète. You have heard of persons kidnapped on the streets of Geneva, of obscure Arab politicians abducted in central Paris in broad daylight, of mysterious aeroplanes and motor-cars. Complaints are sometimes made but, strangely, the inquiries have a way of never finishing. They straggle out to a halt.' His finger mimicked an inquiry straggling out to a halt. There was no answer from the girl.

'Violence will not be offered you. You put me, however, in the position of being compelled to consider you as a criminal. That may entail humiliations and indignities. You understand?' Still no answer.

'I see. You are thinking of being back in England, of telling all your little friends with their flapping ears and quacking mouths all about how dreadful they are here. The horrible way they behaved, and so on. Another mistake. You may not be returning to England. If and when you do, I assure you that you will say nothing at all. You will have learned prudence. But you are very young,' indulgently.

He took the bag and emptied its contents on to the desk top, moving items one by one across the polished surface with a gold fountain pen that lay on the blotter. He took his time over all this.

'Well well – a man's handkerchief. Borrowed from your father perhaps – or not?' He held it up on the end of the pen distastefully, as though it were a dirty dish-rag. Perfectly clean handkerchief, thought Louis indignantly, though he was no longer proud of his silly little trick. It looked nasty and felt nasty, now. The girl stiffened up.

'I've never seen it, I don't know where it comes from, and I've no notion how it comes to be in my bag.'

'You saw, I think, that I did not put it there. Peculiar – not an English handkerchief I should think – that means very little. Can one tell? Perhaps – for comparison – Mr Schweitzer, be good enough to hold up your – handkerchief – which I take it was bought in this country – we might notice a difference.'

'Haven't one,' wooden.

'How careless of you. Paper ones, perhaps.'

'Why? I haven't a cold.'

'Really. How perplexing. You see now, Mademoiselle – it was unwise to make a melodrama at the roadside. You have got yourself in a *fix*.' He sat down behind his desk, refreshed himself with a sip of port, picked up an intercom telephone, and pressed a button on the standard.

'Well? . . . You've had plenty of time . . . nothing? . . . nor in the cases? . . . very well . . . no, leave them where they are.' He put the phone back, thought for a moment, finished his port and laid the glass carefully aside, and arranged his hands on the desk top.

'Be kind enough to stand up, Mademoiselle, and take off your clothes.' He enjoyed the reaction to this. He's a bit of a swine really, thought Louis.

'Oh yes, all of them, I'm afraid. You need have no alarm – there is no unhealthy interest in my eyes. You need not bother about Mr Schweitzer either; he will look, naturally, even if he pretends not to, but he is quite gentlemanly. Besides, he has other things on his mind. Thank you. Come and stand over there by the bookshelf if you will.' He got up and walked over to where the girl had been sitting, looked at the chair, picked up the clothes one by one, shook them out and folded them neatly like a valet in an expensive hotel. He went back to the desk then and sat meditating. The girl stood like a block of wood, face showing nothing but stubborn rage.

'I regret that this should be an embarrassing position for you, but you have only yourself to thank.'

'Don't give yourself the pleasure of thinking you embarrass me' – her voice wobbled a little but she had herself under good control. Her body was rounded and solid, with strong bones and good muscles, clear healthy skin, a clean pungent smell of an athletic and well scrubbed body. 'I'm accustomed to nudism, and I don't mind men looking at me so I don't care – just too bad for you.' So yah – there was a childish element in her resistance, but there was something admirable about it too.

'How fortunate,' absently; he wasn't even looking at her.

'Now, Mr Schweitzer, you and I are old friends. I am quite disappointed in you. I gave you adequate time for reflection, I was careful to place no restriction on your movements – you have not played very fair with me, have you? And now of course you see how futile your little manoeuvre was. I give you my confidence, you abuse it, and it hasn't helped you to do so, has it now? Have you still got it?'

'What on earth makes you think I ever had it?'

'And what then is the significance of the handkerchief, pray?'

'Find out.'

'I see,' pleasantly. 'Shall I allow you to torment yourself wondering whether I will now cause you horrid pains to make you say, I wonder? However – that can wait – I am not quite finished with Mademoiselle here, who has caused me considerable annoyance.' He changed again to his cutting voice as he swung round to face her. 'I suggest, Mademoiselle, that you had better tell me the meaning of this. If you are thinking of being stubborn I will simply have you taken, naked as you are, and put in a rather chilly concrete cellar where the glow of heroism will wear off.'

'I've got nothing to say. I didn't take it, it wasn't given me, and I never saw it before you took it from my bag. Perhaps that gentleman put it there.'

'Perhaps,' agreed Taillefer with his sideways grin. 'I am going to give this a little thought, and have a talk with your parents before deciding what is to be done. A *little thought* – it will not do either of you any harm. You will be left alone for an hour or two to *think*. Food comes later.' He picked up the girl's clothes, opened the door, and laughed a little. 'You may both think that you are in quite a *romantic* situation. You could try whistling and seeing whether James Bond appears. Though I do not quite belong to his world. *Smersh*,' with a hearty laugh that rang out in the passage. '*Spectre*,' with immense enjoyment, imitating chains rattling with a flip of his elegant wrists before closing and locking the door, still laughing heartily. They heard the steps, light and clear, pass unworried and unhurried over tiled flooring on to the staircase. Able man, thought Louis; skilful man.

The girl did nothing for a long minute. She just stood, naked and wooden, and Louis just sat. Then she walked over behind the desk, sat down unself-consciously, and put everything back into her bag, except the handkerchief which she picked up with momentary interest, examined a second, and tossed on the floor, where it stayed. She looked at Louis, then, with earnest inquiry, an intense look with something of a frown that would in other circumstances have amused him. He did not think she understood. The violent mixture of adult and child that made up this girl would have very little grasp of what a man like Taillefer might be capable of.

'It's true then,' she said suddenly. 'You have something, or did have – gold or diamonds or something. You've hidden it somewhere. And you were trying to use us to cross the Swiss frontier – handy, that accident, wasn't it – no, it was too good, you planned something – anybody could have found out at the hotel that we were aiming for Switzerland. Good cover, since you knew this fraud-squad lot had an eye on you.

'I didn't believe it for a second, I must say. Looked a lot more like gangsters to me. Peculiar behaviour, and this is a peculiar house – look at it, it belongs evidently to rich people. Not the place for police.

'Perhaps there is a secret police after all; I mean in England anyhow one never really believes in it, despite all the books – it always seems singularly little use, that's all I can say.'

'Things are slightly different here,' said Louis gravely. It was, he had decided, a good thing that she should believe in the secret police. The belief might yet save everybody's life.

'I suppose the Swiss are smarter. I mean there is gold, all those numbered bank accounts, and there's the O.A.S., isn't there, and Zürich full of spies – at least, that's what one always hears, and I do recall that case of the man the French kidnapped and left in the street in Paris tied up with rope, wasn't it, in the back of a car.

'I suppose nobody ever does really believe in these people, or knows what they're like, till one falls headlong into them.' She had a naïve freshness that plainly was leading her to take a certain pleasure in the situation.

'They make one take off one's clothes and just leave one to it. Hm. Plainly they're no surprise to you, you seem familiar with all these tricks. I must say it seems quite sensible now, the way you behaved there at the road – I thought you were just a wet.

'They would hardly have made me strip at the roadside, of course – always have to be very discreet of course and avoid all publicity, and that's why they have this place – I mean you expect them to have some dingy office, import-export or something, but that's all dead stale now of course, corny as hell.

right back to Robert Hannay – no, isn't it James Hannay? Now what *is* it?'

'I'm afraid I've no idea,' said Louis politely; he had never heard of the chap.

'So you're a smuggler. What is it then, diamonds?'

'You know,' seriously, 'there's very likely a microphone, and a tape-recorder.'

'Oh, of course; I'd forgotten.' Her face went serious a second and then cleared again. 'Well I don't care, really. There's nothing they can do to me. I'll give them anything they want to listen to, anyway.'

It was assertive, defiant even, realized Louis, but above all confident. She was confident in herself and in her world. Born after the war, of course – she could not be much over twenty. To her as to the other children of this age we are all cowardly imbeciles, trapped in outworn supersititions, the memories of conventions that are to her ridiculous. Had his child lived – it struck him suddenly – it would be five years older than this child, of course, and Fabienne would have taught it something. She knew!

The girl got up, walked over to the window and stood with her bottom sticking out provocatively. Louis studied the bottom and thought of Paule Wisniewski. She stood looking out a minute before giving a loud uninhibited yawn.

'I suppose that if we got out of the window – there doesn't seem to be a lock or anything – there'd be a man to herd us back. I've half a mind to try – I've plenty of clothes in the car. I don't even believe there is a man – nine-tenths of this lark is bluff, I'm still sure of that. You don't seem to have the courage to try,' she added with a contemptuous intonation, 'and yet you're the one he's after, aren't you?' She turned round and stretched luxuriously, with elbows above her head and massive breasts aimed menacingly at him. Louis lit a cigarette defensively in face of all this: it was not unpleasant; in fact in many ways it was very nice but he could feel no very hot enthusiasm.

'Perhaps you'd like to make love,' she said with a manner of being quite indifferent herself. 'It would help to pass the time.'

This amused him despite everything.

'Is that when you make love then? – when the time hangs heavy!'

Very determined to be *modern* – it sounded so extremely dreary . . .

'What do you think – that I'm in love with you or something?' she returned crushingly. 'You don't seem to be all that stupid, and I suppose you're not altogether unattractive, but you seem pretty sentimental to be in a business like yours.' That was what he didn't understand; these children loathed and feared romance, and considered emotion as something rather shameful, apparently.

'You find it exciting being arrested by the police?' he asked maliciously. 'Why don't you offer to make love with Monsieur Taillefer?'

'Him! – a cold fish, that one. You know his name? – yes of course, you've been caught by him before.'

Yes, she would naturally think Taillefer cold – the man to whom, before Louis, even more than Louis, the possession of the Dresden diamond was a passion. A thing for which he had killed and would kill again – he wasn't afraid to show emotion!

She appeared nettled by the faint mockery in his voice and perhaps on his face.

'You plainly think that because my parents seem conventional and dim we're all stupid. I can tell you I'm not, and neither are they either really, for all they act it – that's their generation that they just don't succeed in shaking off. You're the same of course – not only too old but too frightened to be any good.'

She was walking about now, still in the unself-conscious graceless way that was singularly unaphrodisiac, though he had to admit she had a kind of crude dignity, perhaps even integrity. He felt all the confusion and uncertainty that had slowed his feet and fogged his mind since it all started. I sit here, he thought, smiling indulgently at this preposterous child, and very likely she is right – she's certainly not all that far wrong. It is true, I am old and frightened. For twenty years and more I have been frightened not only of every emotion and every passion, but of every loyalty, every generosity. I am the prisoner of my absurd notions just as she is of hers – but mine have been out of date for twenty years. Why don't I just sweep my mind out? Set the mouldy straw alight and burn it all away? What I should really do here is burst out laughing, strike a spark of sympathy from this girl, who would be attractive if you gave her a chance, make love to her, get rid of the whole tangle in one breath. Taillefer will be back in half an hour.

And then? Why, give him the diamond. A catalyst. Rid himself of a burden that had eaten into him, rubbed and ulcerated and inflamed his whole being, festering in him for twenty years. Fabienne was dead and nothing could bring her back. Dresden was dead and Taillefer was right. Setting stones above one another in the same old pattern would not bring back the old Dresden to life. What was the phrase the man had used – flying in the face of history? Refusing to accept the future and come to terms with it? – something like that. Yes, he could understand – the old Dresden stood for everything the man hated, and everybody like him had welcomed the fire when it came, seeing old slaveries crumble into calcined stone.

Something held him back; what was it? Surely not Paule Wisniewski, another figure of the past, with her middle-aged sentimentalities, her trotting to church to have her scruples calmed after yielding to impulse – natural enough impulse, he supposed vaguely, after being ten years without a man. It was all dead – he was dead too and perhaps this girl would bring him back to life.

But he could not do it. Idiotic, but it felt like a sort of betrayal. He felt like Razumov, who handed the political assassin over to the police and then sat down in his room to try and work it out, to schematize his certainty that he had done the right thing after all, only the right thing. What had been the list that Razumov had written in his notebook? History not Theory. Patriotism not Internationalism.

Absurd, was it not? Was there any real philosophical basis for holding on to the diamond so obstinately? Of course there wasn't! He didn't own it, he had no claim on it. It meant nothing to him but a memory to which he was not even true. It had no significance, it could not feed the hungry nor shelter the homeless. Surely the truth was that the diamond possessed no more than a little corner of insanity in Louis' mind. Very similar to Taillefer, who also burned with an intense desire – was it worth so much to him? For how long already had he searched for it – and was it that protracted search that had so burned into him that he so hungered now to see it and hold it?

Monday Afternoon

It was a feeling of having come back from a long distance. The girl was still sitting there on the other side of the room, smoking a cigarette – fresh, comic, delightful, this naked girl sitting on a chair, amazingly beautiful, smoking. The room was full of silence: rather sadly he reflected that it was a bored and sullen silence, that of two people who are too far apart and can find nothing to say to one another, rather than the peace of two people who are close and have no particular need of words. It seemed a long time before the light quick steps sounded again in the passage and Taillefer came in with his jaunty expression.

'A good lunch,' he said with satisfaction. 'That is most important. I am sorry to have deprived you but I find that while eating sharpens my wits hunger generally clarifies the ideas of people I have to deal with no end.' He handed the girl her pile of clothes, still neatly folded. 'Very well done, my dear, very well done indeed. I am quite satisfied that you are not keeping any secrets from me. Would you like some dinner? Your father and mother have had theirs.'

'I like choosing myself where I'll have dinner,' with a return to the manner of sullen rudeness, starting to put on her clothes.

Taillefer laughed. 'Dear dear. But I'm afraid you will have to put up with us a little longer. You have to persuade Louis here not to be so foolish.' He looked at Louis with gaiety, and shook his finger with a pretence of conspiratorial friendship.

'You do not understand these modern young ladies. Now if you're ready, my dear, if you care to accompany me we are going to rejoin Dr Harvey and Mrs Harvey, and we are going to have a little session of self-criticism. Lessons. Do tell me,' to the girl, 'what kind of school you went to. One of the progressive ones, was it not, where you called the teachers by their christian names? Since I am to be your teacher for a little while I must learn to make you like me.' More merry laughter. 'This way then. Down the stairs.'

He's talking too much, thought Louis. He has plainly listened to the conversation, but what has he learned from it?

It was like a waiting-room to any doctor's surgery, bare, with painted grey walls. There were ten or so metal chairs with plastic seats and backs, and in the middle a metal-legged table with a shiny plastic top, on which stood nothing but an inefficient little ashtray, but there were no magazines or calendars presented by pharmaceutical industry. Harvey, with a pensive expression, was staring out of the window; it faced a depressing yard where a car was being washed – a little blue Simca familiar to Louis. Mrs Harvey was sitting with her elbows on her crossed knees, resting her chin on her hand with an air of it being her turn next, doing nothing.

Taillefer picked up the table and set it near the wall, sat himself behind it on one of the uncomfortable chairs, and beckoned to Louis.

'You come and stand here, Mr Schweitzer, and everybody else please sit over there facing me. You can observe – it will relieve your *boredom* – we are going to have a sort of little People's Court. I am satisfied that you do not possess the object of my interest, and that you have no idea where it is to be found. You wish now to continue your journey – I'm sure I wish you a most agreeable stay in Switzerland. All you have to do is to persuade Mr Schweitzer here to say what he knows.'

'I'm sure,' said Mrs Harvey in her soft warm voice, 'that I've lost all interest in going to Switzerland. Are there many more like you there?'

'Very sad,' amiably, 'but you have yourself compelled me to these steps. I find you in Mr Schweitzer's company, you resist my attempt to clear the matter up on the spot – you have only yourselves to thank. I intend to keep you here until I find out where this object is.'

'This is really an intolerable abuse of power,' she said angrily.

Harvey said nothing. He was looking at the scene with intelligent, somewhat puzzled eyes, as though faced with an obscure virus.

'You are mistaken,' replied Taillefer politely. 'No hardship is inflicted on you. You were asked to take your clothes off – would you have preferred the humiliation of being stripped by a woman official? You will be supplied with food and drink. The room is warmed. That door leads to a washroom. To regain your liberty you have only to persuade Mr Schweitzer to see the light.'

'Utter rubbish,' with a pooh sound of disgust.

'An outrage, you are thinking? That would never happen in England? Once more you are mistaken. An acquaintance of mine as innocent as you are was detained not long ago for seventy-two hours in a room less pleasant and draughtier than this one at London Airport, with ham sandwiches and tea, his attempts at self-justification disregarded. You are luckier. However I will make another attempt to lighten your burden.' He turned back to Louis, who was standing there indifferent.

'Now my friend. You have not got it on you – that I know. You have certainly not confided an object like that to your little Polish friend – you are not that stupid. She has, I learn with pleasure, gone back today to her valuable work; it is therefore not in her house. You have very foolishly persisted in clinging to it, and you have somewhere found an opportunity to conceal it. Not in the taxi, which has since been searched. It was not given to these admirable people, despite your little attempt to lead me astray with a handkerchief, but for a little while – I am quite frank – after you entered Dr Harvey's car you were lost sight of. You hid it somewhere – you may even have tossed it into some bush by the roadside thinking to spite me. What have you to say? You know, I think, that your failure to co-operate may still have most unpleasant consequences for these friends of ours. I think you understand, no? Well – what have you to say?'

'Nothing. You know me; I know you. The thing is not mine – neither is it yours. I have never admitted your right to have it. It is gone beyond your recall. As for you, be careful not to overstep your precious powers. It might recoil on you. Keeping me and these people here will not get what you want. I can probably persuade them that they would be well advised to stay silent, and that any appeal to embassies or consulates would be useless – you had better simply let us go.'

For a second the man looked nasty, with the whitish lines in his face, before he regained his self-control.

'Stubborn,' thoughtfully. 'Needs educating.'

'So do you. You talk too much.' For Louis had come to a conclusion, that he had been right to resist. He thought, too, that he had penetrated Taillefer. Was he not a man of absurd vanity? Would he not look tirelessly at his own reflection, never weary of listening to his own voice?

The man got up calmly.

'There is there on the wall an electric bell. I have time. When you have seen sense enough to begin your education, ring it.' He walked out and the key turned in the lock.

'Are there *microphones* in this place, do you think?' asked the woman. She looked very like the girl, but was smaller, more fragile.

'*He* says there are,' jerking her nose irritably at Louis. 'Disgusting man that – thinks himself funny.'

'Well if he's listening it hardly helps to abuse him,' answered the mother. 'I have no cigarettes left, dear– give me one of yours.'

'I'll give you half what I've got. Better make them stretch, since you don't know how long you'll be here. . . . I couldn't care less whether he hears me abuse him or not. Why bother hiding my opinion? A lot of good that would do.'

'I think perhaps if we're not *rude* . . . I don't suggest we all keep *silence*, but if we're abusive it puts us in the wrong, surely, even if only a little. The man must realize sooner or later that he can't just keep us here, but the feeling of helplessness is rather hard to bear – I was just saying so to Malcolm – I still can't quite make out what we're supposed to have done.'

The girl shrugged and made a face expressive of disgust at all this stupidity but neither parent told her to mind her manners: probably neither had done so for a good many years.

'First we were supposed to have known or seen what this man did while he was with us – now we're supposed to guess,

or to get him to say. He's a perfect boob, I found that out upstairs, and since stupidity is the worst of evils I warned you
you'd better go easy with the cigarettes, that's all.'

Still nobody told her to mind her manners, but secretly they
will be agreeing, thought Louis.

'I find all this *interesting*,' said the father, speaking for the
first time. Harvey had a serious, intense voice, like an admirer
of television discussions saying to his family, 'Now be very
still and we're all going to listen to the Brains Trust.' 'I agree
that it sounds shocking that we should be in this position, but
moaning about it or our companion helps nobody. This officer,
police inspector or whatever he may be, must be within his
legal rights or he'd never dare do this. I must say I *have* heard
of similar things happening to strangers in England: I dare say
they were quite undesirable individuals but one must realize
that from this man's point of view that is what we are.'

Louis liked Harvey. The slow sententious voice was a scrap
pompous but at least he could make an effort at detachment.

'It's true, too, that he's not even mistreating us. Shutting
people up like this is a form of torture, of course, but I believe
it's quite common in all European countries and that's just our
bad luck. He's nothing to bring us to trial for, of course – we've
committed no *crime* after all – but perhaps that's just as well;
I've heard that even quite simple cases of overstepping the law
can take absolutely months. What he's holding us for, even if
it's only a pretext, is suspicion of guilty knowledge, and we
have to convince him we haven't any. We mustn't be too quick,
either, to judge the attitude of our companion – er, Mr
Schweitzer, isn't it? I forget whether I ever introduced myself
properly; my name's Malcolm Harvey. Now I got the impression that you refused to answer that man out of a certain feeling of *principle*, and I can only applaud that, of course. It is
none of my business, but I understood that you don't admit to
being in the wrong. It's not just a matter of contraband?'

'No,' said Louis. 'A matter of information that he main-
tains belongs to his government. I deny that. I'm not going to tell
you more, because the information couldn't do you any good.'

'I *see*,' largely. Man thinks I'm an Armée Secrète agent,
thought Louis with amusement, or at best a spy.

148

'You hear, Stephanie? You mustn't be so hasty in making up your mind.'

The girl shrugged rudely and looked out of the window, unimpressed.

'You're no relation to Albert Schweitzer?' asked the woman with social brightness.

'It's quite a common name in Alsace,' said Louis composedly.

'I suppose it means originally just the man from Switzerland,' decided Harvey. 'One thing that strikes me – have you ever read Sartre?'

'No. I've heard of him – didn't he refuse the Nobel Prize?'

'That's the fellow – peculiar chap, but remarkable thinker, I should imagine. I haven't read him myself much, but I do recall a play of his that was all about hell. There wasn't any hell of course – he doesn't believe in such rubbish any more than I do, but there were three people shut up in a room, rather as we are, and the point was that by talking and quarrelling they created and added to their own torment. Perhaps this Mr Thing has the same notion.'

Louis looked at him with more respect.

'He has, yes.'

'So we must be careful to respect one another's ideas, and principles – non-intervention, if I may use the term. Perhaps we should talk about books, or paintings, or some *abstract* subject.'

'I know nothing much about either, I'm afraid.'

'I told you he was a fool,' muttered the girl, shifting irritably.

'Stephanie, please do not be destructive. Your beliefs and interests are not shared by everyone. That is not their *fault*.'

'I don't think it makes much difference,' said Louis slowly. 'You don't want to force me to do anything, but sooner or later you will, just to get away from here. That's his whole idea. Sooner or later,' smiling acidly, 'you'll be jumping on me and beating me up. First you will try to be reasonable, to convince me. Then you will try to seduce me – your daughter tried that already, upstairs. Then you'll beg me. Lastly you'll attack me.'

'I'll do no such thing.'

'You will, you know. I've been in prison before.'

'One can be rational.'

'Not a bad idea if you ask me,' said the girl. 'He's quite right. We ought to get him to say what he knows and have it over.'

'Did you, Stephanie?'

'Oh yes, I offered to sleep with him, upstairs. He's probably one of these church-goers.'

'He may simply have thought neither the time nor the place well chosen,' said Harvey reprovingly. 'We must certainly *not* show aggression.'

'What we should really have is a party,' said the wife amusedly, with a warm friendly smile at Louis – perhaps to convey apology for her daughter, he could not tell. 'We obviously have to get to know each other. I'm Leah; I'm not really Jewish but my parents thought it a good idea to call us all by Jewish names – a way of showing solidarity, don't you know. My sisters were Rachel and Rebecca. Stephanie isn't being her most forthcoming, but really she feels about people exactly the same as we do and that is why she offered to sleep with you: I would have done the same.'

Louis could not help staring with big glassy eyes, but was rescued by Harvey.

'You're embarrassing Mr Schweitzer, Lee – he's not accustomed to the way we express our thoughts. You see, Louis – forgive me, but I heard that chap call you so and I agree with my wife that formality is useless: worse, it's a definite barrier, in the situation we're in – we have what may seem to you unconventional beliefs, but we do think that what holds the world back is a blind quite unreasoning attachment to old outworn superstitions: clinging to religion is the most glaring everyday example.'

He stopped and looked to see how Louis was taking this. Louis was taking it very well. He was schooled by now. Encouraged, Harvey went on in his tone of enlightened pedantry.

'Since you might say quite justly that we're all in the same boat here, my wife wants to express to you that she feels solidarity with a fellow, and the best way is to show that she is ready to share all she has with you. I would do the same in her place. So would Stephanie, though she has her own individual ways of showing things. It is by sharing one's pleasure and one's pain that we create progress.' He paused expectantly.

'I don't know how to answer you without sounding discourteous,' said Louis lamely.

'There you are,' in triumph. 'Learning is painful later in life – *that*'s why the early formation is so important: the Jesuits knew that well, of course. All this kind of embarrassment and anxiety is not natural at all – simply instilled into the child at an age where it is completely plastic and moulded for life as a consequence. Have you never noticed that a child is totally free of anxiety about the excretory functions. . . '

But a vague plan was beginning to crystallize in the back of Louis' head, somewhere behind the peculiar humming noise. Paule was out of the house, but would she be out at work this afternoon? It was a great effort that had to be made, to disentangle himself from the diamond pressing on his brain, to wipe out the buzz of these good people, and to recover the details of another, even more idiotic and unreal world with which he had lost all contact.

Of course – it would be committee work preliminary to the debate that was due to start – tomorrow, yes. Paule would be interpreting, effaced and unnoticed, stooping awkwardly with her head between two ministers who were playing at being pally – a worse job than simultaneous translating any day. The ministers felt that out of the debating chamber they had to appear unbuttoned – it invariably annoyed him, the making of jokes and trotting out of proverbs – the beloved pose as the simple countryman. The technical experts who accompanied His Excellency at these meetings, ready to jog his elbow if he had not learned his script thoroughly, loathed it as much as he did. They would stare ostentatiously at the ceiling making faces at their wisps of cigarette smoke when the inevitable point was reached that began 'Of course I'm only a simple Franc'Comtois peasant' (nonsense: his father had been a notary from Ornans, the little town where there are more lawsuits to the square centimetre than anywhere else in France) 'and we peasants have a saying about cheese which will illustrate my point, Your Excellency' – and the other excellency listening with an inscrutable face (in a little he would be inventing imaginary proverbs about cheese too, from the Tatras instead of the Franche Comté, but there was little difference in the cheese). The experts would try and blow smoke-rings, while Paule strained to put the rubbish into some language that made sense. No, she would not be back before six.

It was a simple plan, though desperate, and it depended on Taillefer's vanity. He had to bring him to the flat, and he had to get him to come alone.

He came back to earth with a start, wondering what on earth to say to these people. But they had given him up. Seeing him go glassy-eyed at the words of the evangelist they had written him off as an uncircumcised philistine, a Boeotian. They were all three clustered together now, chattering like jackdaws. He tried to make an effort and listen to the difficult rapid English: it was all about Nature now, and the doctor's long handsome face was pink with animation over alpine flowers. Louis could see him clearer now; he was the type to go long walks in the countryside talking the whole time, and then he would suddenly freeze and say ' . . . Hush. Listen . . . you hear that? . . . you know what it is? . . . a lesser crested stonechat!' When out himself in the Jura Louis had often met these people, who claimed him as one of their own; they were always very voluble and prolix. Their great enemies were the state Forestry men, who prosaically put stamps on tree-trunks and refused to let the woods go wild: people who like nature prefer the tree-disease to the tree; it is more picturesque. But of course their greatest hate was Electricité de France, putting awful pylons in meadows and shoving barrages into the Jura rivers, the vandals. Almost these people could convince one that they would vastly prefer lighting their own homes with pine-branches dipped in resin.

And of course they were quite right! One had to have people like that; one had to have everybody. . . . They were the only ones who complained about polluted water, who always dug neat holes to bury refuse (scouts all of them, expert at lighting fires, pitching tents, tying knots and identifying toadstools). They had a real respect for life. Take this one now; plainly an alert and intelligent man, certainly an excellent doctor. And he had a lot of sense; pitchforked into a situation of which he had no understanding he was most wisely refusing to let himself be nagged. He had scrupulously refused to try and hustle Louis. He was not setting up an egoistic scream that it did not matter what was done, provided he himself was instantly set free to go galloping up hillsides – he was English; it would be in those amazing long baggy shorts – getting rapturous about sunset, birdsong, or gentians.

They would have concluded that he was offended by the remarks about religion. What would their contempt have been for poor reactionary superstitious Paule – poor Paule with her confession and her Madonna with the little light under it? And yet they were so comically like Paule, who had known the danger by instinctive recognition and had not stopped to think of the trouble or anxiety her instinct would bring upon her; who had been able to think of no way of helping him but to go to bed with him – to prove solidarity? Paule who was like Fabienne – so strangely like and so comically unlike. Was it not outrageous that he, who thought himself enlightened, should feel himself on the side of superstition against the forces of progress? They had offered to go to bed with him too, but it was not for his aloneness: it was for theirs. . .

He had to get them out of this, though . . . he didn't know how he was going to do it, but something . . .

They were talking about music now, which they owned, naturally. 'Of course,' came the woman's voice with loud emphatic certainty, 'Klemperer *is* Beethoven.' She must know: she had probably slept with Beethoven.

He had to hold out some hours still; the longer he held out the riper Taillefer would be to chuckle at his own cleverness. The plan was clearer in his mind now. He had to persuade Taillefer that the diamond was still out in the woods, try to persuade him to come alone, let him dig up the army shirt – and try and punch him in the adam's apple. Then what? Or if it didn't work? Louis didn't know himself.

He tried to think about music too, but all that came to him was an absurd notion that he was like Ariadne, stuck tiresomely mourning on that tedious Naxos, with the comedians capering about her unable to understand how she can possibly be so stupid. The afternoon wore on. At last he could stand it no longer; he got up suddenly and rang the bell. They stopped talking then and looked at him with a kind of muted reproach. What had he done wrong now? It was his neck.

The ginger man answered the bell.

'I want to see Monsieur Taillefer.' No reaction; all the man said was 'Wait'. And he was kept waiting, for more than half an hour, before the ginger man put his head in at the door, said 'Come' and Louis came.

He was taken back upstairs to the room where he had been with the girl, and as he came in the heart went out of him. He had wanted to do something heroic. . .

Taillefer was beaming with pleasurable anticipation and Paule Wisniewski, in her dowdy coat, was sitting lumpishly on the chair with her hands in her lap and an expression of anxious pain.

'She's been here some little time already, your little Polish friend. She got nervous at lunchtime and rang up your apartment – was quite upset to hear you weren't there and hadn't been seen. So being, of course, deeply attached to you' – little ironic bow – 'down she trots, to the auto you had told her was keeping an eye on things – you had warned her, of course, that if she went to the police you would not live another ten minutes – and asks very politely to be brought to me. She is obstinate, of course; she knows perfectly well where the diamond is but refuses to say before seeing you. I was in no hurry – I felt quite sure that you would shortly be appearing with some ingenious proposal. And here you are. Very nice.'

'I'll give you the diamond,' Louis said dully.

'That's a sensible chap.'

'She comes with me.'

'Oho no, that's a little too easy. No, my friend, you come with me – she stays where she is. When our little business is settled then we can talk about these matters. You have both given me a lot of trouble. She can stay here and meditate. If there is one more half hour's waste of time, then her life is forfeit. And if I do choose to release you both, assuming that I am completely satisfied within that half hour, I will invite both of you to think about what will happen if there is the remotest peep from either of you. My arm is long, I assure you both.'

'What about these other people?'

'Ah, I have no further need of them; our little Madame Wisniewski here is an even better guarantee. They served their purpose, of course, though they are nothing but a pest. So *sensible* of you, Louis, to say nothing, to allow them to think that they were in the hands of the police. It saved their skins. So sensible of you but so *stupid* of you – had you had the courage to allow these imbeciles to disappear, as for a moment I feared, I might have found you more troublesome. But as soon as I saw you had a sentimental regard for them I knew I had you palmed, my dear Louis, and that an hour's thought would convince you of the fact. Oh, I will give them a little talking to, enjoin them to *prudence*, ha, ha, they will not dare squeak. The Official Secrets Act! We have a better mouse – she's in love with you, my boy, and I seem to recall too that she is sensitive to feelings of suffocation, ho ho. I never would have guessed it – delightful, delightful.'

'Come on and let's get it over with.'

'Certainly.' He got up. 'You will accompany me, Madame Wisniewski.' They went out and Louis was left alone.

He tried to collect himself, to restore movement to his stunned mind, but he was sapped, all will and energy cut off. Even if he choked Taillefer with his bare hands that would not now save Paule.

There was a dry click in the silence and a murmur of voices and movements, filtered through some metallic intermediary. Louis understood at once – these things were quite familiar to him – and went round behind the desk. A drawer stood open; the sounds were coming from a grille in a metal box the size of a portable typewriter. Taillefer had switched it on to tease him a little.

'You will be relieved to learn,' the silvery voice was distorted by the microphone to a disgustingly false imitation silver made of baser metals, 'that Mr Schweitzer wishes to be reasonable. Naturally his proposals will be verified. I hope that these restrictions will not last much longer, but perhaps it might be as well to temper optimism with prudence for just a little longer. Please do continue your interesting conversation – I have brought you a new companion.'

'Sorry to have kept you waiting,' back again, polite and silvery. 'Now – to facts.'

'If you have an auto handy I can bring you to the place.'

'We have everything handy.'

They went downstairs and out the way they had come. The Mercedes, and the gingery man, were waiting: Louis stopped.

'No.'

'What is it now?' He might have been talking to a small child whose shoe-lace has come undone.

'We have to go out into the country. I'm not having any acolytes. You might decide to leave me under a bush, like the Russian. I'll accompany you and you alone. What guarantee have I that you won't try and get rid of me directly I've served your purpose?'

'None,' almost gaily. 'I had offered a generous recompense and adequate time for thought. You chose to abuse my confidence. You tried to dodge, to hide among these English people. It convinced me of your bad faith and your guilty knowledge.'

'Take my offer or not as you wish,' shouted Louis in a querulous, exasperated tone. 'It's either that or land yourself indefinitely with five prisoners. You can murder one. Five will increase your difficulties, not diminish them.'

Taillefer did not hesitate.

'No, Louis,' in a voice that was almost affectionate. Louis got meekly into the auto. He was beaten. But still – they would have to leave the Mercedes in the lane. There was still a chance that Taillefer would choose to be alone to climb the field. He would not want too many eyes.

'I don't need to tell you the way,' said Louis. 'You know whereabouts it was the Russian left the road, even though you yourself didn't go further.'

'What are you telling me?' indifferently, with his eyes out of the window.

'I'm telling you that you don't know where the thing is. Neither do I, but I can only convince you of that by taking you there. I can show you whereabouts you have to look, no more. I haven't got it. I've never had it.'

Taillefer said nothing and appeared to meditate on this remark. But at the crossroads the auto turned left towards the town instead of the country.

'Now where are you going?'

'We have some unfinished business that cannot be settled in an auto.'

Suspicion grew into certainty. Had Paule talked, thinking to save him? Had he made her talk? What had happened? The auto stopped at the Quai Louis Pasteur, a minute from Paule's home.

'Wait in the car – I won't be long,' to the ginger man. That was that much gained, but would it avail him, now? Hardly. 'You know the way,' to Louis with a return of that ominous gaiety.

Could Paule have changed the hiding-place of the diamond? Or even thrown it away, thinking that way better than none? He could imagine her going to the greengrocer's stall, tucking it under a cauliflower for the first housewife. Not a bad solution, at that. The drawback was that it would condemn them both to death. The flat showed no sign of disorder.

'Now we can talk,' cheerfully. 'Sit down then – make yourself at *home*.' The word had an uncomfortable meaning – how much was he at home, here?

'This is a waste of time,' crossly.

'Is it? You have again attempted to deceive me.'

'What makes you think that?'

'We have been over this all before.' But he was enjoying himself so much that he showed no sign of impatience. 'You shot the man I had there, which was clever, since he was a man that knew his business. Since you were able to shoot him, you felt able to underestimate me. A mistake. I did not find it difficult to reconstruct what had occurred. The Russian gave you certain confidences, otherwise my man would not have left his hiding-place: he was there for no other purpose than to listen. The diamond was concealed in the little wood. So was my man. If he left his hiding-place it was because you knew too much. That knowing too much has been your undoing, I am afraid.'

'Look, I may know too much, but I still don't know enough.' Louis was holding himself steady still, though he knew it must sound empty bluster. 'I know the hiding-place, but no more.'

It was a kind of paying out of line. If only he could pay out enough to make Taillefer over-confident. If he could just get him to take his hand off that gun there in his pocket. . . . 'He came out a bit prematurely.' It sounded terribly unconvincing. 'I had made no move towards the hiding-place and I still do not know exactly where it is, so I repeat, you've got to come with me to those fields if you want to lay your hands on that diamond.'

'What?' mockingly. 'Have you so little knowledge then of human nature? Curiosity is the strongest of instincts, Louis. You were alone there with two men who no longer interfered with your movements,' laughing heartily at his own wit. 'You expect me to believe you made no effort to find it, and I, with regret, do not believe a word you say.'

'I don't care. I've said so and repeat it. I maintain it. Two men had just died for this thing. I'm not a fool: I know when a thing is too hot to handle. I tell you I left it where it was. Believe me or not, the only way you can find out is by coming out to that wood to see.'

'You are hoping against hope that a farmer has discovered the bodies and that the police will be there to greet us,' sniggering. 'No, Louis, I am loath to spoil your enjoyment, but you have not spoiled mine. The diamond is not above fifteen feet from us now at this moment.'

'What?' said Louis panic-stricken. Paule had betrayed him after all. It was no bluff; the man sat there too relaxed, too confident: the smile was too broad – the man was playing with him.

'You have hidden it, for sure, more or less painstakingly. It would be quickly found in a search by my men – still, you insisted on being accompanied by myself alone, and I agreed. You will have to get up and hand it to me, for I am not going to bury myself in the coal-scuttle for your convenience.'

With bitterness Louis realized that he had made exactly the mistake into which he had hoped to entrap Taillefer – over-confidence. He had been an imbecile, after all! This man had hunted patiently for the Dresden diamond for many years. He had known how to wait, and how to take action. How many others, before Louis, had thought to prove to themselves that a treasure was the property of the man that found it?

Taillefer did not try to break in upon a train of thought he must consider smilingly as highly salutary. The rattle of steps outside was too sudden and innocent a noise to disturb either of the two quiet figures: Taillefer was too poised, too certain to be put for even a second off his balance, and Louis was too near utter surrender to be able to react, and when the door opened with a bang and Carlos came in, in a hurry as usual, his school bag ready to throw gratefully on the sofa, neither man moved, neither the loose confident panther nor the limp prey. As the boy stood staring at them Taillefer spoke gently, politely.

'Come in, my young friend, come in. Be so kind though as to shut the door.'

Wild thoughts raced through Louis' mind, lurching erratically. He wanted to say 'Run – bunk – quick' – as though that would have helped. He had an absurd momentary stab of the pathetic hope that never leaves a man – that notion that the prison walls might fall down, that the heavens will open suddenly, that the angel with the flaming sword might still appear. Just so will react the man being led to the guillotine, should one of his guardians that hold him pinned by the upper arms slip suddenly on the greasy cobblestones of dawn.

It might have worked, perhaps, in a film. That the boy might have thrown his heavy briefcase in the man's face – that the man, momentarily rattled, might have turned his eyes and his pistol towards the boy long enough for Louis to spring, to throw him over backwards in the chair off balance and helpless – these things happen in dreams. In real life people are more like rabbits. Or an excitable movement, a nervous shout, on Taillefer's part might have galvanized the boy into a bolt – but he was too good, too quiet. He simply said 'Come in and shut the door' in his silvery conversational tone. The boy glared at Louis, lost, frenzied.

'Is that . . . ?'

'Yes.'

'And mother?'

'She went to them.'

Taillefer seemed to turn over this fragment of conversation and peer at it with leisurely amusement.

'That was very foolish, Louis. I was deceived, for some little while, by such naïveté. You told the woman – and now I find that even the boy knows. Quite a little family conspiracy. I am astonished – yes, astonished – at your double foolishness. A boy of fourteen or so – and a boy can never keep his mouth shut, can he?' He shook his head sadly. 'We shall have to *see*, shan't we? However, it makes the immediate problem even simpler. You stay quite still, Louis. Tell the boy where to look for it – unless indeed he already knows,' with an indulgent smile. 'Tell him then to be a sensible child and bring it to me.'

'It's in the other room,' dully.

'Splendid,' crossing his legs in comfort. 'Open the doors wide, my lad. That's right. The curtain as well, if you please. Well, what are you waiting for? Tell him then, Louis.' It was like the man in the spinney, the chubby man. Was there not a touch of sadism in making the boy get it?

'It's in the table drawer, Carlos. In that silver box. You thought it was a paperweight.'

'A paperweight!' chuckled Taillefer with delight. 'That's splendid – quite perfect. I must remember that one.' Really he was no different from a business man in a bar, shaking the ice-blocks round in the hope of getting a taste of whisky still, while laughing heartily at the latest De Gaulle joke.

Carlos opened the drawer slowly with his head bowed. He put both hands in it to open the box; Louis, watching wretchedly, recalled that the hinges were stiff and the lid tight-fitting. He fumbled. 'This what you mean?' dragging the words out of himself.

Taillefer had his eyes on Louis, his eyes wrinkled up with the concentration of pleasure.

'No doubt,' amiably. 'Bring it here and we'll see. It's not very likely that there would be two.'

Carlos raised his other hand slowly. Louis had left the pistol in the drawer in a faint notion of camouflage; the boy had carefully put the catch down with his thumb while it was still in the drawer, and now had plenty of time to sight carefully at a man sitting comfortably with his knees crossed, one hand in a trouser pocket playing negligently with a key-ring, the other in his jacket, holding the pistol that was pointed along his eyes at

Louis – for one never knew. However limp the fellow looked, it had been just that second of careless over-confidence that had led to the downfall of the chubby man: he was not going to *underestimate* Louis.

Carlos drew a long breath, held it, and pressed the trigger, far too hard. The pistol jumped in his hand, and went off twice. The man jumped in the chair and his eyes turned with an expression of indignation more than surprise, as though what Carlos had done was not fair. The pistol fell on the floor; the man lurched forward with his hands still absurdly in his pockets, and fell after it. Louis stood up slowly.

The boy stood there with a hand pressed against each side of his head as though in an illogical attempt to close out the sharp noise the pistol had made in the small room. There was a strong firework smell; the boy's eyes were wide and frightened. A passer-by might have thought that the boy had put a banger under the headmaster's chair, and was now aghast at his resounding success, and the probable consequences to himself.

Louis picked up the pistol; there was a long silence. Taillefer got his hands out of his pockets; the boy stood frozen.

'He's not dead.'

Louis had had the usual sensations – the observing through binoculars that were somehow back to front, the world cut off by blinkers, the immense oppressive silence, the feet in a slight quicksand, accompanying the body with pain, the perfect lucidity wrapped and swaddled in stupid confusion. Was he to start with the boy, now crying silently – going rapidly into shock – or was there anything to be done with the man? He knelt by the figure on the floor. The boy had aimed low, exactly as though he had *known* how the pistol would jump. Two seven-sixty-fives close together in the stomach – no. Taillefer lay doubled up with hands crossed over his belly, pathetically. The position had something of a small child in bed.

'He's not dead,' slowly, 'but he's probably not far off. Hit in the nerve centres. Vital places.' He wanted to get the message to Taillefer. The hiding-places of life . . . yet life is tenacious . . . a quick treatment against shock – one dies of shock quicker than one does, very likely, of this kind of bullet-wound.

Poor Carlos, standing there blubbering, without the remotest clue – what was there to be done about what? Give him something to do, like sending him for a doctor. That would be dangerous – the boy might very easily get run over crossing the road. Feet still dragging in the quicksand he asked himself stupidly what it was one did. One telephoned Police-Secours, that was it. With a second shockwave, malicious because delayed, he recalled that he had forgotten the ginger man. Did he know about the diamond? No, but he might have instructions. What might he be doing – getting impatient? Was there any cognac in the house? But it is a bad idea to give cognac to people in shock – or with stomach wounds. They should not even have water.

'Do you want me to get a doctor?' in a stupid mutter.

Taillefer was perfectly conscious, and replied with a peculiar smile. He was lucid all right.

'Did the Russian ask for a doctor?'

'He asked me to shoot him in the head.'

'Yes, of course.' He might have been asking for a telephone number that had slipped his mind.

'I can't do that,' said Louis apologetically.

'No. I see that.'

'Is he going to die?' asked Carlos, who had stopped crying.

'Go and get some water.' Louis didn't know what else to say.

'Yes,' said Taillefer. 'Yes. You made a good job of that, young man,' though Carlos was no longer there, but fumbling about in the kitchen. His voice was peaceful, oddly good-humoured. If Paule were here, Louis was thinking drunkenly, she would say go for a priest, but the ginger-haired man . . . Paule was in danger . . . would be as long as Taillefer neither returned nor telephoned . . . those people would be frightened, with their brain, their commander, missing . . . frightened people were dangerous people.

Had he spoken aloud? He had no idea.

Carlos came back with water.

'Drink it yourself,' said Taillefer kindly, and closed his eyes. 'The Russian asked for water too.'

Was it a kind of pride that made him refuse? There was a melodrama about the way the scene repeated itself. But that is the essence of farce. Farce is the inevitability of scenes you know are impossible. As in Feydeau – you *know* that the husband will get into bed with his own wife thinking that it is his mistress. The inevitability of every entrance and exit forces laughter. You stupid bastard, thought Louis; you're in shock yourself.

He took the glass from Carlos and was annoyed to find nothing in it: the boy was standing there with the empty glass in his hand.

'Get some more water,' crossly; he had no idea that he had drunk it himself.

He took a cushion off the chair, lifted Taillefer's head and put it under him.

'Thank you.' There was a pause. 'I want no doctor, no water, no help – I want the diamond. Give it to me – t is only for a little while,' politely, even apologetically. Louis went and found it.

'Thank you. I give it to you. It's yours.'

'But it's not yours. To give.'

'Where will wants not, a way opens, we say. Take it from me when I am dead. No, take it now . . . it hurts,' he said like a child; his face was twisted with pain, but he stopped himself complaining. 'There's a man outside . . . Louis.'

'Yes?'

'Don't let the police hear. The others will kill the woman – and the English people . . . Ah.'

'Is it very bad?'

'No. It's going off.' He clutched the diamond in his fist, opened it – the thing lay on his palm; the palm was sweaty. Louis and the boy were both on their knees beside him.

'What am I to do?' whispered Carlos – but why whisper?

It was extraordinary; pain left the man again while they watched and when he spoke his voice was quiet and reasonable; that of an elderly man who has good advice to give.

'Louis, can you drive the car?'

'Yes.'

'If I were you – I would dress up in these clothes. You see' – and again that astonishing good humour – 'all the bleeding is inside.'

'But the man!'

'What man?'

'The man,' stupidly. 'The one with the ginger hair.'

'Oh. Him – he's unimportant. Hit him on the head,' exactly as though he were speaking to someone slightly mentally deficient. 'You can't get a stamp to stick like that, dear: you have to lick it, first.'

After that there was a long silence. The shallow breathing did not alter perceptibly.

'Good-bye,' said Taillefer suddenly in his normal voice.

'Good-bye,' said Louis, and in a gesture of conventional stupidity he gave the man his hand, which was an unpleasant feeling, for the hand was sweaty and the diamond still stayed between the two palms. The man turned his head and looked at Carlos. Something of the old malicious amusement came back to his expression.

'You are a young man with courage. I wish you were mine.' He closed both eyes, having said all he had to say. Louis held on to the hand, ashamed to let it go. He was still holding it after perhaps three or four minutes when he realized that the man had died, had been dead already all the time.

Carlos looked better. He could not yet be over the dose of shock, but at least the glare was out of the eyes and the stunned, stupefied expression had lessened. Now he had to see about the boy, first.

'Are you all right, Carlos?'

'I don't know.'

'Can you listen? Can you do as I say?'

'Yes.'

'I have to go and get your mother.'

'Yes.'

'I don't know the address, but you tell them the Montagne Verte and they'll understand. One of the houses with swimming pools. They'll know then.'

'Who?'

'The police.'

'Do I have to go to the police?'

'No,' stupidly, the quicksand again. 'But if I don't come back. Stay here and watch me go. Don't leave the house. Then give me – yes, give me an hour. You phone Police-Secours. From the café – you go to Roger. When they come here you tell them to send a car with guns to the Montagne Verte. You say your mother's there. You understand? Can you do that?'

'Yes. What's the time?'

'Ten to six.'

'I haven't done my homework.'

Yes, that was important too; life was full of problems. Louis tried to think.

'Your mother will write a note. We'll say you were ill or something.'

'All right.'

'I'd better write a note, and you give it to the police – but not till after an hour, not till I don't come back. Understood? No, say an hour and a half – can you hold out that long? Do you know how to phone them?'

'Of course,' quite indignantly. 'Roger did it once when there was a fight on the pavement outside. An Arab got knifed.'

'O.K.,' said Louis.

He wrote a note. It would read very strangely, and his writing was quite uncontrolled – odd, the letters would not accept the shapes he wished to give them; his fingers seemed frozen. But it was legible – and it would fetch them.

'There. At eight o'clock, then. But I'll be back. For sure.'

'Yes,' said Carlos with the same confidence.

Since it is Taillefer's idea it is probably a good one. At least I will be able to get up closer without them noticing. I hope.

He took Taillefer's pistol; it was a nine-millimetre, a professional's gun, and would look more fierce than the other. Getting the suit off the dead man was not easy; it was too small and too short, but wearable; the bullet-hole did not show. With the expensive oyster-white raincoat and the hat at first it looked better, then it looked worse – the farm-hand in the hired dinner jacket – but it would have to do.

If it doesn't work it's simple; they kill me. I will join Taillefer, and the Russian. It is only the diamond that survives.

He left it by the body, horrible in the shirt and bare white legs, with the socks held up by beautiful elegant suspenders! He didn't know what to do with it; he didn't want to touch it.

He lit a cigarette and then put it out again; it tasted revolting. And Taillefer – did he smoke? – or not? Louis could not remember.

Carlos was watching him in silence. Louis was at the door, shaky, ready to go, when the boy spoke.

'Are you my father?'

As pertinent a question as Louis had ever had to answer – and as difficult, but he did not hesitate more than a very little.

'Yes.' He shut the door behind him.

Monday Evening – Monday Night

It was so easy – Louis could not get over his astonishment at how easy it was to make people do as one said . . .

The ginger man was reading the newspaper. As Louis approached, terrified, thinking how unlike his stiffened totter was to Taillefer's easy, jaunty steps that were so neat and rapid, he did not even glance up. As Louis loomed alongside, wondering whether just to wrench the door open and clonk – or should he simply point the pistol he had clutched in the raincoat pocket? – suppose there were passers-by? – somebody was bound to see – no no, no clonk in any case; one would never get him out of the driving seat – damn it, to listen to Taillefer anybody would think such things were easy, but this stealthy stuff, the solitary Hawkeye, Skorzeny the Terrible – no, his days were definitely over, and no one could have been more astonished than Louis that he should have been capable of flooring that horrible fellow with an empty Vittel bottle.

The gingery man flicked his eyes up for a trustful half-second and started to busy himself folding up the newspaper. As anybody knows who has ever tried, folding a paper small enough to go in one's pocket while sitting at the wheel of an auto is a frightful job and claims all one's attention. Louis, advancing on a path of roses, got in, shut the door, and stuck the big pistol into the other's ribs. He looked *then*, perfectly thunderstruck.

'Start the car and just drive it normally.'

166

'But where am I to drive it to?' So disconcerting was this apparition, insolently dressed in the clothes of invincibility, that he had no thought of offering argument.

'Back to the house; where else? Get on.'

Presumably the gingery man spent the trip wondering how Louis had managed it, but he did not ask, and Louis had nothing to say either.

One piece of heroics left to perform, with distaste – he had lost the last shred of his desire to go through life sloshing people. As the Mercedes slowed in front of the doorway Louis, who had thought it out, hit the ginger man on the top of the head, jammed his foot over the other on the brake pedal and let the motor stall by itself. He looked long enough to make sure that the poor chap would stay hit for a few minutes, switched off and got out, leaving him collapsed in his corner. He ran the few steps to the door, for if anyone was going to be trigger-happy now would be the time. Nobody was in the hallway; there were, as far as he knew, three, and three he found, next door to the waiting-room where the Harvey family was presumably peacefully drinking coffee and playing cards, still sitting. Louis shut the door behind him with the soft movement, unworried and unhurried, that Taillefer would have used, and they just gawked.

They simply did not believe their eyes. Once more he found himself full of admiration for Taillefer, who must have reached an enormous ascendancy over these people, because plainly the sight of him in these clothes was monstrous, so outrageous that none of them dreamed of the violent reaction he had been so frightened of. Had Taillefer known that? Had it perhaps amused him? Why else should he have said 'Wear my clothes' in that innocent voice of a man preparing a good joke. He had had understanding, and probably contempt, for his subordinates, for he had guessed, Louis felt sure, that at the 'Yoo hoo: it's Santa Claus' they would just gawk.

One noticed the pistol in his hand and made a nervous movement: Louis, who had decided on the way that the every-one-the-hands-in-the-air performance was not in his character, threw the pistol on the floor. Certainly a sound instinct; it banged heavily on the wooden floor and skidded into the corner under a sideboard; and they gawked even more. The one who might have been tempted to shoot it out with the cops went on holding on to the back of his chair, another got half-way up and sat down again discouraged, and the third simply went on sitting, imagining that the witch-doctor had already turned him into a toadstool.

'Taillefer is dead,' said Louis. 'I have come to let all these people go. You have about a quarter of an hour, I should think, before the police are here. They have been warned, and will be sure to close the frontier. If your papers are *very* good you might all be able to cross separately; I should split up if I were you. I don't know any of you and don't want to. I won't give any descriptions: I'm not interested in you, but remember there's been a murder and if the French police get you you all face perpetual. Your ginger pal is outside in the car.' He walked on, opened the door, and shut it again behind him. Trust them! Five minutes to fill their pockets and it would be a puzzle landscape in a children's magazine. Granny has lost her umbrella, her hat, and her shopping basket in the high wind. Can you find them for her? No no, one tells the triumphant six-year-old: I can't see *any* of them!

Everybody was sitting much, as far as he could judge, as he had left them. Paule had a studious, puzzled expression, like someone doing a crossword; the three faces of the Harvey family turned towards him with varying degrees of indignation.

'This has gone quite far enough,' said the doctor in lieutenant-colonel's tones: the Senior British Officer in the prisoner-of-war camp.

'I quite agree.'

'What are you doing in those clothes?'

'Oh, mine got wet.'

'But what on earth is the meaning of all this?'

'I can't explain. It would take me a week and you wouldn't believe me anyway. Look, Harvey, you are a very intelligent and reasonable person; try and just accept what I tell you. You are free – all those people have just gone. They weren't police at all – they were bandits – you've heard of the O.A.S. Their leader has been arrested, and the police will be here very shortly. I wouldn't stay. It would take a month and you'd never get away. As it is you've only lost a few hours and nothing very dreadful has happened. Take my advice and go straight to Switzerland, and don't make any complaints or remarks: you'd never hear the end of it. Keep it for a party story for when you get home. Don't worry about me. I'm a government agent and officially the police don't even know I exist. I apologize very sincerely for all the trouble you've had: I'll buy James Bond a drink next time I see him. Your car's outside – at least I hope it is – they might have pinched it.'

He had a sudden sinking feeling – he hoped they *hadn't*. It was all right; Harvey's face had an expression that was almost amusement.

'We will certainly have a *story* to tell. I doubt, though, whether anyone will believe it.'

'Very likely not. But it's the best you'll find. If you mention it to any consuls it would likely become a very nasty story, though. I'd lose my job, and be in very bad trouble, and other innocent people, like this lady here, who is a refugee from the Communists, would have their whole lives ruined.'

'Well if that's so . . . ' said the dreadful Stephanie – he could rely on her to be tiresome – 'but that's really the only reason why I would keep quiet. I know *your* sort – agent provocateur.'

'Yes,' said Louis humbly. 'But you see I'm only small fry. I have my orders from the Swiss government.' Not very fair – first Taillefer and then him! Switzerland, though, would survive these successive libels. He was only repeating the lesson he had learnt! 'If you follow the road down the hill, and turn to the left at the crossroads, you'll be back at the Swiss frontier within two hours, and I promise faithfully nobody will look twice at you – not even a customs man.'

Harvey was looking at him shrewdly. 'There is evidently a great deal more behind all this than you have chosen to tell us.'

'Yes, but for lord's sake hurry up before the police get here.'

'Quite true,' said the woman firmly. 'Do come on, Malcolm. I have *no* wish to meet any *more* policemen.' Harvey collected his dignity. Luckily he had plenty, and it fortified him now as it had all day against kidnappings, threats, humiliations, and being kept nearly eight hours in a beastly waiting-room.

'I must say I'm extremely hungry,' he announced firmly. 'I think the best thing would be to look for a good restaurant.' He looked at Louis with a glint of humour. 'I remember I invited you to lunch, Mr Schweitzer, isn't it? – no, it probably isn't – but you will forgive me if I do not renew the invitation.'

'Quite right, I will,' said Louis: he wanted to laugh – the atmosphere of farce was still so strong.

By a merciful deliverance not only was the Mercedes gone – they had all tumbled into it and driven hell for leather to the station for sure: the police would find the auto late that night and tow it away with irritation – but the Humber was still there: no, they would not have taken it; it would leave an unnecessary trail. Off went the Harvey family, Stephanie still glaring suspiciously at him: thoroughly tiresome girl, but no fool. They *would* make a tale of it when they got back, and never again would any of them ever give a lift to a stranger. He was left alone in an empty house with Paule Wisniewski. She was crying a little but had stopped.

They found Taillefer's black Peugeot in the garage. Paule wanted to walk, at least till they reached a bus route, but agreed when Louis told her that Carlos was alone at home waiting to call the police if they did not get back soon. He did not tell her that Carlos was alone with Taillefer's dead body.

Louis had not driven an auto for several years, and his biggest fear was of having a bump and being asked to produce his identity and insurance cover, but by going very slowly, very *prudently*, they managed to reach the station where they abandoned the Peugeot – one more would make little odds and when it was traced it might with any luck be presumed that Taillefer had made a getaway with the others – walked a hundred metres, and took a taxi to the corner of the Quai Louis Pasteur, where Louis threw the keys of the Peugeot in the river under the cover of the coming darkness. It was half past seven, and there was nothing to eat in the house, but nobody felt hungry.

Carlos had not been able to stay in the house with Taillefer. They found him in a corner of the café, watching the television in a glazed, listless way. He got up quietly when he saw them and came along calmly, but no sooner was he at home than he broke down into fits of sobbing, shivering, and clinging to Paule. It was no harm, Louis decided; it kept Paule from worrying about the supper, about the thing on the living-room floor, about her not having gone back to work that afternoon (Mr Meatli would be in an uproar) – about a number of other things. Louis picked up the diamond and put it in his pocket, got a sheet to cover the body, and went out to the nearest apothecary for the most powerful pills he could get without a prescription. He left Carlos in Paule's bed, with Paule herself lying on it next to him, and went to the café.

It was the kind of café where there is stale bread, cheese, and hard-boiled eggs on the counter. Even apart from the television there was a lot of noise, hearty laughter grumbling, a strong smell of beer, and at least forty people; nobody noticed him at all and he had two of that morning's rolls and two hard-boiled eggs, and three glasses of white wine. After that he had no wish to eat, no remnants of shock (nothing like hard-boiled eggs for shock), and a very faint idea of what it was he still had to do. He went back to her house, but she was asleep and so was the boy – he had filled them both to the brim with pills. He covered her with blankets and sat down to the writing-table, where he could find nothing better to write on than one of Carlos' exercise books: he felt guilty at tearing pages out but decided it was a minor crime compared with some of the other events of the last days.

Darling Paule,

I have gone off to draw the last line under this – I don't know what to call it – not an affair, or a business, is it? I will be back by eight tomorrow morning. If I can't get this job done in twelve hours I would have an even poorer opinion of myself than I have now, and it hardly *could* be poorer.

You will have realized that you – neither of us – are in any further danger, but you might be thinking that a dead body on the living-room floor is even worse than a diamond in the bedroom drawer. I think I know how to get rid of both in one breath, and will explain this when I see you.

I have plenty of experience of shock, and Carlos will be none the worse tomorrow morning. It is important that everything should be normal for him. Send him to school as usual with a note about his homework (he was worried about this and I promised him a written excuse) and he will be quite all right – a wonderful boy.

There is no reason why you should not go yourself to work tomorrow. I intend to go myself. Our dear Mr Mestli's little displeasures at your absence yesterday afternoon (you simply tell him that the boy was taken ill) will be quite effaced by his joy at seeing me return faithfully to the fold in time for Mr Tsara's speech! I dare say I will be short of sleep, but that will hurt nobody. I will still be

Your very loving
            Louis.

He put on his coat but left his suitcase where it was. Packing would have to be done tomorrow anyway! He propped the paper against Paule's alarm clock, wound and set it, and shut all the doors quietly behind him.

It was a strange feeling, back there in the Avenue du Jura. After the two flights to Paule's flat the six here felt very long, the flat itself very high, very large, and very cold, and the contents very alien – he did not recognize these familiar objects as belonging to him at all! – and it had only been since Friday morning . . .

There was an unpleasant smell, such as all old houses get even if left closed for only three days, and a damp chilly feel, which he got rid of by lighting all the radiators. Taillefer's men had not made too much mess, even though a cold chisel had been used on the big bureau – ah well, it had never been an object of beauty. It had contained him, Louis Schweitzer, and everything that concerned him, for many years now, but that was no longer true.

He had to take stock. He went and had a shower and changed all his clothes, putting on his good suit, the one he used to visit Marie-Claire in. He felt able to smile at that idea – Marie-Claire would miss him, and wonder for two months anyhow what on earth could have become of him. He cut his finger-nails, looked at his watch, and was agreeably surprised – it was not yet ten o'clock. With decision he ran down the stairs and headed for the telephone on the corner. Mr Mestli was at home and reached hungrily for his receiver after only two rings.

'Hallo? Louis Schweitzer here. No no, I'm fine. I rang to tell you I'd be back for the debate tomorrow. Yes yes, thanks, my business is cleared up. You never have any confidence in me. I did not want to say it would take a week and then find it took a fortnight – that wouldn't have pleased you at all.'

'Well, that's very good news, Louis,' came Mestli's querulous voice down the hollowness of the line. 'There's only one thing, and that is that I felt I had to warn Mr Tsara that you would not be able to translate his speech. He was not too pleased, but I finally got him to accept the notion. But I'll look foolish when he notices tomorrow that you're there after all. He'll ask himself whether I was falling down on my job, hm?'

'I can't see that that's any problem. You've got his phone number: I'll ring him myself. That's one of the reasons I rang you – his number won't be in the book.'

'But he'll very likely be out.'

'Very likely he'll be in,' with a familiar, momentarily forgotten irritation at the man's incredible capacity for getting more and more fussed about smaller and smaller details.

'Well then, he lives in the Rue du Cervin. One moment; I've got to look in my book for the phone number.'

'Just give me the street number,' said Louis. 'That's only five minutes from me; it's as easy to go there as it is to phone.'

'That would be just as well.' Mr Mestli was audibly relieved. 'You see, Louis, after all, these telephone numbers are supposed to be confidential after all, and he might be none too pleased at my giving it, though of course I know I can make an exception in your case . . .'

'Just give me the street number.'

'Twenty-five; second floor.'

Agreeable surprise to find it so near; Louis had had a gloomy suspicion that Mr Tsara might well live in a grand villa out in the Montagne Verte – a neighbour of Taillefer's! One never did know with Russians. As it was he had a little stroll, about twice as far as it was to Marie-Claire. He wondered with amusement whether Mr Tsara knew Marie-Claire. Louis had given her address to other delegates! No – the Russians were far too well trained – they knew all about bawdy-house gossip.

These streets, a series of short streets off the Avenue de Neuchâtel dense with wealth and respectability, were like his own but narrower, lined with the expensive English autos affected by the high bourgeoisie in France and smelling strongly of money. Noiseless heavy green rubber marble steps, edged with red, led to a little lift smelling of Diorissimo and panelled in mahogany, and the row of brass pushes was glitteringly free of greasy fingerprints. Second floor, thick Turkey carpet, a brass bowl with a large elegant palm, and a tremendously thick forbidding tight-fitting door. A tiny oval silver medallion said 'Tsara' in Russian script. Louis rang and waited some time before the door opened on a thin bald man-servant all veins and muscles with big pointed ears that stood out like bats' wings, whose eyebrows made a polite interrogation mark, or would have if he had had any.

'Is Mr Tsara at home?'

'I could not say, monsieur. C'est de la part de . . . ?'

'Louis Schweitzer. He knows me.'

'Be so kind as to wait: I will enquire.' A kind of little lobby, panelled like the lift. There was nothing to steal, neither fur coat nor jade-Buddha-on-the-hall-table. Carpeted silence and another fairly long wait, before Bat-Ear came back in a soft pad, bowed very slightly, and said, 'Will you follow me, please? Mr Tsara will receive you.'

Corridor: Persian prayer-rugs, Venetian glasses. Chinese water-colours on narrow vertical strips of silk hung on wooden rollers. Thick heavy door again; a big warm room like a colossal jewel-box, bursting with subdued glitter, and Mr Tsara, who matched all this to perfection.

Mr Tsara, the permanent delegate of the Soviet Republics, was a diplomat out of a full-page colour advertisement in the *New Yorker*, drinking Harvey sherry and Calvert's Reserve out of the same cut-glass decanter while toying nonchalantly with his solid silver spurs, the hand-carved walnut butt of his shotgun ready to repel boarders. He might easily have been sixty – Louis had no idea – but was so tanned, so athletic, so fit, that his black and silver hair arranged in a Napoleonic mèche looked absurdly old over an Aznavour face: bright, wicked, sparkling. Black eyes snapping and burning with vitality, face as smooth and brown as a cigar with little lines drawn in with India Ink, tennis-player's shoulders, tango hips. He had a rapid easy way of getting out of autos like the gunslinger in a western sliding off his horse, and was the press-photographers' darling.

At work he wore narrow black business suits and horn-rimmed glasses, and carried a briefcase unexcelled by even Monsieur Couve de Murville, and strictly no jewellery. His silky voice was less soft than Taillefer's, but had an incisive edge, a chased silver paperknife from Tashkent that looks innocent till you cut yourself on it, exactly like certain types of grass-blade. Here at home the voice was the same but the clothes completely different. No glasses, no black suit. No conventional sapphire-blue velvet jacket, either. Mr Tsara was dressed in an ordinary black cotton tracksuit and looked as if he had just finished his limbering-up exercises.

'Hallo Louis: grand to see you – sit down there. Have some whisky – one always kept whisky for Anglo-Saxons before the vodka craze started – then that got corny and they switched to white rum, but the French insist on whisky.'

'Is it Calvert's Reserve?'

Tremendous laugh. 'The most attractive thing about you, Louis, is your ability to make jokes. Boring old Johnny Walker I'm afraid. I'm going to drink whisky too; I'm bored with those old Cuba libres.'

There was a vast silver tray and a perfect artillery-battery of cut-glass decanters, but the Johnny Walker was straight out of the bottle and the peanuts straight out of their vacuum-seal tin. That was what Louis liked about Mr Tsara – at all times he had a flair for the simple, the direct, the unpretentious. His phrases escaped from the silken cocoons of diplomacy and flew like butterflies. He was very easy and very difficult to translate, and hated being translated by anybody but Louis. Last week after an interminable discussion about oilbearing seeds he had remarked, 'We sound like a pack of suburban budgerigar-breeders.' It had come out in English as 'smalltown pigeon fanciers'. The French had laughed but a delegate from Wales who *had* raced pigeons in his trade-union days had glared, thinking himself the victim of Russian espionage, and Mr Mestli had been furious.

Louis accepted a great deal of whisky in a Scotch thistle glass gratefully. No damned ice or water or anything to spoil it at all. Worry fell off him like a squashed mosquito and he started to look about him. The glitter came from French furniture, rosewood and satinwood and maplewood encrusted with chiselled bronzes: huge commodes, a cylinder bureau, a map table, a Caffieri clock; the rich grave glitter of Louis XIV. There was a Lurçat tapestry on one wall and a picture by Marc Chagall on the other, and a great deal more bronze everywhere. Louis felt like the Duke of Buccleuch.

'I invented a new breakfast this morning,' said Mr Tsara comfortably sipping whisky. 'Banania with brandy and whipped cream.'

Banania is a French children's drink made of cocoa with dried powdered banana added.

'I'll try it tomorrow,' promised Louis. 'No, I didn't just drop in for a chat – it's serious.' He put his hand in his pocket, drew out the Dresden Green, and laid it on the table. It went very well with the furniture.

'Good heavens, is it a diamond? By all the patron saints of Europe . . . ' Mr Tsara got up, went over to his bureau, and came back with a big magnifying glass. Dissatisfied, he went back and got a loupe. 'But this is a historic piece – unless I'm so gravely mistaken I deserve to be birched this is Augustus the Strong's diamond.'

'It is.'

'And now Louis turns up with it. We were supposed to have stolen it. There were endless investigations and complaints. Last year only in Dresden they told me they'd little hope of ever tracing it, but that they hadn't given up. Might have known it would reappear – you don't just *lose* these things. And you – you haven't a nice picture by Georges de la Tour you're willing to part with by any chance? Seriously though – ah, I can see there's a drama behind this.'

'I don't know. I only know the very last act. But I would guess that somebody made approaches to them, to attempt or pretend to sell it back, to create some atmosphere for making money out of it. I mean it's worthless, isn't it? You couldn't just walk into the jeweller's with it and ask for ten thousand francs. You'd need to find a dishonest cutter to split it up and then remount it and so on. That wouldn't be very easy – or I wouldn't think so.'

'I don't know very much about diamonds,' with regret, 'but I should imagine that good ones with that peculiar colour were excessively rare and might arouse comment in any knowledge-able circle – not only anybody in the trade but insurers, art historians – any amateur of collections, even me, humble as I am – I recognized it at once.' He looked at it again through the loupe. 'It's not even scratched.'

'It had been carefully preserved.'

'It really ought to be back where it belongs. Not that those bastards deserve it.'

'Your reasoning,' said Louis smiling a little, 'is much the same as mine. I don't intend to give it back to them.'

'Why not? You speak decisively – you've a reason.'

'They killed the man I got it from. No, they didn't kill him – I killed him – they'd blinded him. They very nearly killed me. They would have, but they were in too much of a hurry to lay their hands on the diamond first.'

Mr. Tsara's face became hard and still. The clinical edge appeared to his voice.

'Why do you come to me?'

'Can I tell it bit by bit – my way?'

'Yes. Help yourself to whisky.'

'You know the Germans – not our pals here *en face* but those from *d'rüben*. And you know a lot about art – your interest in antiques, objects of beauty – it's public property. Have you ever heard of a man moving in both circles calling himself Taillefer?'

'Mm ... I'm not sure, but I believe it's possible that I might – what does he look like?'

'A bit thinner and smaller than I am. Soft-spoken, very elegant, snappy dresser.'

Mr Tsara had lit a small cigar. He waved away a bunch of smoke with his left hand and said decisively, 'Yes. Met him once in Leningrad. Some art commission belonging to that crowd – for us too, remember, they're *ceux d'en face*.'

'So it was true.'

'What about him?'

'He's dead on my living-room floor.' Louis never noticed that he said 'my'.

'Because of that diamond?'

'Yes. Two more are dead that I know of. A Russian and another of them.'

'I'm not a bit surprised,' said Tsara flatly.

'You're not surprised?' Louis was surprised.

'No.'

'You know something then – about this Taillefer?'

'No. But I know something about the diamond. I'm from Courland. That means nothing to you – it's a province on the Baltic – it's the little tongue of land that forms the western side of the gulf of Riga. Between Lithuania, Latvia, and Estonia. A godforsaken place, an ice desert in winter and a stinking marsh in summer. Not the place one would choose to be born in – less still the kind of place one would choose to live in – the proof . . .' with a wave of the hand round the apartment. He gripped the little cigar between strong white teeth and drew his lips back in a smile that held no amusement. 'The history of Courland was one of the main factors – perhaps the chief factor – in my interest in diplomacy. You want to hear a brief sketch?'

Louis lit a cigarette and stared at the diamond, an icy fire on the table between them.

'Go on.'

'The wilderness was settled first by Germans, from the Hansa ports – twelfth century perhaps. Our brothers started early. They were kicked out by the Danes. In the thirteenth century the province was bought – I have always admired the word "bought" in this context – by our old friends the Teutonic Knights. You've heard of *them*.'

'Yes.'

'We also learn, with some satisfaction, that they were busted at Tannenberg – a name that Russian children know – in the fifteenth century. Their *estates* got carved up. Russia got some. Sweden got some. Poland got the rest. Skip to the eighteenth century. Sweden invades and forces the Russians to withdraw. Poland, well thrashed by the Swedes – been naughty customers in their time, these Swedes – no longer counts. Our friend

Augustus the Strong – King of Saxony – the owner of *that* – even walks about calling himself King of Poland. No match for Charles the Twelfth of Sweden. Who in his turn was not a match for Tsar Peter. The last so-called independent Duke of Courland is married to a young Russian Grand Duchess – Peter's niece. She is left a widow at an opportune moment. Augustus thinks that one of the good candidates for re-marriage – and succession to a reigning dukedom – and something to underline Polish influence in this part of the world – meaning German influence – would be one of his favourite bastards, Maurice de Saxe.' All this between puffs at the cigar. 'But the Russians weren't having any. What conclusion do you draw from your brief history lesson, Louis?'

One had to be careful. Never can one quite know whether it is the man talking, or the accredited representative, who does not have personal opinions: he 'puts forward the views of his government'.

'What you're saying is that the Poles are not having any nonsense from Germans about the famous lost eastern provinces – and neither, by the same token, are the Russians.'

'Just so, Louis, just so, that is the book answer. But I was born in Courland. One would say that the eighteenth century was finished, that the time when provinces were owned by men who married the right girl had passed – and yet we have seen in our times German troops take possession of Courland by what they thought of as divine right. If you want me to find a diplomatic word it disquiets me to see that diamond there. For that diamond, Louis, you could in those days buy a cavalry regiment, a town, a province. The people who lived on that land, and their forefathers before them, were of little consequence, were they? What importance had they, as long as Augustus of Dresden could call himself King of Poland, and his son Duke of Courland? That is why I tell you that I am not surprised to learn that this diamond carries a train of dead men in its wake. There have been more, many, many, many more. The thing makes me sick to look at – and it is beautiful, beautiful . . . '

'You don't want to let them have it back?' asked Louis stupidly.

Tsara took off his glasses, which he had put on to examine the beauty, and rubbed his eyes wearily.

'No, Louis. You and I are men. You know that I can upon occasion act as spokesman for my country, upon economic affairs. When it is a political question, you know that the Minister comes and sits in my chair. It is not as a Russian but as a European that I speak. You know that our much-criticized management of affairs in Eastern Germany is designed for one purpose – to neutralize for good the corrosive acid, the insatiable appetite for other people's provinces. We want no kingdoms in Dresden – or in Berlin . . . '

'Taillefer told me that they would never rebuild Dresden as a symbol of the old days of conquest and vainglory.'

'Perhaps we would not let them, Louis,' softly.

'You think . . . ?'

'He was a German – whatever he chose to call himself.'

'He wanted the diamond, I think, for himself. What his plans were for it he did not tell me.'

'Perhaps he wished to make himself Duke of Courland.'

'What shall we do with it?'

Mr Tsara looked at him with amusement, picked up the whisky bottle and refilled the glasses.

'Have some more peanuts. They're easier to pass from hand to hand.'

Louis kept silence; into it came a crunching noise from Tsara's strong white teeth.

'You are naïve, Louis. You offer me your green diamond, and in return you would like me to use my *influence* to get rid of a dead body for you.'

'I don't want it. I thought I wanted it. My wife and child were killed in the destruction of Dresden. And it was a town I loved.'

'For the beauty? For the buildings? For all the splendours? So did I. It is a price we have to pay. I too would say rebuild – if in the rebuilding I could bring your wife and child back to life. Together with all the others – *all* the others. As it is, my advice to you is to keep your diamond. There are other wives, other children. Perhaps the diamond brings you luck.'

'I've changed my mind. I don't want to keep it. What will I do? – give it to the police? – say I found it?'

'What will a republic do with *crown* jewels?' spitting out the words with a shred of cigar, mashing the stump in the ashtray.

'What else can I do with it? I would like to bring people to life too. But what use is the Dresden diamond to charities, to organizations, to works of goodwill? It cannot be sold, it cannot be cut – you could not even make earrings for a girl. It belongs in a crown, maybe, but nowhere else.'

'You begin to understand.'

'You mean it will feed no one, clothe no one, house no one, make no man happy.'

'It is not like a picture, Louis. A picture, even if stolen or looted, even if paid for by the blood of hundreds, pays back its price. It continues to instruct, to elevate, to unite, to construct. It is of no importance whether it is a revolutionary picture or a court picture – a Goya, a Delacroix, a Fragonard, a Hubert Robert – its value stays absolute. You can hang it in a state gallery, putting a notice "Property of the State" – it remains the property of every man that takes the trouble to walk up and look at it. The same with music, with a book – yes, a building, perhaps! But that – what would you do with it? Put it in a case. Write: "This is the famous green diamond of Augustus the Strong, King of Saxony, temporarily King of Poland, nearly Duke of Courland. It is impossible to state its value in monetary terms. A cavalry regiment, a hospital and three schools?" Your first peasant would smash the glass case and trample on it – and he would be quite right. A pity – it is very beautiful. intensely seductive, I desire it intensely. Looking at it, I begin to understand the mentality of Augustus... you had better take it away. It reminds me too vividly of the Dresden I knew as a young man. With knights – Teutonic knights – on the stage of the opera house. Put it in your pocket. It's yours. Will we see you tomorrow, by the way? It will not be myself who makes the principal speech, but I will be making an opening statement. You will back me up?'

'Yes.'

'Good. What's the address of that flat of yours – in case I wish to get into touch with you? Your Mr Mestli has all the details of the protocol – he regards that as a state secret, of course!'

Louis gave the address of Paule's house.

'I don't know the number, I'm afraid. But it's next door to the café, between the café and the dry-cleaning depot.'

'Excellent neighbours to have,' said Mr Tsara. 'But you don't know the number – oddly incurious of you: do you never get letters?'

'It's not really my flat,' in confusion. 'It's Paule Wisniewski's. Uh, Madame Wisniewski, works as translator for the Poles – you know her perhaps by sight.'

'Yes, indeed, the little Polish woman, I know her well.' The smile was sly. 'I must ask you to excuse me, Louis – I have a little paper work to do, and I must be up bright and early – breakfast with the Minister! Oh, these political breakfasts . . . ' He threw up his hands in mock anguish, laughed heartily showing all his splendid teeth, and accompanied Louis out himself without bothering to ring the bell for Bat-Ear.

Louis walked back to the Avenue du Jura. He did not want to take the diamond out of his pocket, to look at it. He had left the radiators full on, and the flat was glowing with heat and welcoming quiet. He went to bed, solitary. He did not bother with any of the chores he had trained himself to for many years. The whole place was dusty and messy, but he did not take the dustpan and the little brush; he did not pass the vacuum-cleaner. There was nothing to eat but he did not peel the onions for soup, he did not set the beans to soak nor write a shopping list for next day in his little black notebook. His shoes were dirty but he did not polish them. His suit was crumpled but though he only had to push the plug of the iron into its socket he could not be bothered: he did not even brush it; he just went to bed in unaired sheets.

He was out of bed at six, and left everything the way it was – bedclothes in a tangled heap that no longer smelt fresh, everything lying about: a dirty mess. He walked down the six flights of stairs without jumping the way he had always done to keep his ski muscles in trim. Outside in the street it was still dark and there was a thick lazy drizzle of rain from a lowering sky that one could only guess at. It was cold too, so cold that one could almost imagine that one was back in February. The day, say, of Louis' birthday, or the night Dresden was bombed – only then, of course, there had been a clear sky and a full moon.

He walked all the way to Paule's house, at first through streets half dead and yawning with sleep, but with animation beginning as he progressed. Doors opened letting out gusts of light and warmth and coffee, shopdoors creaked and clanged before floods of the heartening pungent stink of fresh bread; the street-cleaning lorry went growling softly along the gutters, its hard round brushes mumbling and masticating a day's refuse. After the slam of the doors came the infantile putter of the Solex being pedalled into life. When he came into Paule's quarter the vegetable market was in full spate and the regular crash every three seconds of another crate of cauliflowers being unloaded told him he was there before he turned the street corner. The café 'Roger' was full of Arabs having breakfast and that meant that Paule too would be making coffee – he ran up the stairs with a renewed vigour. He had to be gay, quiet, confident.

They were waiting for him in the corners of the room, cobwebby shadows, but the presence they had brought was real, heavy, violent. The figures might be veiled and dim but the meaning was precise. He could smell them there in the half-lit room where the strengthening daylight seeped through the still-drawn curtains: a smell of fear and hatred: the smells of cheap hair-oil, sweat and over-pungent aftershaves: the smell of cheap mediocrity never more spiteful and more vicious than when it has been recognized and knows it has been recognized.

Three of them. The fourth, his old acquaintance the gingery one, would no doubt be waiting in the auto, on guard and ready for a smooth unnoticeable departure after they had done what they came to do.

Louis stood still, very like Carlos the day before who had also come running into this room glad and confident and gay. He was old and stiff and very tired; he had no reactions left. He could only stand dully and wait for it; they would make him wait for it, seeing it, knowing it, recognizing it, for they were like that. They were carrying no guns, for guns make noise, and in this crowded quarter might attract attention. Yesterday, Louis thought dimly, Carlos' two shots had attracted no attention but that had been just luck. There might have been a heavy lorry at that instant in the street – here between the vegetable market and the abattoir there was a constant stream of them. Or perhaps at five o'clock in the afternoon there had been no near neighbours at home: such things were a matter of luck, weren't they?

He did not ask – either them or himself – where Paule was. She would be in the back room still, and Carlos with her. They might have tied her, tormented her, holding her head with the brutal dirty thumb under one ear while the other hand slowly brought the edge of the knife nearer. They would not have believed she would not know where it was, where he was, but they would have searched and found nothing – except the note he had left, and after that they had had nothing to do but patiently to wait, knowing that he would come, savouring it, loving it, licking their lips at the sound of his innocent feet on the stairway.

Had she died quickly? And Carlos? To stop any yelling or struggling they would have finished with him first – it was just one more troublesome little chore, of no importance to them but as eyes and ears and mouth, a witness, a little cockerel that would run out on to the street and crow. They could not know that it had been Carlos' hand that had held the pistol and fired the shots.

Had it been quick, or slow? How could he know? and what difference could it make, now, or indeed at any time in twenty years? Had he known how Fabienne had died? Had she died quickly, struck in a flash of shock and light, hit direct? Had she suffocated slowly under a pile of plaster rubble? Had she lain in pain with both legs broken under a wooden beam, watching the slow pale flames lick at the burning roof, waiting for them to reach her? Had she been kicked down and trampled to death in a shelter all egress from which had been blocked by masonry? Had she died in a cellar, safe, untouched, unhurt, from lack of air? From thirst, from hunger? People had been killed by nothing but the blast of air. People had been cut by a glancing sabre of broken glass and quietly bled to death.

People had been run over and left lying by the equipages of would-be savers, fire-fighters, ambulance men. People had died of burns and unreduced fractures, of pneumonia and typhoid, of lack of resistance from malnutrition, of hopelessness and despair. People had been lynched by mobs, shot by the police, struck down by others who had no potatoes and no piece of bacon. People had died saying their prayers, pillaging shops, making love, trying to save others. People had died long after it had all finished, from walls, rafters and doorways that just fell down on them.

Paule had died too, and Carlos, just two more of the Dresden dead. And now it was his turn, after the Russian, the chubby man, Taillefer, Carlos, and Paule. Perhaps the Dresden death-roll would never end. How many had died in the years since, of tuberculosis or syphilis, or just of slow degeneration and disintegration? Or of trying to run away?

He was part of all that. He belonged among them, not that he had ever done anything special. Acts of heroism, for which he had been decorated – oh yes, there had been occasions on which he had been most heroic. He had saved the lives of comrades, heaven knew why. And the other times? The times when he had lain foul and shivering in holes too scared to move, when he had let people die, comrades or not. All his innumerable acts of meanness and cowardice, of selfish sloth and of sly opportunism, the times when he had always managed to save his skin. True, he had never betrayed anybody to the Gestapo, probably because he knew nobody to betray, but there had been people executed by firing squads for doing less. Well, it was his turn Now was the time to pay for all that. Was there any-after life? Which would he meet there – Fabienne? Or Paule? Or neither. When they both knew all the things that he had done, neither of them would look at him. Or was there any forgiveness? Perhaps this was it, perhaps this was the crowning mercy. He would never know.

The four of them had been frightened off, but not sufficiently, he supposed. Over-confidence again, his old enemy. He had thought that without Taillefer they would be helpless, bereft of sense and thought even assuming they had ever had any. Taillefer would not have been scrupulous about the tools he used, but neither would he have neglected all precautions. If he had chosen vicious helpers, he would have been at pains to ensure that they were stupid. He would have known how to protect himself, how to feel confident that no one would ever betray or doublecross him, that in case of accident or capture by the police none would ever know enough to compromise his rulers nor even himself.

Louis had not even believed that they knew about the diamond. Taillefer might have told them any cock-and-bull tale, but he would not have said that the trophy they were after was one so precious, so anonymous and so recognizable, so easy to steal and so easy to hide – and so difficult. A thing with a knack of never being totally lost, a thing with a curse on it, as though Augustus the Strong had brought down a terrible lingering inexorcizable vengeance on the whole of the race that had destroyed his wonderful, his beautiful city, his magnificent Dresden.

They must have known, guessed, found out. They had listened at doors, or Taillefer had been careless, trusting too much in his own deadly skill, his ascendancy over them – he must have known enough about each to hang the lot twice over!

They had run, but not far enough. They had seen or realized that the police had made no move, that the police knew nothing, that Louis had routed them with an insolent piece of bluff. They had waited all night. After listening to the late radio bulletins – nothing – they had waited for the morning paper – nothing. And they had felt sure enough, then, to close in and wait.

They might even have been sufficiently frightened of what had happened – Taillefer's death had certainly *routed* them – but a greater fear had turned them back. Might they not have been even more fearful of the welcome that would await them at home, when they came back with no treasure, no Taillefer, their hiding-place lost, their resources broken and scattered, their network destroyed. All that money wasted and nothing to show for it. . .

And they might simply be acting as unthinkingly, stupidly, helplessly as the bombs that had killed Fabienne and the other two hundred thousand. Bombs had no brain either.

They knew. The three closed in on him on soft feet, grinning awkwardly, maliciously, stupidly. You fools, Louis wished to say, do you think it stops here? Do you think it will lift its hand from you? Do you think that the possession of this thing will save you from a death as sudden and as sordid as this death you give me? But he could say nothing; his mouth was too dry, watching the knife in the dirty hand, the scared hand, the greedy hand. He smelt the stink of them all around him, felt the hands fumbling at his clothes, patting at him. Still no sound, not even the little sigh of content when the hand reached and found the diamond, scrabbled into the pocket and got it in his fingers. Louis hated the hands more than anything else, those disgusting hands that stripped him of manhood. Had they fingered Paule in that way, pulled her clothes off, amused themselves with her? He shut his eyes and there was nothing but the squeaky breath of the man in front of him, who had a slight cold, unless it was just adenoids. It was the last impression left with him before the tearing wrench of light and the crunch of the expert boxer's punch, the left hook to the liver that was the knife knocking him apart, and he went down on the floor to join Taillefer and Fabienne.

Tuesday Morning

Light burned: there was the smell of coffee and the pot was standing there on the stove keeping hot, and there were two cups in the sink. But there was no Paule, no one in the flat at all, nothing but silence and disorder. He went through to the bedroom; there were the imprints on the pillows that had been made by her and by Carlos – not him this time. The bed had not even been stripped: there might even still have been warmth in it.

'Paule,' he yelped in a voice hardly above a whisper. No answer. He ran back into the living room, his breath coming heavily, his heart banging laboriously, all his tired muscles scraping on the racked bones. No sign of her. He pushed the sofa back: there Taillefer lay still peacefully stretched out on his back, with the old rug over him. No signs of any blood on the carpet, no sign of any struggle or sudden attack or anything at all. He put the sofa back. They had got her?

A sudden patter of steps sounded through the door from the landing, and in a convulsion he gripped the pistol, the one he had carried for hours, the one that had shot Taillefer – he had no idea what had happened to the nine-millimetre – would it not be still on the floor under that sideboard thing? – had it been a sideboard, or a filing cabinet, or what? – he had not even noticed – out there in the abandoned villa of the Montagne Verte.

But it was Paule, Paule tight and grey around the face, very pale around the wings of the nose, with a raincoat on and a scarf wound around her hair. She managed a sort of papery smile when she saw him.

'You're there. I hoped you would be. But I hoped I might be back before you came. I was in the street – I don't know how I missed you. It must have been while I was just paying for the bread.'

She had a paper-bag with half a dozen croissants, fresh and crackly, their undersides still sticky from the metal: they would be steaming slightly still when one broke them open. Their smell chased that of hair oil and that foul aftershave, the suits that needed to go to the cleaners, the breath stale with beer and cheap white wine and patent aperitifs and rotted teeth, the underclothes tainted with sweat and urine.

Paule was pouring him coffee with jerky awkward movements.

'I got Carlos off to school all right. You were quite right – he had got over it. He has no idea the thing is lying there behind the sofa.' She did not spill any coffee though; she was in good command of herself.

He sat down and drank half a bowl of coffee – it was not so hot any more, but perfectly drinkable – straight off. He put a cigarette in his mouth and lit it.

'Don't you want croissants?' There was a childish note of her disappointment: they were a treat. She always finished yesterday's stale bread for breakfast, grilling it if it was too far gone. 'Old Mother Pain Rassis', he had heard Carlos call her rudely, jokingly.

'Of course I do. This is for you.'

'Thank you. Yes. I want that.' He ate his first croissant. His hands were thicker and more awkward than hers had been; when she went to strip the beds he held his arm out and watched the hand shake – he didn't want her to see. He had to regain command.

'Sit down,' after the second bowl of coffee and the third croissant: it was going better now. She sat obediently opposite him.

'Louis – what if they come back? I've been thinking about it all night.'

'But they won't – they'd never dare. Their one idea is to bolt for a safe hole. I've taken steps anyway – I've told the whole story. If they had been hanging about – if they had chosen, say, to follow me – they would know by now who I've seen and who I've spoken to.'

'Who?' She needed reassurance above all things and he had to give it to her quietly. He lit another cigarette for both of them.

'Mr Tsara He knows something of these people. He pulls a lot of weight, what's more. He will know how to handle that crowd.'

'You gave him the diamond?'

'Yes.'

'And what will he – what will the Russians – do with it?'

'I've no idea. I didn't ask. I don't care. Whatever they please.'

'Thank God for that. God – Louis. . . .' He put his hand round her shoulders and shook her gently.

'What we have to do is to do the housekeeping – I must shave – and then go off to work exactly as usual. We must do everything exactly as usual.'

'But – that thing.'

'It'll be gone when we've come back, and never ask how because I don't know myself. It'll just have vanished. Trust me.' He trusted Tsara – that far – didn't he?

'And Carlos? Now, this morning, it's vague and shadowy in his mind; he'll half think he almost dreamed it. But he'll remember. Things like that mark one one's whole life: you never

189

get away from them, never, I know, I should know, I've done it, I've been there, it's happened to me.' She dragged at the half squashed cigarette and fought the hysteria back.

'You know what Carlos said to me – almost immediately after he shot the man – after the man died – just after, I mean just before, I went out of the door to try and get you: I'd told him to go to the police if we weren't back by eight.'

'No. How could I? You mean had he said anything to me? No.'

'He asked me whether I was his father.'

'And you said?'

'I said yes, of course.'

And there it would stay. They would go to work, and stay there all day – a hard day's work, with a heap of extra delegates, special delegates, Ministers of this and that come from all the countries of Europe for the debate on the Oder-Neisse line that people hoped would lead to a final settlement of the German question. Radical, but so had been the final settlement of the Jewish question. The Germans and the Poles, the French and the Russians, the Czechs and the Hungarians would be there in especial force. Sweden, Switzerland and Austria would only have *observers* – it wasn't their business. Such a busy day – all translators hard at it and Mr Mestli in a perfect orgy, and even the Under Secretary pale and tense – that neither Paule nor Louis would have time to worry. Louis would find time for a handshake with Mr Tsara, very dynamic in his black suit (his Minister, superb with a rose in his buttonhole, was posing for the press with other ministers, all beams and jolly jokes).

'Ah, hallo, Louis – glad to see you back. How goes it? Everybody well wound up, what? By the way I thought of how to fix that little affair you mentioned to me – the Minister agreed with my opinion, which was a big help.' He stretched his big fine muscles under the narrow coat that sat so well on the powerful shoulders. 'The Swiss tell me too in confidence that their people picked up a couple of members of what they suspect is a spy-ring – ja, slipping across the border. But they're sitting on the information *very* tightly – they don't want any embarrassments while these delicate negotiations are in progress, ha. No publicity. But they were grateful for a tip. Well bye-bye, *mon vieux*, see you later.'

And later that morning a nondescript van would be stopping outside Paule's house. Two men in overalls, one of whom had ears that stuck out under his dirty beret, unloaded a big cardboard carton that had 'Refrigerator – Fragile. This way up. European Dynamics S.A.' stencilled on it. They carried it up the stairs but they must have made a mistake or got the wrong address, because five minutes later they were down again: the refrigerator was heavy and they cursed the narrow stairs.

During the lunch break another van – they all look like each other; for all anybody noticed it could have been the same – passed the big notice saying 'Chantier – No Admittance' at the huge site outside the town where the new hospital was going to go up. Not that there was much sign of it yet – a wilderness of trenches and huge holes, with bulldozers and excavators standing idle where everybody had gone for their sacred lunch break. They were making a beginning there with the foundations, driving deep steel piles and pouring concrete over, but one would have needed to be an engineer or an architect to make much sense out of the wilderness, which looked like Troy Seven, or a bombed town several centuries later.

The two men in the van were electricians, come to fix a defective powerline, and the watchman, comfortable over his little electric stove on which he was cooking a cutlet between swigs of vino, was uninterested; those temporary powerlines were always defective and there was a nasty drizzle outside; let them find their own way. Louis had put the diamond in Taillefer's pocket. You keep it for us, old chap. The foundations of a new hospital – quite near the engraved stone that a few months after, when everything was *tidy* and the summer was arrived, would be patted by a silver trowel in the hand of the Minister for Public Works, his other hand held by the Prefect – was not a bad place at all for the Dresden Green to find peace.

And Louis would go home with Paule, and they would a few weeks afterwards get rid of both flats and find another in their place, rather larger and handier, near the University, which would be nice a year or so from now for Carlos. And a few weeks further on they would go together to the Mairie, and to the Préfecture, Bureau of Aliens, and they would take steps for the legal adoption of Carlos.

It makes a better ending than the other. It is certainly the ending that Louis would have preferred.

Wolfisheim: Strasbourg. January 1966.